Boo!

^A Tiger Lily's Café_{TM} Mystery

by Kathleen Thompson

Boo!

[A] Tiger Lily's Café[TM] Mystery
by Kathleen Thompson
© 2015

ISBN-10: 1507820321

ISBN-13: 978-1507820322

Cast of Characters

Annie Mack, with the help of her "kids" and a talented staff, owns and manages a B&B, a cafe and other businesses on the south side of The Avenue.

Candice is the head waitress at Mo's Tap. She and George can't decide if they are dating or not.

Carlos is the manager and baker at Mr. Bean's Confectionary. He supports his mother and younger sisters in Mexico.

Cheryl inherited The Marina from her parents. It's a small deep water marina with basic amenities. Cheryl is married to Ray.

Chris is the Officer in Charge of the Coast Guard Station. His sketches – in charcoal, pencil and pastel – are sold for charity.

Clara owns the flower and gift shop, Bloomin' Crazy. She grew up in a tropical climate and is influenced in that fashion.

Diana is the chief instructor at L'Socks' Virasana (Veer AHS ana). She is Mem's daughter; they have a tenuous relationship.

Felicity is the chef at Tiger Lily's Café. She is young, perky and extremely talented in the kitchen.

Frank recently moved to Chelsea to open an antique shop, Antiques On Main. He and Mem and getting to know one another.

George is the bartender and manager of Mo's Tap. His only ambitions are to live simply and enjoy life.

Geraldine Foxglove was the leader of the "it" crowd in high school. Somehow, life didn't turn out quite as she expected.

3

Ginger is the daughter of Pete, the Chief of Police, and Janet. She is a senior in high school and works at L'Socks' Virasana to save for college as well as for high school credit.

Greg is a progressive realtor in Chelsea. His goal is to get the right property to the right owner, always moving Chelsea forward.

Hank is a member of the Town Council. He opposes Annie in every way.

Henrie manages the KaliKo Inn. He never speaks about his background. He runs the B&B in an elegant manner.

Holly and Jolly, twins, own DoubleGood, an electronics and hardware store. Holly lives in a wheelchair.

Janet is Pete's wife. She spent 20 years as a Marine officer's wife. She traveled the world and is now living in Chelsea. She is an outsider, not having grown up here like Pete.

Jennifer and Marie, sisters and nurse practitioners, own The Drug Store and The Clinic. Folks call the sisters before calling 911.

Jerry learned how to make candy in a minimum security federal prison. He was not an employee.

Jesus manages Sassy P's Wine & Cheese and also selects the wines. His family makes wine; he prefers to choose them.

Joan is a member of the Town Council. She opposes Hank in every way. Clara's pet name for her is "Joan of Chelsea."

Laila owns Babar Foods. She has three children, the youngest of whom (Carl) has Autism. James is in high school and Ava is in junior high.

Mem owns the health food store and cyber café, CyberHealth. Her wisdom is reassuring to everyone, including her daughter, Diana.

Minnie chooses perfect cheeses to accompany the rotating wine selections at Sassy P's Wine & Cheese.

Nancy and Sam are Annie's mother and step-father. They have been married since Annie was a child.

Pete is a native of Chelsea. He retired from the Marine Corps and is now the Chief of Police. He and his wife Janet have three children, the eldest of whom is Ginger.

Ray owns and operates The Escape, a yacht fashioned into a cruiser for fishing, diving and pleasure. He is married to Cheryl.

Teresa pastors a small church, Soul's Harbor. She came to this community to serve.

Trudie is the barista at Tiger Lily's Café. She is from Jamaica and ended up in Chelsea quite by accident.

Guests At The Inn

Mystery guests take three rooms at the Inn for several days during their murder mystery cruise entitled In The Weeds. They are joined during the same period of time by a mysterious businessman and a group of three friends.

Alec and Jessica Minor are guests at the Inn, twins — brother and sister — have come for a fun getaway with a friend, Herb Taylor.

Herb Taylor is a guest at the Inn. He recently suffered the loss of his significant other and is here with his good friends, Alec and Jessica Minor, for a getaway.

Hirsch and Linda Stone are part of the mystery crew. In their mid-50s, they have the look of well-healed professionals. They play the parts of Brad Spit and Mary Monroe for the murder mystery, In The Weeds.

Jeff Bennett is a guest at the Inn. He is in town to promote his business, which he never really clarifies to Annie and Henrie.

Spencer and Hannah Smith are part of the mystery crew. They appear to be a mismatched couple of a handsome, athletic man and a mousy, aging woman. They play the parts of Onstair Royds and Alabaster Pearl in the murder mystery, In the Weeds.

Tom Miller and Susie Benton are part of the mystery crew. They are in their mid-40s and have the look of a casual, family-oriented couple. They play the parts of Dr. Mortimer Bong and Sparkle Shine for the murder mystery, In The Weeds.

And The Companions

Annie has seven cats. Most people would call them "rescue kitties." From Annie's perspective, each of them rescued her.

Tiger Lily is a beautiful tabby cat with soft green eyes. She is the titular manager of Tiger Lily's Café, the main gathering place for Chelsea. She is generally calm and logical.

Little Socks is a bright-eyed black cat with white socks. She has a commanding personality and is small and sneaky enough to serve as a cat burglar. She spends time at the yoga studio, L'Socks' Virasana (Veer AHS ana).

Kali, Ko and Mo are litter mates. They shared a secret language as kittens; Kali and Ko now speak "cat," but Mo still speaks "secret." Kali and Ko can be found at the KaliKo Inn, a lakeside B&B. Mo spends time at Mo's Tap, an upscale blues bar.

Sassy Pants is aptly named; it's difficult to keep this little girl's attention. She is overly sensitive and will react out of emotion instead of reason. She entertains at Sassy P's Wine & Cheese.

Mr. Bean is the baby of the family and is mostly gray with traces of tiger. He has two speeds: fast and love me.

Claire is a blue point Himalayan cat whose human is Frank. She's beautiful and loves people. She is stand-offish with other cats.

Cyril is an English setter whose human is Pete, the Chief of Police. Cyril is friendly and calm. He is an excellent hunter.

Honey Bear is a large, golden, long-haired mutt of a cat who believes it is his perfect right to be anywhere. Other cats hate him.

Jock is a Portuguese water dog whose human is Ray, the captain of The Escape. Jock is spirited and affectionate; he loves children.

Chapter 1: Boo!

"Boo!"

Mr. Bean executed a perfect mid-air pirouette, back arched into a perfect "u," hair standing on end, tail straight up in the air, four legs straight out, and mouth wide open, too scared for a sound to come out. When he landed, headed the same direction he had been, he yelped a silent screech, turned around and ran back to the bedroom. This took some effort, as his little claws were not making purchase on the parquet floor.

Two older cats came out, hair at the back of their necks standing straight up, fangs bared, growls and snarls at the ready. They were prepared to protect their home. And possibly Mr. Bean. But probably just their home.

Annie, whose coffee cup had stopped halfway up, said calmly, "Tiger Lily, Little Socks, say good morning to your Uncle Honey Bear."

She heard snarls in response. Honey Bear lay still, not having moved an inch with the exception of his tail, which on occasion would curl luxuriously around his body, then twitch out. Curl in. Twitch out.

This had become a regular morning routine. Honey Bear arrived sometime early in the morning and lay passively next to the kitchen island. Annie, too bleary in the morning to see much of anything, would make coffee, not realizing she had a guest on the other side of the island. One or another of the cats would make the discovery, and the daily fight would be on.

Honey Bear was Annie's brother. Oh, more appropriately, Honey Bear and Annie shared a Mommy. Nancy, married to Annie's step-father since Annie was very young, was a newcomer to the world of cat lovers. She hadn't progressed past loving this one cat, a large, golden, long-haired mutt of a cat.

Nancy and Sam were visiting for the month, and of course, they brought the baby.

Annie lived on the third floor of the KaliKo Inn, a Bed & Breakfast in the lakeside resort town of Chelsea. The town was situated on the east coast of one of the Great Lakes and was nestled into a state park.

To the back of the Inn was one section of the park; the west side of the Inn opened to a large private beach of purest white sand fronting the lake. From the beach, one could see the town's deep water marina to the left and a city park to the right. Beyond that was the other section of park, encircling its arms around this part of town, sheltering it from the outside world.

The Inn was situated at the end of Sunset Avenue, known as The Avenue to everyone in Chelsea. The Avenue started at the town square and ended, one long block later, at the lake.

Annie owned several businesses on this side of The Avenue, all the way up to the town Square. Annie's group of intelligent and talented cats managed the businesses. Well, to be honest, there were human managers as well.

Kali and Ko, dilute calico siblings, were responsible for helping Henrie maintain the KaliKo Inn in tiptop condition. They rarely left the Inn, being perfectly content to roam the common areas and guest rooms, using cat doors to come and go as they pleased. They made sure Henrie kept the rooms clean, checked on the treats he left out for guests at night, and were especially mindful that breakfast was on time and fabulous.

On the other side of The Avenue were businesses owned and operated by Annie's close friends. The cats had free access to all of the places on The Avenue. Let's face it. They were close friends to the cats as well!

With plenty of room to spare at the Inn, Nancy and Sam had taken up residence in the guest room on the ground level. It was in the back with direct access to the lake. Annie imagined her mother was already out there, taking her hour-long morning walk. She assumed Sam was having coffee in the kitchen with Henrie, chatting and reading the morning paper while Henrie prepared and served breakfast for the guests of the Inn.

It was a perfectly dreadful October day. The kind of day to remind Annie that autumn, while her favorite season, did have its dreary moments. She couldn't wait for her mother — all 70-some years of her — to bounce into the kitchen and announce what a perfectly wonderful walk it had been, and Annie, you need to join me tomorrow morning!

Annie took another sip of coffee and debated. Breakfast with edible food of some variety up here with the kids? A fantastic breakfast downstairs with Mom and Sam? She turned to reach for the refrigerator door, decision made, when the intercom interrupted.

"Annie, honey, Henrie has a perfectly wonderful breakfast ready. Come on down. Bring Honey Bear with you."

Would this month never end?

Gritting her teeth, she took another drink of coffee, then answered her ringing cell phone. It was Chris.

"Good morning. I think. Is it a good morning there at the Inn?"

"Let's see. We've had our morning Honey Bear scare, my mother is bouncing around in the kitchen following her walk on the beach, and apparently Henrie has a perfectly wonderful breakfast ready. And now I'm on the phone. It's barely light outside. You tell me."

"I only call in the morning while your mother is there. I'm trying to wake you up a little. When she's gone, I'll revert to the standard never-talk-to-you-until-lunchtime routine."

"Thank you. I can't wait."

Annie and Chris, after 10 years of a perfectly nice friendship, had recently embarked on an exploratory venture into "something more." The venture had been interrupted by this extended visit. They still saw one another, and Chris was getting to know Annie's parents, but alone time was limited. Annie thought to herself, this, too, shall pass.

Chris continued, "When can I plan on seeing you today?"

"I'm not sure. I'll have to get back with you."

"Okay. Enjoy breakfast. Wake up."

Annie rinsed her coffee cup and raised her voice so all the kids could hear, "We're having breakfast downstairs."

Sassy Pants and Mr. Bean came running. They halted at the kitchen island, unsure if it was safe to go on. Annie leaned over, picked up the offending Honey Bear and said, "Come on. Down we go."

Mo followed at a stately pace. Tiger Lily and Little Socks sulked in the back of the line. Kali and Ko were already downstairs, supervising the preparation and serving of breakfast.

Annie got into the elevator, not wanting to carry Honey Bear down the stairs. Her cats took the opportunity to rush down to the first floor via the stairs, to say good morning to everyone before Honey Bear arrived to ruin it for them.

As the elevator opened on the first floor, Nancy greeted Annie with a hug and a kiss while she took Honey Bear onto her shoulder. "He is such a love in the morning. He just wants to cuddle!"

Honey Bear was indeed cuddling into Nancy's neck. Annie gave her mother a smile. Half a smile. The right side of her mouth slowly inched up while she brought her chin down, trying to help the kind of smile along.

Nancy chirped, "Come on into the kitchen. Henrie has a wonderful breakfast made. We can have a little bit of all that good stuff after a nice bowl of oatmeal with fruit."

Annie craved the good stuff. She could smell what was probably cinnamon bread or cinnamon French toast. As they walked through the dining room, Annie saw Kali and Ko, bookending the sides of the buffet, looking alternately welcoming to the guests and guarded for potential intruders to the feast.

Nancy smiled at everyone and went on to the kitchen, Honey Bear still on her shoulder.

Annie stopped to give each girl a quick full-body rub and to speak to the guests already gathered at the table. "Good morning! This is your last breakfast with us, isn't it?"

Four heads nodded, mouths full of what proved to be cinnamon French toast, or a bacon and egg casserole, or, Annie noticed, Brioche Au Chocolat. So far, no one had touched the oatmeal. It was very good oatmeal, but it wasn't cinnamon, bacon or chocolate. Her mouth started to water.

Finally, bite swallowed, a large man, taller than most with broad shoulders and a solid trunk, said, "We're leaving after breakfast to go home, but we've already made reservations for next year. We love coming to Chelsea this time of year, and this is the best B&B we've found. The private beach is outstanding, but the food would bring us back, no matter where in town you were located."

His wife, a slim 5'2" added, "This time I got recipes from Henrie. Last year I tried to replicate the breakfasts we had here, and it didn't work, but I asked, and he printed them out for me. I know some of these come from the Café and the Confectionary, but he got those recipes as well. Everyone here is so generous and friendly. Anywhere else we go, recipes are guarded like Fort Knox."

"Well, we aim to please. Did you get to do everything you wanted to do this time?"

The other woman, a medium-tall, large-boned woman who looked like a roller derby queen, said, "We did, but we weren't thinking big enough. Last night we talked about booking even more of your rooms next year to try out one of those mysteries that you have coming up this weekend. We checked; you still have a few rooms available the week we plan to come back."

"Yeah! We never thought about doing something like that. We had a fishing cruise this time on The Escape, but it sounds like fun to have a few days and nights on the boat and around town doing a mystery play."

Annie laughed. "This will be our second one. If it works out well, we'll run it for you next year, or you might want to pick another theme. We'll need a couple of months advance notice, and of course, we'll have to make sure The Escape is available."

"We checked with Ray. Right now, he has the days available. We're going to start calling people as soon as we get home. You'll hear from us within a couple of weeks."

"Great! I'm looking forward to it. Have a safe trip home, oh, and here are a few cards to take to your friends."

Annie noticed that Sassy Pants, Mr. Bean and Mo had taken up residence around the guests. Sassy Pants had decided the really big guy would be a push-over. She didn't want any food; she wanted to have her tummy tickled. She jumped onto the table and found room in between plates, bowls, silverware and glassware to get onto her back and offer her tummy to him. He happily obliged, using four very large fingers to tickle along the bottom of her belly.

"Sassy! Get off! It's rude to be on the table during breakfast!" Sassy Pants just looked at Annie with a glazed expression.

Mr. Bean and Mo jumped to the laps of the women of the group. They were happy to have one hand taking care of their needs while the women continued to eat.

"It's a wonder any guest returns with this kind of reception," Annie sighed.

"It's great. We've gotten used to seeing these cats around town, but we've not been honored with their presence at breakfast. Kali and Ko usually run a pretty tight ship."

Annie finally got the three of them moving and went on to the kitchen to face her own breakfast ship. It would be pretty tight as well, with her mother in charge.

Kali and Ko jumped off the buffet to join the family. They didn't want to miss out.

"Good morning, Sam, Henrie. What is everyone planning to do today?"

Any response was immediately stifled by an unexpected flurry of snarls, claws, quickly moving small bodies and a high-pitched screech.

"Kids!" yelled Annie and Nancy at the same time.

Everyone stopped. Nancy said, "You'd think they'd be used to him by now. Honestly, I don't know why other cats don't like Honey Bear. He's a perfectly wonderful cat."

"He gives off a vibe, Mom."

"A vibe?"

"A leave-me-alone-I'm-the-King-of-this-place vibe wherever he goes, whether it's his home or someone else's."

"Well, they should still get used to him."

With a sigh, Annie asked again, "What is everyone planning to do today?"

Sam, who loved being away from all responsibility for a month, said, "I'm going out on The Escape with Ray. He's got some guys going on a late season fishing expedition, and he invited me along. I'll do a little fishing, but mostly I'll just enjoy the lake, either on deck or from inside, looking out."

"Did you bring the right kind of gear to go out on the lake this time of year?"

"No, I wasn't thinking about it when we packed, but Ray said he has everything I'll need to stay warm and dry."

"It will be a great day, I'm sure. If the weather starts to turn, he won't be so far from shore that it will be dangerous."

Nancy chimed in, "Dangerous? It could be dangerous?"

"This is a turbulent season for being out on the lake. That's why fishing season has officially ended by now. But seasoned captains, like Ray, know how to stay safe on the lake. He'll stay shallow, and not very far from shore. If something kicks up, he'll get to land and tie up. It may not be at Chelsea, but it will be a safe harbor."

As Annie talked, she helped her plate to the good stuff, paying no attention to the bowl of oatmeal Nancy had placed in front of her.

Nancy rolled her eyes but said nothing.

"Mom, what are you going to do?"

"I was hoping you would come with me to Antiques On Main. I told Frank I would help him sort through some of the items that have been arriving from his storage places. He's seeing things he purchased years ago and he needs a second set of eyes. Also, I haven't had an opportunity to see the living quarters yet. Frank said he would love to give me a tour."

"Great. He's been doing a lot to it, and I haven't seen it yet. I probably won't stick around for the antique sorting. I wouldn't be any use to you there. The cats will be disappointed they can't come along."

"Why not? You let them go everywhere else."

"They don't leave The Avenue without human supervision. They've been to that building when it was a diner, but not since Frank bought it and moved in. Frank's cat is – personality wise – another Honey Bear. She's a one-cat cat. No other cat can cross that threshold now that it's her domain."

Speaking of leaving The Avenue, Tiger Lily was in the process of reminding Annie that she was being unfairly detained inside the Inn. She should have been at the Café over an hour ago. The breakfast rush was on, but she was locked in! No one else seemed to mind, but Tiger Lily knew what was expected of her.

Tiger Lily stood by the cat door in the kitchen, securely locked so Honey Bear couldn't get out of the house. She looked at Annie with cat eyes, willing her to look in that direction. Eventually, it worked. Annie's head turned to find that gaze full on her.

Annie said, "Sorry, big girl. We'll be leaving in a few minutes." Annie turned back to her mother. "I haven't taken a house-warming gift yet. After we have the tour, let's go shopping and find the perfect whatever. You're so much better at that than I."

"Good idea, honey. What in the world is she doing?"

Annie turned to look. Tiger Lily was now standing against the door, holding on with one paw while she slapped at it with another.

"She wants to go to work."

"Honestly, Annie. The things you let these cats do!"

By now, Tiger Lily was throwing herself at the door. It was a standing-up full-body slam. One. Look at Annie. Two. Look at Annie. Three. Four. Glance back and get ready for five.

"Okay! Okay! Don't hurt yourself, big girl! Who else wants to leave?" Suddenly there was a mad rush to the door. Little Socks, Mo, Sassy Pants and Mr. Bean, all of them wanting to get as far away from Uncle Honey Bear as possible.

"Mo, you go to the Confectionary first thing this morning, alright? Wait there until George gets to The Tap."

Mo gave a roll of his eyes that went unnoticed by the humans in the room.

Annie turned to make sure her mother had a strong grip on Honey Bear, then she unlatched the cat door. Five cats rushed out, and she closed and latched the door behind them.

18

"I think the kids are getting tired of being locked in."

"I appreciate that you are locking the doors, dear. It won't be long before things will be back to normal for them."

On the other side of the door, the cats gathered before walking up The Avenue to their respective places. Tiger Lily said, *"One more week of this and I'm going to go crazy."*

Little Socks looked sick. *"We have another week to go?"*

"I think so. I like Grandmommy and Grandpoppy. But that cat!"

Mr. Bean chimed in, *"What happened to him? Why's he so mean?"*

Little Socks answered, *"He's not mean. He just IS."*

Sassy Pants, confused, asked, *"What is is?"*

"'Is' means that Honey Bear just exists in his own world. He doesn't give a flying fig for any other cat, and he gives off a bad vibe." Tiger Lily always took time to explain things to the younger cats. Unlike Little Socks, who had no time for them.

Tiger Lily looked at Mo. *"You heard what Mommy said. You're supposed to go with Mr. Bean."*

"Trill?"

"Carlos is making new pet treats. Maybe he'll let you sample them."

Tiger Lily couldn't understand Mo, but sometimes she pretended to respond to him if she could make a statement that appeared to be in context. She decided she had guessed correctly about an appropriate response. This time. Because Mo had already taken off at a run, Mr. Bean hot on his tail.

Sassy Pants scooted along after them. She could go to the winery a little later as well; she decided a taste test of new treats would be fun.

19

Tiger Lily and Little Socks walked at a more sedate pace. *"I'm already late. No sense rushing and getting there out of breath."*

Little Socks answered, *"No sense rushing for any reason. There's no sun. I'm going to have to find a nice jacket for my nap."*

Having hurried along, Mo, Mr. Bean and Sassy Pants were soon sitting on top of the counter of Mr. Bean's Confectionary, buttering up the candy maker, Jerry, and the baker and manager, Carlos. Carlos reached into the display case to pull out three of his newest creations, cat treats made using recipes supplied by Annie's best friend.

Each cat, mindful of the awesome responsibility of being a personal taste tester, approached the job in the most professional manner possible. Sassy Pants sniffed the treat carefully before taking a cautious nibble. Mo bit the treat in half, taking one slow taste and one quick one. Mr. Bean gobbled the entire piece and looked around for more. Regardless of the method, the treats were a success.

Little Socks entered L'Socks' Virasana – her personal yoga studio – with a flick of her tail in farewell to Tiger Lily. Diana, the manager and main instructor, was leading a class. Little Socks walked slowly past the benches set against the windowed wall, sniffing jackets and purses as she went. She stopped when she came to an unusual smell. *"Pleasant. Possibly a Chihuahua,"* she thought. *"This will do."* She kneaded the jacket until it was suitably softened, turned around two times and lay down in the center with a contented sigh.

By the time Tiger Lily got to the Café – Tiger Lily's Café, the gathering place for all of Chelsea, townsfolk and tourists alike -- the breakfast rush had slowed to a fast-paced crawl. She walked in as several guests were leaving. She heard choruses of "We missed you, Tiger Lily," "It's good to see you," "I was worried about you," and "I had to choose breakfast all by myself this morning."

She acknowledged all with a polite nod of her head, a purr, and a flick of her tail.

As she jumped to the hostess stand, Trudie, the barista, came around to give her a hug. "My goodness, girl! You're late today!" Trudie turned and gave a shout to the kitchen. "Felicity, you don't have to call Annie. The big girl just got here!"

Felicity, the chef and manager, came around the corner and rushed to the hostess stand. "Tiger Lily! I was worried about you!"

Tiger Lily showed her appreciation for the concern by rubbing her head into Felicity's hand. They all turned to the business of serving the best darned food in town.

Chapter 2: Come On Up. Coffee's Ready.

Frank answered his intercom from the third floor. "Come on up. Coffee's ready."

Annie and Nancy were at the front door of Antiques On Main, the newest addition to the Chelsea business community. It was not open to the public yet, so the front door was kept locked, with an intercom system connected to each of the three floors.

Frank was a newcomer to Chelsea. Recently retired, he was fulfilling a life-long dream to own an antique business. Frank had an inauspicious beginning in Chelsea, but he settled in and became a fast friend of everyone on The Avenue.

He purchased this building, which recently housed a diner on the ground floor, to serve as his home, office, carpentry shop and display area. The store itself was ground level, with storage and carpentry on the second floor. He had nearly completed the renovation of the upstairs living area.

Annie walked around while Frank poured coffee and chatted with Nancy. Odd, thought Annie. Ultra-modern digs on top of the antique store. Perhaps an antique lifestyle 24/7 was a bit much.

She could tell Frank enjoyed this new lifestyle. He was working in his retirement, yes, but working at his avocation. He purchased antiques for years, mostly furniture items but other, smaller items as well. He filled one atmosphere-controlled unit after another. He couldn't remember all that he had, although he kept a meticulous inventory.

In earlier visits to the downstairs area, Frank shared his ideas regarding floor displays. Not knowing exactly what he had, and not knowing how items would come and go over the years, he designed the display floor much like an artists' showroom.

He purchased temporary walls that could be moved to accommodate larger and smaller groupings as needed. The floor was sturdy tile that could take a lot of punishment as furniture was moved from one part of the building to another.

The walls, both permanent and temporary, were painted eggshell, to keep the emphasis on the antiques. Frank placed ceiling hooks throughout the building; no matter where the walls stood, lamps, baskets and other items could hang from the ceiling.

He added a combination of can lighting and display lighting that could be adjusted to illuminate in the direction needed.

Now, as Annie walked around the converted apartment, she noted again the sense of light and color, this time mingled with glass and chrome instead of cherry and oak. Window coverings were minimal, letting natural light predominate. The walls, as the walls downstairs, were a neutral eggshell, but around the rooms were splashes of color. Modern art. Colorful metal wall sculptures. Comfortable furniture with splashes of color either on their upholstery or in the pillows and throws that adorned them. Coffee and end tables of glass and chrome held colorful lamps and pieces of art.

The bedroom was decidedly modern mannish, but with two large walk-in closets. One closet was empty. While she looked around the room, having stepped into the master bathroom, Frank came in. Annie smiled and asked, "Why are you keeping that closet empty, Frank?"

He laughed. "You probably know the answer to that."

"But your bedroom furniture is so…manly."

"Bedroom furniture that is going to be shared is best chosen by the two people that will be doing the sharing. We haven't gotten there yet. So I just brought what I had in Indiana."

"Nice to know."

"Yes. Nice to know. And you can keep it to yourself."

"Mum's the word."

"Are you talking to me, dear?" asked Nancy, coming around the corner. "Oh, Frank. This room looks so different from the rest of the place."

Frank and Annie just looked at one another and smiled.

"Let me show you the best room in the house!"

"Yes!" Annie knew where they were headed. The kitchen had two doors. One set of glass doors led outside to a deck adorned with a gas grill, table and chairs and a low storage cabinet that could function either as a low table or a bench for sitting. It was a great deck.

The second door from the kitchen led to a narrow stairway leading to the roof garden. Garden, in this case, was a misnomer. Frank had no intention of puttering around with vegetables and flowers.

He did, however, have a low brick wall surrounding the space with a higher u-shaped brick wall along each side and to the back, so parties or intimate encounters would be private from the rest of the town. Just inside the higher wall was what appeared to be a small storage shed.

Because the state park surrounded the town, Frank's roof garden looked out on the park to the right, straight down to the businesses on the north side of The Avenue, left and down to Annie's businesses with the park behind them, and over, straight ahead, to the lake. And the sunsets. The glorious sunsets.

The sunset could be viewed from the kitchen windows or from the back deck and would, Annie decided, be beautiful from that vantage point. But from up here, they would be fabulous.

Annie lived on the third floor of the Inn, and her sunset deck was on the same floor. This was a floor higher, and a bit further removed from the lake, but with nothing in between to hamper the view. And no one on either side of Frank had yet to come up with the idea. His was the only roof garden on the street.

He added all-weather rockers, Adirondack chairs, benches and end tables. No adornments, no potted plants, no silk flowers. It was a place to enjoy the moment. The right kind of place for a no-fuss-no-muss man.

Frank said to Annie, "You know, now that I'm on the block party committee, I thought we could have the next meeting here. I know we planned to meet at Sassy P's, but what about here? And at sunset? It's a little cool this time of year, but we could dress warmly, and it would be a kind of housewarming party."

"That's a great idea! I'll have Jesus put together some chilled white wines and a crockpot mulled cider. We can get some snacks together and have a great time. Hopefully we'll get some work done too!"

Frank looked at Nancy. "You may not have planned to go to the block party meeting before, but you're welcome to come to this one. You don't have to work, just enjoy the sunset."

"Well, I've been enjoying them so much from the Inn, I can't imagine how beautiful they will be from up here! Sam and I will love it!"

They went back through the apartment, leaving their coffee cups while heading to the main floor. Nancy had already spied some bins she would sort through, so she went toward them as Annie waved good-bye to head toward the Café. On her way out, she let Mem in.

"Good morning, Mem! You're making my first call easy! We're moving the block party meeting to Frank's rooftop garden. We'll start at 6:00 so we'll be able to watch the sunset after our meeting. Well, during our meeting. Well, maybe we'll finish early."

"Great! I'll bring some carafes for hot water and several different teas. Is your mother here? Frank said she would be helping him sort through some things."

"Yes. She's already going through some bins."

"Great. I wanted to spend some more time with her. She's going to be a good friend, I just know it. Even though she's only here on occasion."

Once inside, Mem looked first for Frank. He was working on a temporary wall, setting it in place, and hadn't noticed she had entered. What he did notice was a low hiss.

Claire, his blue point Himalayan cat, normally loved people. However, she hated cats. She had picked up on the scent of Honey Bear on Nancy. Honey Bear seemed to find cats that didn't like him without even leaving a building. Claire had taken up residence on a table near the bin Nancy was sorting through and had decided glaring wasn't enough. She added the sound effects.

26

Frank admonished Claire. "Claire, darling, be polite."

When Mem answered with, "Yes, Claire, darling, do be polite," Frank's heart gave a lurch and he was certain he jumped five feet off the ground.

Nancy turned to say, "Mem! It's so good to see you!"

Frank wiped the top of his forehead with a handkerchief.

Mem laughed, gave him a kiss on the cheek, and went over to help Nancy sort while they chatted and gossiped.

"Women," said Frank, including both Claire and Mem in the statement.

Mem and Nancy spent the rest of the morning going through small items, deciding where and how to best display them, and getting that accomplished. As they worked, they chatted.

Nancy, suddenly looking at her watch, said, "Oh, my! It's nearly lunchtime. Can I treat you to lunch at the café?"

"Oh, no, but thank you. I need to be at the high school by 12:30. I'm teaching a lunch-time class on social media. It's not anything that students receive credit for attending, but every now and then I go in to catch as many students as I can – those that want to be caught, that is – to bring them up to date with the changes in technology. The good and the bad."

"Oh, how fascinating. I need to learn more about all of this stuff. Facebook and that new thing that Annie has – what she has her meetings with now – Skike?"

"Skype."

"That. Yes. What do you know about that?"

"I set that up for Annie and her staff, and actually, for all of us on The Avenue. I even added Frank to the group."

"Can you show me what I need to know? So I can stay in touch with Annie when we go home?"

"Certainly. It's easy to set up. I'll come over this evening and show you everything you need to know.

"Thank you! Why don't you come over around 6:00, and I'll have a little something ready for supper. Either something I whip up or something from the Café."

"I was going to spend the evening with Frank. How about I bring him along with me. He and Sam can keep one another company.

Mo and Sassy Pants stayed as long as they felt welcome at Mr. Bean's Confectionary. Actually, they started feeling unwelcome as soon as Carlos decided they had eaten enough treats to last a week.

Sassy Pants looked at Mo and said, *"Let's blow on this place."* Mo, knowing that once again, Sassy Pants had screwed up a reasonably good human phrase, just shook his head. But he agreed with Sassy Pants.

Mr. Bean had been making a perfect fool of himself in the windowsill, dancing around, inviting people to come in, and they bought it! Mo couldn't believe how many people came in just to pet that darned kitten and then wandered over to the display counter to purchase something.

Mo couldn't tell Sassy Pants what he was thinking, because only Kali and Ko could completely translate what he trilled. But he thought, *"I don't have to work that hard at my place. Women just come in and want to be with me. I'm a love magnet."*

As if Sassy Pants was thinking in sync, she said, *"I don't dance neither. I rolls on my back and gets tickles."*

Mo looked at Sassy Pants in amazement, and they walked out together. Before hooking a right, Mo stopped to watch Sassy Pants hook a left and walk away. He then moved on to the business next door and stepped into the cool, muted atmosphere of the upscale blues bar, Mo's Tap. Sassy Pants went to the next building on the other side of the Confectionary. She stood back to wait for a couple walking into Sassy P's Wine & Cheese, then followed them in at a trot, angling for a good place to wiggle her stuff.

Annie decided to check up on the kids before going to the Café for lunch. She went first to Sassy P's, calling Chris from her cell phone while she walked.

When he answered, she said, "What time can you meet me for lunch at the Café?"

"1:00 would work out pretty well. Is that good for you?"

"Sure. Gives me time to check on the kids and help Felicity through the worst of the lunch rush. "

"See you soon."

She hung up just as she reached the winery. The bell jingled as she walked in. Minnie looked up from behind the bar and waved. She was talking to a middle-aged couple, finding out their tastes in wine before deciding which bottles to open. Annie could see she had already stocked the display cases with crackers and a wide variety of cheeses for the day.

Annie didn't see either Jesus or Sassy Pants, so she walked through to the back garden area. The garden was still open, even though it was late in the season. Only one of the window walls had been pulled partially shut, keeping most of the breeze out but still allowing fresh air to permeate. Soon, though, they would have to pull it completely and then pull the second, matching wall as well. This made for a two-layer closing, and with the use of an infrared space heater, a smaller, cozy back dining room would be available for tasting and snacking all winter long.

Jesus was at the back bar, stocking some reds, while making sure the customers at three tables had everything they needed. Sassy Pants was enthralling – and being enthralled by – the women in the middle of the room.

Annie went to that table first. "Holly, Jolly, it's good to see you." Holly and Jolly were twins who survived their childhood with constant teasing. They continually asked their parents for new names. As adults, however, they enjoyed the unusual nature of their naming and made light of it. Together, they owned DoubleGood, a combination hardware and electronics store on the other side of The Avenue.

Sassy Pants, as all of the cats, was especially drawn to Holly, who, since the age of eight, lived in a wheelchair. Jolly was used to it.

"Hey, Annie. How's the visit going with your folks?"

"I really enjoy having them here. The kids don't like their Uncle Honey Bear, but otherwise, it's been great. What are the two of you doing here so early? Is your store closed already?"

"No," answered Holly. "We're trying to break in some new counter help, and it was time for us to leave the store and let him sink or swim."

"So what happens if he is sinking and the two of you are deep into your second bottle of wine?"

"We don't go that far in! At least not when we're doing a test run."

"By the way, we've moved the block party meeting to Frank's rooftop garden, so we can do a little sunset gazing while we work."

Holly and Jolly looked at one another. Jolly said, "Okay, so, how do we get up there?"

"Oh!" said Annie, surprised. "I'm sorry. I thought everyone knew, but then again, how could you? Frank extended his elevator. It goes all the way up to the top. He intends to use that garden for all kinds of neighborhood and charity parties, so he wanted to make sure everyone could use it."

"You're kidding!"

"No. That's one of the first things he did. There was an old, small elevator in the building, but that wasn't good enough for his furniture. He replaced it with a freight elevator and, while he was at it, put a shed on the roof and took it all the way up. It's a sturdy shed, to withstand wind gusts, and it gives him a little bit of storage space as well as a sheltered area to get on and off the elevator. He's got a generator for his building, so if the power goes down, it will still work."

"I'm liking him better and better," said Holly.

Jolly chimed in, "Me, too. I hope he and Mem are still getting along well."

"I think it's going along as well as can be expected for two independent people of their age. They both know what they want out of life."

"*Meh!*"

"Oh! Excuse me, sweet girl," said Holly to Sassy Pants. I forgot I was supposed to be paying attention to you. Forgive me."

Annie stopped by to say hello to Jesus on her way out. I just wanted to check on the kids. They've been a bit beside themselves with their uncle visiting.

Jesus laughed. He had visited the Inn to meet the infamous uncle and had nothing but sympathy for Annie's kids. "I understand."

"We're having the block party meeting on Frank's rooftop. Do you know if it will be you or Minnie attending?"

"Not sure yet, but I'll make sure you have everything you need."

"Great. Chilled whites, a crockpot of something mulled, and some crackers and cheese?"

"You got it."

"There's a freight elevator, so maybe I'll stop in at Bloomin' Crazy and borrow the wagon. As long as everything fits in there, it should be a breeze."

Annie's next stop was at Mr. Bean's Confectionary. Mr. Bean had danced himself to a frazzle. He was sleeping it off on top of a soft, much loved pillow in the windowsill. He didn't even wake up when Annie entered.

Carlos came to the counter when he heard the bell. He smiled when he saw Annie and called Jerry to the front. Jerry, a shy, talented candy maker who learned his skill on the wrong side of the wire in federal prison, had an assignment to complete every time Annie was near. Per instructions from Carlos, Jerry was to initiate a conversation about something – anything – until Carlos was sure he had broken the shyness gene.

Jerry came out with a slice of "safe conversation" in his hand. "Hi, Annie. I've made a new chocolate for you."

"Another one? How do you come up with them?"

"I like to surf the net when I'm not working. I go over to Mem's and settle in with a pot of tea and just surf around. I find a lot of my best ideas out there. But this one, I got this idea from Laila."

"Laila?"

"Yeah. When she was here helping Carlos with his new pet treats, she gave me an idea for this truffle."

"What is it?"

"This one has dark chocolate – I made some with milk chocolate too – sweet curry powder and coconut."

"Oh, my. Can I have a few? I'll take them over to the Café to have several people taste them at lunch."

"Sure. I'll get a box."

When Jerry was gone, Annie said to Carlos, "He's an absolute genius."

"I know. Thank you again for giving him a chance."

"I'm not giving him a chance. You hired him."

"You know what I mean. You could have flipped the switch at any time."

"Hey, change of subject. Whichever of you is coming to the block party meeting, we're having it at Frank's rooftop garden."

"Oh, well, I guess both of us will be there! We'll be closing when it starts, so I'll send Jerry on and join you as soon as the last customer is gone."

"Great. Bring some chocolate. Anything. Candy, cake, pie…."

"Done."

Annie stopped at the window on her way out, waking the little guy up to stroke his cheek. He was stretching his way back into the world of the living as she left.

At Mo's Tap, she first saw George behind the bar. She stopped to say hello and let her eyes adjust. A few tables had lunchtime customers. The kitchen served small plate lunches, the menu varying with the whims of the cook. The cook, called Cookie, just because, really wanted to be a chef. He spent as much time as he could learning the trade from Felicity; her flair for the unique was rubbing off on him. Annie had a hard time getting to know him. She finally decided he didn't want to be "known" by the owner, so she stopped at "hello" whenever she saw him.

Today the menu included bruschetta with ham, olives and oranges, and roasted, browned red potato slices seasoned and served with mango salsa. Annie's mouth was watering again. It was a wonder she wasn't a 300 pound behemoth.

"George," she said, "we're having our block party meeting on Frank's, rooftop. Which of you will be coming?"

"I'm not sure. One of us will be there. I hope it's me!"

Candice, George's lead server, and, for the last couple of months, George's lead squeeze, was serving small plates and beer to a table in the middle of the room.

And there was Mo. Of course. In the middle of the room where he could see everyone, gauging if someone coming in might be a better mark. But not today. Nope. In the middle of the room, enjoying small plates and craft beer for lunch, were Clara from Bloomin' Crazy, Cheryl from The Marina, and Jennifer and Marie from The Drug Store and The Clinic. All were businesses here on The Avenue. All were in love with Mo.

"So, he's hooked you into drinking with lunch now?"

Clara laughed. "We're stopping at the one, but gracious! These craft beers are so good!"

"And how does it taste with long cat hairs?"

"Mo doesn't let his hair fall in."

"Oh. Well, I don't want to keep you all from eating; I was just checking on the big boy. His uncle is driving him a little looney these days."

"At least when he's here, he can forget that golden ball of fur," said Clara. She had the pleasure of meeting Honey Bear on a few occasions. "I haven't seen Kali or Ko since he came to visit. I think they must be upstairs hiding when he's downstairs. He's a beautiful cat, and he is very loving. If you're a human."

"That's the key. Humans love him. By the way, ladies, we are having the block party meeting at Franks' place, up on his rooftop garden."

"Just in time to see the sunset! I can't wait!"

"He expects to make it a party place."

"I think you can count on 100% attendance!"

Annie waved good-by and headed next to L'Socks Virasana. She didn't intend to stay long there. A) Little Socks didn't care to visit. B) Diana was usually busy with a class. C) Annie didn't care to do yoga. But she wanted to stop in.

Diana was, indeed, busy with a class. Annie sat on the windowsill next to Little Socks, who was curled up in a jacket. Annie didn't know it was her third jacket of the day. She pulled out her cell phone and sent a text to Diana, saying hello and letting her know of the meeting location.

Annie gave Little Socks a long, deep pet, and Little Socks responded by doing absolutely nothing. Didn't even open an eye.

Chapter 3: I Need Help In The Back!

As Annie got to Tiger Lily's Café, she saw almost perfect bedlam. One of her most steady servers arrived at the kitchen window to yell, "I need help in the back!" before hurrying to the coffee station with drink orders.

Tiger Lily sat stiffly at the hostess stand with a worried expression on her face, looking through the dining room to the back area.

Trudie didn't even respond to Annie walking in. She was busy listening to two servers, reading notes in front of her for orders for other servers, pouring, mixing and brewing.

Servers rushed from one table to the next, frazzling the customers with their own haste and confusion.

Cooks threw plates onto the serving counter, yelling, "Order up!" giving servers no clue as to whose order it was.

Annie quickly saw the problem.

Two tour busses arrived at the same time; apparently neither of them bothered to forewarn the Café. In addition to a full dining room of regulars, the back room was quickly set with two long tables to accommodate an additional 50 to 60 people.

Hurrying in behind Annie were two servers on their day off, called by Felicity to come in "right now." They were followed by an off-duty cook who looked like he needed at least two more hours of sleep. And a shower and a shave.

Annie knew what to do in a crisis rush. Her first stop was the kitchen. "Felicity, do you need me back here?"

"No, Annie, thanks. Most people are ordering specials, and we prepped for lots of those. I think Trudie's in the soup, though."

"Got it."

On her way out, she stopped to give a pep talk to the cooks. "No one will leave until you have served them the best meal they are going to have all day. Remember, you can't think if you're not breathing. When you realize you're holding your breath, let it go, take in one big one, and start breathing again. Work with your servers. They need you now."

One by one, they got back to work, calmer, more relaxed.

At the server station, she did a quick version of the same speech. "Take a deep breath. Take another deep breath. You are the best servers on the planet. You can do this. Work with your cooks. Work with Trudie. You're doing great."

Annie got behind the coffee bar. Trudie was running out of supplies. She said, "I'm going to stock up first, then you can tell me what you need me to do."

Trudie nodded in Annie's direction.

Felicity had been right. Her specials today sounded so good, almost everyone ordered them, locals and tourists alike. That was both a blessing and a curse. Annie decided to concentrate on the blessing part.

She and Trudie worked together for the next hour, making drinks, often taking them to the tables to help out the servers, and continually filling up supplies.

Tiger Lily, calmer now that Annie was present, returned to doing her job, greeting guests and making them feel welcome. She decided the tour bus groups needed a little special "something," since they had been greeted so rudely in the beginning. She slid down from the hostess stand, trotted to the back room, and jumped up to several table ledges – made especially for her – to say hello, give a purr, or accept a pet here and there. She knew how to work a room.

At some point, Annie saw Chris from the corner of her eye, but it was just a glimpse. Funny, it looked like he was taking photos. When she had time to look around, he was gone.

A little later she saw a purple day lily at the hostess stand with a note attached. When Trudie no longer needed her, she went to the stand. Tiger Lily was back; she had placed her body lengthwise on the flower, from stem to bloom, rolling her head every now and then into the petals.

Oh, well. Annie took the card – it had a few tooth marks in it now – and saw it was to her from Chris. It read, "I'll call you later."

Realizing she was on her own for lunch, she asked Trudie and Felicity if they had time to sit down with her. They didn't have time, really, but they certainly had the inclination. They were beat! Felicity told everyone to take a break if they could. She then plated up portions of the daily specials.

Everyone had a cup of roasted pumpkin soup, and they shared what was left of the parmesan black pepper biscuits and the spinach and tomato puffs. Before long, one of the cooks came out with several bacon grilled cheese sandwiches on sour dough bread cut in half for sharing. While servers and cooks rested tired feet, Trudie made several cups of pumpkin spice latte and s'mores coffee. Annie brought out the box of chocolates for dessert and cut them in half so everyone could enjoy a taste.

Tiger Lily, as tired as everyone else, lay sound asleep on top of the hostess stand, having enjoyed several bites of spinach puffs and bacon.

All good things must come to an end. Eventually, customers started to drift in for mid-afternoon snacks. Tiger

Lily roused herself and one by one, cooks, servers, Trudie, Felicity and Annie got up, cleaned up after themselves and got back to work.

Annie pulled out her cell phone to call Chris, but before she could dial, he walked in.

"Thanks for the flower."

"You're welcome. I didn't put it in a vase for you."

"It was better this way. Tiger Lily loved it."

Chris looked down and noticed for the first time the crushed blossom. Tiger Lily sat on the stem while pushing her head into Chris's hand. The purple day lily petals were scattered on the stand and the floor.

"Well, I'm glad it was a hit. So, you were pretty busy over the lunch period."

"Apparently two tour companies conspired to hit us at once without notice. Generally they're pretty good about letting us know they're coming, but sometimes these late season tours are handled by guides in training, and they don't always remember to call ahead."

"Did you say something to them?"

"Didn't have time. I'll give the companies a call in a day or two, so they can make sure to include this little courtesy in their training. We love it when they come; it would have been great to have enough staff on hand before they got here. And food. We squeaked by with the food. There were some leftovers for us."

"Do you think I can see you this evening?"

"Let me give Mom a call and see what she and Sam are going to be doing. It seems like I'm always putting you off."

"It does indeed." Chris gave her a kiss on the cheek and started to leave.

"Hey, when I saw you earlier, it looked like you were taking pictures?"

"I meant to ask you first, but I certainly would have asked before going much further. I have an idea for some charcoals to sell at the block party. I thought doing charcoals – with a splash of color somewhere – of the local companions might be a good idea. Cats, dogs, turtles, ferrets…I know most of the companions here on The Avenue, but I could branch out and get to know some of the others in town as well."

"That's a great idea! And by the way, Frank is hosting the meeting on his rooftop garden."

"Nice. Well, if I don't see you before, we'll at least get a sunset in."

As Chris left, Annie moved over to the hostess stand to hold Tiger Lily close. "It was a busy lunch, wasn't it, big girl?"

Purring, Tiger Lily replied, *"Yes, it was. You should have gotten here a little earlier than you did."*

"I probably should have come straight over from the antique shop. I didn't pay any attention to the tour busses today."

"You were probably visiting those silly kids who don't work nearly as hard as I do."

"I wonder if you ever wish you could spend more time at the yoga studio and nap all day long."

"That would be boring. But a little less busy would be good."

"I saw you go to the back and work the room for a little bit. You really do have the charm needed to be a great hostess."

"I know. You need me."

"I really need you."

"Are we having a moment? Do you understand me?"

"I sure wish I could understand you."

Suddenly, the hostess stand was filled with a great big dog.

"Cyril! It's good to see you! Let me get you a treat."

Pete, the Police Chief, stood at the open door, holding it for a couple as they left.

"Man, I love this fall weather. Cool, crisp, well, kind of dreary today, but much nicer for walking around outside. Cyril likes it, too."

"Is anything exciting happening around town today, Pete?"

"No. Boring. A few tourists, but that traffic is slowing down, and no crime. Sometimes I wish we had a little crime. It would fill in the hours."

"Well, maybe we can get some going for you. I'll do my best to cook something up."

"No, thank you. Last time you got involved, it was a little bit worse than exciting."

"Pete, all of your kids are old enough to stay by themselves for a couple of hours in the evening, right?"

"Sure, as long as it's just a couple of hours."

"Why don't you bring Janet to the next block party meeting? Frank is going to have it on his rooftop garden, and it will be kind of a housewarming / sunset party."

"She'd love it. I don't think she has anything else on that evening, so she can probably come."

As Pete moved on to a table, Nancy came in.

"Have you had lunch?"

"Yes. Henrie and I had soup and a sandwich at Mr. Bean's. That little kitten is a hoot."

"He is. He is a bundle of energy. Sometimes more than the other kids can handle. Are Sam and Ray still out on the lake?"

"I got a call just a few minutes ago. They're at The Marina. After they clean a few fish, Sam will head back to the Inn. We're going to have supper with Frank and Mem tonight. They're coming over, and she's going to teach me a little bit about this Facebook and Skike."

"Skype."

"Yes. Skike. Since you have it, I thought it would be a good idea to see if Sam and I can learn to use it. That way, we could keep in closer touch."

"What in the world brought this up?"

"Well, we were just talking while we worked at the shop. I didn't know Mem was so good with all of this young stuff. I'm only about 10 years older than she. If she can teach it, I can learn it."

Annie tried hard not to roll her eyes. "Can I get anything for you while you're here?"

"I thought I would take something for supper that would pop right into the oven or microwave. I invited them for supper, but I don't want to mess up Henrie's kitchen."

"We have lots of things that microwave well. We also have cold items, like sushi and other appetizers. We could put together several small plates to share."

"That sounds wonderful. Tell you what, I'll sit down and look at the menu. I might get something cold to drink."

"Trudie has been selling her hot drinks like crazy, but she has some great cold drinks also. She has a mango lassi and a pomegranate and cranberry Bellini on special today, or we can get you something straight, like lemonade or iced tea."

"I'll try that pomegranate drink. That sounds about as decadent as I want go."

"As long as you have dinner plans, I may go out for a bite to eat with Chris. Would that be a problem?"

"Oh, no, dear. Do you want to join us?"

"I don't want to intrude. You already have your evening planned." Annie was pleased her mother was comfortable enough to make Chelsea a second home, and these friends – Annie's friends – a second family. And she was pleased to have an evening to herself.

Really, Annie thought to herself, these visits would be very pleasant if Mom and Sam did what they wanted and we saw one another once or twice a day. Maybe this is the start of a new era for us. Or not. There was still Uncle Honey Bear to consider. He upset the kids and disrupted the flow of the household, because they had to keep all the cat doors allowing access to "out" locked. Maybe she could convince her mother to keep Honey Bear in her room. Or maybe she could give them the lower floor of the carriage house. Maybe.

Annie asked Trudie to make the drink and took a tour of the Café to see if she could help anyone. Only a few tables were filled, and the servers and cook who thought they had the day off were gone, back to doing whatever they had been doing before the rude interruption.

Felicity sat at a table, notebook in front of her, trolling the Internet. She looked tired. Or bored.

"Looking for ideas?"

"Sometimes my creativity hits a low point and I have to see what other people are doing."

"That could be creative also. You might find something that's being done in Paris that no one in Chelsea could ever imagine."

"Paris. That's a thought."

Felicity typed in some search terms and suddenly perked up, interested once again.

Annie decided it was time she went on her way. She stopped at Nancy's table to see if she could help in any way, realized Nancy was fine on her own, said good-bye to those within hearing distance, stopped at the hostess stand and said, "Come on, big girl. Let's blow this place."

On their way, they stopped and picked up all of the kids. They didn't like going home early, but there was no getting around it for now.

Back at the Inn, Annie found Henrie tending to the laundry. Henrie was an enigma. For several years, he managed a five-star hotel in New York City. For whatever reason, he decided to leave that life and come to this small resort community where he was chief cook, bottle washer and toilet bowl cleaner of a bed and breakfast. He never talked about his background, his accent was difficult to place, and his manner was unfailingly formal. She loved him.

"Henrie, Mom invited Frank and Mem to dinner tonight, and in return, Mem is going to teach Mom how to Skype."

"How charming. Will you be joining them?"

"No. I think Chris and I will take the opportunity to have some alone time."

"I'll prepare something for your mother."

"No, you won't need to worry about it. She's at the Café picking out some things to carry in. She may use the microwave or oven, but that's about it. She doesn't want to dirty up your kitchen."

"Oh, my. She needn't worry."

"I know. She will, though. She'll be fine on her own."

"How about you? Can I prepare something for you and Chris?"

"We'll go out, but thanks. Who's next on the schedule?"

"No one, really, until the crew starts to arrive for the mystery tour."

It's funny, thought Annie, how we pick up these terms. So many of their guests booked rooms with them and also booked a trip of some variety on The Escape, a small yacht refurbished into a fishing and cruise ship. The experience on The Escape was meant to be a working experience, so participants were also crew members. If there were a combo set coming to the Inn, Henrie, Annie and almost everyone else on The Avenue thought of them as "the crew."

"We'll have guests that evening, but if you can get away, we're having the block party meeting on Frank's rooftop garden. The sunset should be fantastic."

"I will do everything in advance that I can, to be able to get away for an hour or so."

"Where are the girls?"

"I think they're napping on the second floor sitting area. What little sun we have today is shining through those windows."

As Annie started up the stairs, she heard Sam come in.

"Sam. How was the fishing?"

"Cold, windy, cold, and then we had some more wind, but I tell ya, it was fun!"

"Did you catch anything?"

"I did! I caught a big old hunk of plastic bags all wrapped around some trash. I can't believe how people use that lake as their personal garbage can."

"I know. We have to clean up our beach almost every day. It looks so pristine, but we have to work at it. Actually, it's a great job for several high school students. They trade off by the week, so no one has to do it all the time. They get credit in their environmental class, and Henrie pays them a combination of an hourly fee and a per pound fee for trash. And sometimes they find a treasure. It works out well for everyone, but I wish we didn't have to do it."

"I don't suppose you know where your mother is?"

"She's at the Café, choosing items for supper. You and she are hosting Frank and Mem for dinner tonight, and then Mem is going to teach Mom, and you, too, if you want, how to Skype."

"How to what?"

"Skype. Get the word right, because you are always going to be correcting Mom on that one."

"And what is it?"

"It's talking to people like talking to them on the telephone, but you can see them."

"Oh. That sci-fi stuff. I'll probably leave that to her, but by golly, I'll bet I can sit behind her while she does it, and people will think I'm doing it too!"

"That's the idea! Anyway, you're doing that this evening – hope that's alright – and in a couple of nights you're going to come to our block party meeting, because we're having it on Frank's rooftop garden. It will be a real treat to see the sunset from up there."

"I think the only reason you live here is so you can see those sunsets. Mind you, they're awfully pretty, but I don't know that I'd plan my life around them like you all seem to do."

"What would you plan your life around?"

"Pie."

"Pie. That's an idea. Hey, before we plan everything for you without letting you get a word in edgewise, is there anything you want to do?"

"Well, I'm going to meet that real estate fellow, Greg, and we're going to go beachcombing. He said he knows a couple of beaches that tend to get really good driftwood. I thought I would make some things to sell for charity at that block party of yours."

"That's a great idea!"

"I do have a few skills. And do you remember what's coming up in few days?"

"Your anniversary."

"You're right. I want to take your mother someplace special. Now, not that I don't like your places, I like 'em all, but I want to take her someplace different. Someplace special. Do you have any ideas?"

"There's a great restaurant in a town about 20 miles from here, Marsh Haven. It's a pretty drive up the coast. I'll get online and get a menu for you, to see if it's something you'd like to consider. You can take a car from the Inn."

"That's a great idea. Let's keep it a secret for now. Just don't let your mother go planning all kinds of things for that day, or at least for that evening."

Annie went up to the second floor landing, where all seven cats lounged in what little specks of sunlight were left for the day. A couple only had paws in a speck of sun, because Kali and Ko had taken the good spots first. They made room for Mo, but the others had to find sun where they could. Annie sat at the notebook and found the menu for Sam, printed it out and took it downstairs.

As she was going down, Honey Bear was going up. Sure enough, in a matter of seconds, there was enough hissing and spitting to scare anyone who didn't know it was coming.

Annie left the kids to their own devices and continued downstairs. Sam and Henrie were getting ready to share a small pot of coffee while Sam regaled Henrie with his heroic activities of the day. Cleaning the lake of its trash, indeed.

Chapter 4: Mr. Bean Pounced On Her Chest

Annie woke refreshed for the first time in weeks. She was already awake when Mr. Bean pounced on her chest to get his morning kiss, and had nearly finished her first cup of coffee when Sassy Pants rounded the corner of the kitchen island to let out a snarl at her Uncle Honey Bear.

Tiger Lily and Little Socks came running. Again. You would think they would know this would happen by now and come out first thing to rid their home of its unwelcome guest. But, no. Every morning, another cat found him before the older sisters came running to the rescue.

Today was going to be a good day. She just knew it.

She and Chris had enjoyed an evening together – alone – for the first time in weeks. They celebrated by going to the very restaurant Annie told Sam about. It was in Marsh Haven, far enough away they stood a chance of not being seen by anyone from Chelsea. It was pricey. It was "just dark enough." It was a great break from everything she was used to.

Today, she had absolutely nothing planned. She would spend some quality time with her mother. She would help Henrie get ready for their mystery crew. Maybe she wouldn't set foot outside the Inn all day. Just stay in.

Huh. Wonder how long that plan will last.

Soon, her mother was on the phone, yes, it was another marvelous day for a walk, and Annie, you really must start getting up earlier so you can join me, but come on down for breakfast, dear, and bring Honey Bear with you.

And so it began.

Breakfast this morning was simple. There were no guests to feed, so Henrie had opted to fix everything on his own, with nothing added from the Café or the Confectionary.

He fixed oatmeal with cranberries and blueberries. He made "plain old" bacon and eggs and wheat toast. He put out locally-made jam, a pitcher of orange juice and a carafe of coffee. It was delicious.

Kali and Ko, having no guests to take care of, sat in morning sunbeams on the kitchen counter, while Tiger Lily and Little Socks kept Honey Bear sequestered in a corner. Mo, having roused later than anyone else, wandered down when breakfast was almost finished, but soon enough to get a taste of bacon from Sam.

Sassy Pants and Mr. Bean ran up and down the library and television room, one chasing the other. Every now and then humans heard a very loud sound followed by a few seconds of silence. Then play resumed. Henrie closed his eyes and breathed in deeply when this happened.

Annie explained to Nancy and Sam, "I think this is the first morning you've been here when we had no guests. This is typical behavior. They are very polite and quiet – at least on the first and second floors – whenever guests are present. They love having the house to themselves. Sort of. No one but family around. Mr. Bean is still a kitten, and Sassy Pants is barely older than kitten herself.

Sam said, "That Honey Bear has never been a kitten. I swear, his top speed is three inches per minute."

"Sam!" exclaimed Nancy. "He's just very sedate. Well, moving on, what is everyone doing today?"

Henrie responded, "I have to start getting the house ready for the mystery crew. And no, Annie, I do not need any assistance. Enjoy your day doing something fun."

Sam said, "I think it's a beautiful day for Greg and me to go beachcombing. It will give me an excuse to get out and drive around a little, and take a walk on the beach myself."

"You don't need an excuse like that, Sam. You could walk with me in the morning."

"Yes, dear, I could. Or then again, I could walk on my own."

The conversation lagged a little after that last rejoinder.

"Mom, we didn't go shopping yesterday like I'd hoped for a gift for Frank's house. Could we do that?"

"Oh, I'd love to."

"And tell me how the Skype training went last night."

"I think we're going to have fun with it! Sam and I need to get a computer, and we need to get an Internet account, but Mem said we can probably do that with the company that provides our television. If we buy a computer before we leave Chelsea, she'll help us set it up. That way, we'll only have to have the phone company help us get online when we get home."

"Wonderful! Are you going shopping for the computer here in town?"

"She said we need to go to DoubleGood and ask Holly or Jolly to find exactly what we need."

"Do you want to do that today as well?"

"Sure. That way, if they have to order it in, we'll still have plenty of time before we go home. Where do you want to shop for Frank's gift?"

"I'd like to look around here on The Avenue. If we can't find anything here, go into town. If that doesn't work, I'll guess we'll have to do a little driving."

"Certainly we'll find something perfect right here."

The phone rang, and Henrie answered it. "Good morning, Greg. Yes, he's right here."

Handing the phone to Sam, he said, "The two of you were having a moment of Karma. Today will be beachcombing day."

Annie suddenly said, "Tiger Lily, Little Socks, it's time you got to work!"

Tiger Lily jumped up, surprised. She had been so intent on keeping Honey Bear in his place she had forgotten all about the breakfast rush! And Mommy hadn't helped!

"Good grief, I'm going to get an awful reputation!"

"Oh, hush. It's kind of nice to not have to run out of the house first thing in the morning every day."

"I like the rush. And anyway, my work is done by the middle of the afternoon."

"The rest of us have to work a little longer. Think of poor Mo. His place is open until really late."

"But he doesn't stay late. They push him out the door as soon as they start lighting the candles."

Both Tiger Lily and Little Socks started laughing, rolling over on their backs because their legs were weak from the strain.

Mo heard it all. He walked over to sit on Tiger Lily's butt.

"Hiss!"

Mo calmly stood up and moved on. Kali and Ko, watching from the counter, said, at the same time, *"Mo, don't let them get to you." "Mo, they're just jealous."*

Annie yelled, "Sassy Pants! Mr. Bean! Time to leave!"

The two little ones came running. Annie checked to make sure Nancy had a firm grip on Honey Bear, then she opened the door for everyone else. "Mo, go to the yoga studio today for a little while. When George gets in, you can go to the Tap."

"Trill."

Tiger Lily, tired of guessing, looked to Kali and Ko before walking out the door. They said together, *"He's tired of being the one that has to go with someone else every morning." "He wants to go to the Tap and take a nap until George gets in."*

At L'Socks' Virasana, a class was in session. There was sunshine today, so Little Socks didn't need to find a jacket. She went straight to a sunbeam and curled up.

Mo found the class exciting. He wandered around, curling his tail around a leg here, an arm there. Every now and then he found a neck low enough to wrap around. The class didn't seem to mind. In fact, since they were all women, they loved having him. Mo had that effect on females of the human race. He was right. He was a love magnet.

Diana let him be. If anyone had a problem with him, they would say something. Until then, she enjoyed watching him work the room.

Pete's daughter, Ginger, was there today, watching Diana teach the class. She would teach the next one. She was a senior in high school, and they allowed her to go to work a couple of mornings a week for credit. As she waited, Mo noticed her and decided sitting on a lap was preferable to wandering around the room. He hopped up, and as he always expected, she opened her arms to him and made sure he was comfortable.

Little Socks, from her sunbeam, opened an eye and gave out a low growl. They had better not expect that kind of behavior from her. She didn't like bringing the other cats into her place. They raised the expectations of the cat lovers of the world by being friendly.

It wasn't long before the first class ended and Diana prepared Ginger for the next one. Ginger had to stand up. Horrors. That meant Mo had to get up as well. He went to the sunbeam and tried to snuggle with Little Socks.

What a mistake.

After a bop on the nose, some hissing and trilling, he settled down on the next windowsill. Even in the sun, sleeping on wood was never preferable to sleeping with something soft and cuddly. But he got by until, finally, he saw George opening up the Tap.

Mo sprang up. Well, for him, it was springing. He lazily stretched his way to an upright position, licked his privates, jumped off the windowsill, allowed a patron or two to honor him with pets, and ambled out the door and over to his own place.

Annie and Nancy saw Mo amble into the Tap. They were still a few doors down, outside Sassy P's, when they saw him. Nancy, momentarily awed, said, "He just came out of the yoga studio."

"Yes, and?"

"You told him to go to the yoga studio and to wait until George got in."

"Yes, and?"

"He did what you told him to do."

"Sometimes they do that."

"He's a cat!"

"Yes, and?"

"Cats don't do that. Oh, my gosh. What am I thinking. If I stay here long enough, I'm going to become as delusional as you about your brood of children. Cats."

They walked up to the Café then turned and crossed The Avenue to Soul's Harbor, the local non-denominational church. Pastor Teresa was outside, working on a seasonal window painting.

"Pastor Teresa, you're decorating for Halloween!" exclaimed Nancy.

"Sure. 'Tis the season."

"I didn't think churches went in for that kind of thing."

"This may not be your typical church. We minister to the community, tourists, campers, people putting in at The Marina for short or long term…we really are a community church."

"How refreshing."

"What are the two of you doing out and about today?"

"Two things. First, I'm trying to catch everyone I forgot to tell, you being one of those everyones, that our meeting tomorrow evening will be on Frank's rooftop."

"I already heard that, but thanks."

"Second, I'm looking for a housewarming gift for Frank and thought I would take a look at your charity gift shop."

"I'm supposed to be helping Annie find the perfect gift, but to be honest, I just wanted to snoop. I've only been in your shop once and didn't have the time to look around like I wanted to."

"We have several nice things, and everything is unique. Everything is made by a local artist. Well, it could be a camper or a tourist or a boater, but to me, that's still local."

"My husband Sam has been here a couple of times."

"I've talked to him. He's interested in the driftwood art."

"He and Greg are beachcombing today. He wants to make some things himself, to sell at the block party."

"That's great! And if he gets into it, he can always put his work here. What kind of gift are you thinking of getting for Frank, Annie?"

"We were just in his apartment yesterday. Have you seen it yet? It's modern. Very modern. Driftwood items wouldn't fit. I think I'm looking for something that is very simple, but with a splash of color."

"Have you seen Chris's latest work?"

"Chris? He's been talking about doing charcoals of Chelsea's cats and dogs, basically black and white, with a splash of color. Maybe that's why I thought of it."

"He brought in a couple of pieces last week that you might want to consider."

They went into the shop. Annie took the time to introduce her mother to the woman behind the desk, a semi-permanent camper from the State Park campgrounds.

Teresa walked Annie and Nancy to a display of artwork. Several of the items were done by Chris, a collection of charcoal, pencil and pastel drawings. Two of the pieces were new. Annie had not seen them, nor had Chris talked to her about them. They were done in charcoal with splashes of bright color, certainly pastel chalk pencils, but what a misnomer. These colors were primary.

One was a silhouette of a woman, medium height, willowy, walking along the beach at night, with a bright yellow full moon lighting her way. The title of the piece was "She."

Annie stood in front of it, mesmerized. "Wow."

Nancy breathed in, "Is this you, dear?"

"No. Well, it's hard to tell, since there is nothing in the picture for perspective, but I'm either shorter than that or wider than that. Or both. And I don't have that long, flowing hair."

"Who is it?"

"I'm not worried about that. I just think it's gorgeous."

"It is that. But that's not a good housewarming present for Frank. Unless we want him to start fantasizing about her."

"You're right. Let's move on."

On the other side of the hanger was another charcoal from Chris. This was of the lighthouse. The detail of the lighthouse was amazing. You could almost see every brick. But it was night, and a stormy one. Muted gusts of rain drove down at a slant to indicate a stiff wind. In the distance, at the edge of the picture, was a ship, a schooner, dating the picture to sometime in the 1800s. Again using yellow, the splash of color was the beacon of light from shore to the very tip of the schooner. The title of the piece was "Safe Harbor."

"This is it."

"Yes. Frank said this town was his safe harbor."

"It is. You know, I first met Frank at the lighthouse."

"Really? How did that happen."

"I was doing my shift as a tour guide, and he came in on a bus. Got off the bus at the lighthouse and never got back on."

"Did you have anything to do with that, dear?"

"Not really. He was interested in my buildings, not my body!" Annie and Nancy laughed and the two made their way to the front to pay for the picture.

"This is a little pricey," said Nancy. "There can't be much overhead here at the church."

"It's all for charity. Not a penny goes to overhead."

"Well, in that case, let's look around a little more. I might find something to take home."

Nancy purchased a colorful woven hat, one that looked as if it belonged to a rich Chinese peasant, for working in her garden at home, and a pair of gardening gloves made from recycled clothing. They had a quilted look to them.

They couldn't go straight home, though. Now that they were shopping, they had to stop at every store on the way back. The next stop was CyberHealth, Mem's combination cyber café and health food store. They sat down to have a cup of tea. Nancy chose apricot tea while Annie had iced chai.

Annie and Nancy had not had the opportunity to talk – really talk – yet. Nancy approached the subject carefully, as in their lifetime, they had never discussed Annie's father.

"Annie, this life seems to agree with you. I know you put so much more effort into it than you seem to, and it has to be daunting to stay on top of all of these businesses at the same time, but you just glow these days. I just wanted you to know I'm very happy for you. I'm happy that you and your father maintained a relationship, and that in the end, he was able to pass on to you the things that mattered the most to him."

"Thanks, Mom. You know, we talked about you. Once. Only once. Did you know you were the love of his life?"

"Oh, no. You were the love of his life. I was the one that made you possible."

"I think it was more than that."

"Well, that's water under the bridge. History. We made our choices many years ago, and I've been very happy with Sam. I've had no occasion to ever regret marrying him."

"I know that. I can't imagine you and Dad married for the long term. Not after getting to know him as I did in later years. I always wanted to hate him for leaving you, but he never left me, so I couldn't hate him. I actually grew to really love him, like a daughter should love her father."

"And I'm happy for you. I don't really know a lot about your father's family history, but I know he owned the Inn, and the building that the Café and all the other businesses are in, but the other day, when I was sitting on the porch, it came to mind that this building, on this side of The Avenue, looks very much like that one."

"They're almost exactly the same. The differences came later. His family sold this building right before the Depression, and the new owner went under. It went through a few owners, and eventually, dad helped to save it."

"Really? How did he do that?"

"He had an interest, because his family used to own it, and because his own livelihood was right across the street, and because he had a love of history. He and Greg worked together to break it out into smaller pieces. The building was sold in parts, not in whole, and each unit was sold at a good price, so the new owners would hopefully have the cash they needed to renovate and get a business going. Everyone who bought a part saved even more by making the upstairs into their own apartment. And they worked together to paint the outside so it was consistent and flowed together."

"That's obvious. It's very attractive when seen from a distance, as well as being seen close up. And the Inn. What was it originally?"

"It was the family mansion. Then a hotel and restaurant. Dad was a forward thinker. It appears he came from a long line of forward thinkers. He rode that B&B wave from the bottom right up to the top, and now that Chelsea is such a tourist town, it's doing very, very well. If the nature of Chelsea changes, I'll have to find a way to change with it. But for the foreseeable future, we're fine the way we are."

As they got ready to leave, Nancy chose a variety packet of tea bags and a bag of mixed unsalted nuts. "For midnight snacks. I don't want to roam around in Henrie's kitchen."

Their next stop was Babar Foods. Annie's best friend, Laila, owned this grocery store. All of her children were in school today, so she and a part-time clerk were alone in the store. As usual, Laila was elegantly outfitted in the traditional Pakistani trouser outfit, loose but tight at the ankles with a loose tunic top, topped off with a dupatta. In the store, Laila wore the dupatta in traditional fashion, covering her head and draping her bosom and shoulders. Today, her clothing was a butter yellow color with bright orange, green and purple stitching.

And also, as usual, she was working with food, not bothering to put on an apron, and not one speck of food was on her clothing. If Annie lived to be 2,000, she would never understand this.

"Oh, Laila," said Nancy, that smells heavenly. What is it?"

"It's a Pakistani salad, called sweet corn sundal. It has sweet corn, coconut, mustard seeds, black lentils, red and green chilies, fennel and, of course, curry."

"Well, give me a pound of that, please."

"It's spicy, Nancy."

"Yes, that's good."

Laila laughed and dished it up. "What are the two of you doing today?"

"Shopping for a housewarming gift for Frank. And I found – guess what – a charcoal by Chris. It's outstanding."

"Can I see?"

Annie opened the package and showed Laila the lighthouse.

"Wow. Did you know he did that one?"

"No. He just talked to me about doing this kind of combination of techniques, but I didn't know he had done some already."

"You need a man with a little mystery."

"Before I forget, did you hear where we're having the meeting?"

"Yes. Can't wait to see it. The rooftop. And the sunset. Are you coming, Nancy?"

"Of course. We have to get the entire experience before going back to our dreary, land-locked existence."

A customer came in. "Forgive me, I need to tend to business."

"We'll see you later!"

Annie and Nancy walked out the door, turned right, and stood for a while at the window of DoubleGood.

"Well, are you ready?"

"Ready for what?"

"Ready to shop for that computer?"

"Oh! Yes! Let's go on in!"

Getting ready for the total experience, Annie and Nancy deposited their packages behind the counter of DoubleGood while Annie explained to Holly the purpose of their visit.

"A first time computer owner. Alright! Let's get to it!"

An hour and several hundred dollars later, they left the store with the promise that a new computer would be ready for pick-up by the end of the week.

"Mom, we still have two stores to go, but it's time for lunch."

"Where are we eating today?"

"How about Mr. Bean's?"

They first dropped off packages at the Inn, then walked to Mr. Bean's to love up a little boy kitty and to have one of their special lunches, a hearty vegetable beef stew served inside a small loaf of French bread.

When they returned to the Inn, Clara was there with her wagon, changing out the fresh bouquets. Clara, owner of

Bloomin' Crazy, had jet black hair pulled back tight and a bright red tropical flower behind her ear. This flower was fresh, but it was almost the time of year for her to go to winter silks. Clara was from Haiti and spoke with a sassy French lilt.

"I've got something different for you this week. All of the arrangements have a Halloween theme, and they also have a weed in common. They have 'duckweed' mixed in."

Clara and Annie both laughed, while Nancy, puzzled, looked at the arrangements Clara brought for the Inn.

"This looks like broom sedge. You call it duckweed here in Chelsea?"

"Only this week," said Clara. "The mystery crew coming in has a script calling for lots of what is known as duckweed. It plays a prominent part in the play, so I'm accommodating by putting it into all of Annie's fresh arrangements."

Clara had altered the typical vases for the Inn. The oversized vase for the entryway was a bright blue pumpkin – ceramic, of course – that looked almost big enough to hold Cinderella on the way to the ball. Large blue day lilies were interspersed with roses tinted blue. Sprigs of duckweed sprouted everywhere, making the otherwise glamorous arrangement look a bit, well, weedy.

The arrangement for the dining room had a similar vase, but much smaller, filled with white roses. Again, duckweed sprung up inelegantly, and spider webs hung from the weeds and down past the roses, with black spiders clinging to them. One spider had nearly escaped the vase, having a leg on the table, ready to run to the nearest unsuspecting victim.

"Let me show you the others," said Clara. "For Sassy P's, I have this purple and red vase. Hopefully the suckers will stay in until the week is over, but if it starts to look a little empty, I can refill it."

She referred to the lollipops that stood every which way in a metal vase with splashes of purple and red in no apparent pattern. The lollipops – circles of candy six inches in diameter and covered in cellophane – stood on red sticks. The cellophane covers varied. Some were purple with bright red spiders. Others were red with purple witches on broomsticks. Annie saw a red one with a lilac-colored ghost.

And of course, throughout the arrangements were sprigs of duckweed, filling in the empty spaces.

"I have this green one for Mr. Bean's." Clara pulled out a long, low green glass vase with high sprouts of green bamboo sprouting what appeared to be bats. Flowers – small blooms that had been died green – started low and curled up the bamboo. Duckweed again filled up the empty space, starting low and going high.

The arrangement for Mo's tap was typically done in shades of yellow. This week, Clara had a smiling jack-o-lantern with yellow columbine, gold nuggets and a witch's hat perched on top. Duckweed stuck out low, and some sprigs actually appeared to have grown up and through the brim of the hat.

"I had fun doing Little Socks' arrangement. I always do orange for her, so I did this cute thing with a big witch's hat." A black hat, at least a foot tall, was arranged on top of the vase. Clara cut holes in the hat to get flowers down to the water. The duckweed in this arrangement was draped tightly around the hat, like a hat band, and orange flowers and berries curled around the brim and up to the tip of the hat.

"And here is Tiger Lily's." A bright purple pumpkin sprayed with glitter had glittery purple lilies, large glittery black pods of some sort, and duckweed going high and wide. The weed itself had been sprayed with purple glitter.

Annie, pleased with each effort, said, "Clara, what would we do without you?"

"You'd be boring as chalk on a board."

Henrie came through just as Clara made this statement. "Amen, sister," he said, in his perfectly upper class accent, causing all of them to howl with laughter. Kali and Ko came running to see what was up.

Clara exclaimed, "Girls! I was wondering where you were. You have to examine the bouquets. Here, I have your sample."

Just as Clara leaned down to give Kali and Ko a smaller bouquet, with all of the blooms contained in the two arrangements, Honey Bear walked in. Slowly. Princely. Right up to Clara. He took the offered bouquet and slowly walked into the library, taking his time while Kali and Ko spit and hissed.

"Don't worry girls. He did this last week, too, so I brought another one." Clara offered the girls another bouquet.

Kali and Ko purred together, *"We love you, Clara." "Uncle Honey Bear is a weasel."*

Annie, feeling a little guilty about not helping Felicity over the lunch hour, made a cup of coffee in the kitchen. Kali and Ko enjoyed having her to themselves this early in the afternoon, so they did their sunbeam sleeping in the dining room, which was as close to the kitchen as the sun came this time of day.

"Henrie, can I help you some more with your mystery characters?"

"I think I have it in hand, but let's go over it again. I want to make sure we get it right."

"We have six guests for the cruise, three husband and wife couples – or at least three couples of one male and one female. I don't know for sure if they're married."

Annie, looking at the notebook, said, "There are more people booked in, all coming in tomorrow and staying through Sunday. They aren't all on the cruise?"

"No. The gentleman staying in the front room booked a few days after the mystery crew. And because Sam and Nancy are in the back room, we ran out of rooms in the house itself. The group of three, two men and a woman, when offered a large room in the carriage house, said that would work out fine for them."

"It will be nice to have an almost full house." Annie dug around in the kitchen until she finally found a tablet and a pen.

Henrie looked at his notes. "Here are our mystery characters. We have Spicy Pepper."

"Really."

"Now you'll just have to go along with me here. You know how these things go. The names are outlandish. The plots wind around and around and around, and the premise is, well, silly."

"But fun."

"But fun. Yes. Spicy Pepper."

"Spicy Pepper. That would be who?"

"Actually, he's the easy one. Ray will play that role, because he's the one who will die in the first act, and then Ray will go on to become the detective who solves the case.

He is the only one who will know, from the beginning, what happens to whom."

"Okay. Ray. Spicy Pepper. Who's next?"

"Here is the list of characters, and keep your comments to yourself."

Annie laughed. "Okay. I'm sorry. I'm done. I'm serious now."

Henry, as only someone of the very upper crust can do, listed the mystery characters with quiet aplomb.

"Brad Spit, a 60-ish, playboy who, truth be told, has connections with the underworld." Annie sniffed and pursed her lips.

"Dr. Mortimer Bong, a famous — at least in his own mind — scientist who develops duckweed products of fantastic properties." Annie hid her mouth behind her hands.

"Onstair Royds, who hopes to gain Olympic gold in track and field." Annie shut her eyes tightly.

"Mary Monroe, a fading society gadfly." Annie burst out, "Fading? I thought she was dead!"

Henry continued calmly, "Alabaster Pearl..." He was interrupted by a hoot. "Alabaster Pearl, an extremely efficient secretary."

Annie said, "I'm sorry."

"Thank you. And finally, Sparkle Shine, a marketing executive."

"Sparkle Shine?"

"Sparkle Shine."

Annie had been writing the names of the characters on her tablet. "What else do I need to know to help you out?"

"Well, in the play, Onstair Royds and Sparkle Shine are secretly married. I don't know if it's a good idea or a bad one to have a 'real' couple play a 'cast' couple."

"Since it's a secret, it probably doesn't matter. What do we know about the crew?"

"I asked them to send photos of themselves and to send a paragraph describing themselves, so we could try to make the best match. Here they are.

"Couple one, Hirsch and Linda Stone. From the photo they sent, the two of them at some kind of tropical get away, they appear to be mid-50s. He has the look of an executive of some sort, and she looks like either a lady of leisure or perhaps someone who works in a high end jewelry store."

Annie made a couple of notes. "What did they say about themselves?"

"They chose to send a statement that regarded the mystery rather than themselves. They said they were happy to play whatever part they were assigned, and that no matter what, they would play the parts to the hilt."

"Dramatic flair."

"So it would seem. Next we have Tom Moller and Susie Benton. They sent a photo of the two of them with three children."

Annie looked at the photo. A couple possibly in their 40s, fit looking and casual, with three toddlers. They were in what appeared to be a backyard, with a grill off to one side and a swing set and what could be the tip of a treehouse on another. She made some more notes.

"And then we have the Smiths."

"Please."

"That is the name they gave me. Mr. and Mrs. Smith. Spencer and Hannah. They sent separate wallet photos, headshots, I think you call them."

Spencer looked to be in his 40s, handsome, athletic. Hannah appeared to be a bit mousy. Also in her 40s, possibly, but if they were the same age, she had not aged as gracefully as he. Spencer was dressed in a business suit; Hannah was dressed in a somewhat severe dark blue dress with ruffles. Very 80s, thought Annie. She made more notes.

"Did you make an original assessment?"

"Yes. Can we now compare notes?"

"Sure. This is what I have, taking them by character."

"Brad Spit...Hirsch Stone."

"Dr. Mortimer Bong...Tom Mollar."

"Onstair Royds...Spencer Smith."

"Mary Monroe...Linda Stone."

"Alabaster Pearl...Hannah Smith."

"Sparkle Shine...Susie Benton."

Henrie smiled. "It would appear we are in agreement. Wonderful! When they arrive, I will hand each of them their character names and ask that they use those names at all times while in Chelsea. At breakfast, I will give them the introductory pages. They can read and become familiar with their roles, and I will then ask them to introduce themselves to one another. Of course, they will have to do that again for the start of round one at Sassy P's, but giving them a head start, they can spend the day in character. They do not know that Ray will be the one to die, so he will be here for breakfast also, meeting them as tour director and as mystery character."

"Did I hear you talking to Chris about playing a role as well?"

"Yes, well, he will be helping Ray with the entire tour, so he will play the role of one of the investigators. He does not need to attend the introductory session, however.

"Round one has four investigators, but rounds two and three will be on The Escape. It won't be convenient to have four investigators for those rounds. We revised the story so that Chris will be the only investigator on the lake."

"Have you chosen the other investigators?"

"Ray will do that at Sassy P's. They could be local, or they could be tourists. He'll decide that evening."

"It's going to be tough remembering two sets of names. I have a hard enough time with just one."

"That's part of the plan. For the entire time they are here, they will be called by their character names. It will be easier for them to remember their parts, and, truth be told, easier for us to be polite."

Chris came to the kitchen door and knocked once. Henrie got up and said, "Please come in."

"Thanks. Hi, Annie." He gave her his standard kiss on the cheek. He had a camera in his hand again. "I was hoping to take photos of Kali and Ko."

"They're in the dining room. How about Honey Bear?"

"I should take photos of him, too," said Chris. I'm sure all I'll have to do is wait until I hear some hissing, then I'll be able to find him."

"I saw your charcoals with color today," said Annie. She pulled out the package with his artwork and showed it to Henrie.

Chris came around to her side of the table again. "Which one did you get?"

"Safe Harbor. I got it as a housewarming gift for Frank."

"This is outstanding work, Chris," said Henrie.

"This and the other one at the church are the only two I've attempted to date. I just used yellow, but I want to use other colors with the cats and dogs."

"What are you planning?" asked Henrie.

"I want to do charcoals with a splash of color of the local – famous – cats and dogs to sell at the block party."

"I can't wait to see them. I will probably purchase at least one each of Annie's kids, and maybe even more. I'll have to start saving!"

"I could save you some money and do a grouping."

"Oh, please do!" said Annie. "Please do at least two groupings, and maybe more. I would give one to Mom for Christmas, and buy her one of Honey Bear. And I'll buy one of each of them individually to hang in their own places."

"I'd better get busy! If I do a good job, these will go like hotcakes. And the block party is just around the corner. I won't have time to do many."

Henrie left to plan menus for the week with Carlos and Felicity; Chris took his photos; Annie went to the library and called Kali and Ko to come take a nap. They slept for about an hour, until Sam and Greg came through the kitchen door.

"Annie? Nancy?"

"Here, Sam. Did you get enough driftwood?"

"I sure did! Come take a look."

Piles of driftwood lay outside near the beach-side door to Nancy and Sam's room. There were pieces big enough to paint, small enough to weave into something larger, and interesting enough to almost stand alone as a piece of art.

"What are you going to make?"

"I don't know. I'll need some inspiration, I guess."

"Where are you going to get your ideas?"

"Well, Greg and I are going to go get a piece of pie at Mr. Beans' place, and then I'm going to do some cloud gazing."

Annie smiled to herself and left them to finish their day with pie.

Annie and the kids enjoyed a quiet evening alone. Until Honey Bear arrived. "This is absolutely enough!" said Annie. She picked the big boy up and took him downstairs to Nancy. Nancy and Sam were on the porch, drinking a glass of wine and watching the sunset.

"Mom, could you please lock Honey Bear in your room this evening, so we can enjoy an evening alone?"

"Oh, honey, he hates being cooped up all night!"

"Well, how about cooping him up until you get up to go to the bathroom. You still do that, right?"

"Oh, all right. I guess it won't hurt him. For one evening."

"Thanks, Mom."

Back upstairs, Annie sat in her overstuffed chair with a book in her lap. Soon, she was joined by Little Socks, then Sassy Pants. Mr. Bean finally jumped into the chair, and after some wiggling around, settled down. Mo, Kali and Ko tried their best to fit in, eventually settling for nestling in a pile on the sofa. After a while, Annie looked around and called, "Tiger Lily? Tiger Lily? Where are you, big girl?"

No response.

Huh, thought Annie.

Chapter 5: All The Rooms Are Dank And Dreary

At 10:00 the next morning, long after the kids had gone to work, Mem, Frank, Clara, Holly and Jolly arrived at the Inn. Nancy, Sam and Annie were waiting for them.

Henrie had a pot of coffee ready, but he was off with Kali and Ko, making sure rooms were ready for the guests who would arrive early in the afternoon.

Nancy said to the group, "I went downstairs this morning, and you will not believe the great rooms down there. Once you get past the laundry room – now Annie, that laundry room is wonderful, but it's just not Halloweenish – all the rooms are dank and dreary. They're small, there's the old coal room that's pretty big, and the stairways are just awful."

"Perfect!" said Clara.

"We'll be able to use the outside cellar entrance. It's big enough, and Chris already made a ramp for one side of it. It's not really ADA approved. Someone will have to help you, Holly."

"That's not a problem, as long as you don't forget and leave me down there."

Annie told the group, "We actually have a 'safe suite' down there. Most folks have a safe room in the basement for waiting out storms, but Dad went full tilt. We have to consider having guests during weather alerts, so it makes sense.

"Of course, our laundry facilities are down there, and the main room is really big. At least 10 people can sit comfortably. We have storage for supplies, and a full bathroom and a bedroom. But you're right, Mom. We don't want to use it for the haunted house. It would be a great room for teenagers to use for a sleepover, though."

"We got a little off track, dear."

"You're right. So we'll have food and drinks up here, in the library and dining room, and downstairs we'll have the haunted house. We'll have to find a way to greet people at the sidewalk and send them around the house to the cellar door, figure out the haunted house part of it, and then bring them up the stairway into the kitchen. Or the elevator. I'm glad Dad thought to put it all the way down to the basement."

"We'll have to do spooky stuff outside too, from where people leave the sidewalk, around the Inn and into the cellar."

"We can do something at the beach area too, up close to the Inn."

"That will track sand through."

"That wouldn't be a problem, really."

"Well, let's keep it as a thought if we think we need more 'stuff.' I'd hate to make more work for Annie and Henrie. There will be enough set up and clean up to do without adding sand."

Everyone made notes and some people had quiet, private conversations about ideas while the rest of the group talked.

At the end of every other month, this group of friends from The Avenue hosted a block party for the town, tourists and campers. The parties were typically held in the grassy area behind Annie's building or in the catering hall at Tiger Lily's. This year, they had decided to move the Halloween party to a new venue. The basement of the Inn was going to become a haunted house.

The date of the party was October 31. They decided to ask the Town Council to declare the early hours of that evening the standard "Trick-Or-Treat" hours for the community. That would allow kids – of all ages – to be comfortable dressing in costume for the party. They could continue the trick-or-treating at the party as well, with bowls of candy monitored by a ghoul or goblin.

Annie said, "I'll call Joan and ask her about the town's set time."

"How is Joan getting along, now that she's in charge of the Council?"

Clara had to answer this one. "Joan of Chelsea? She's gettin' along just fine. She's in her element!"

"Who's going to take care of the upstairs menu?"

"Henrie, Felicity, Trudie, Laila and Carlos. And we'll have plenty of people to help serve and keep platters refreshed as well."

"I think your charity idea was great, Annie!"

Annie smiled. "You know, it was really Mom's idea. Every year, when I was a kid, Mom took me to this church in town, and the kids would go out trick-or-treating for UNICEF. The town was always ready for us. They had their change ready, and no one gave us any candy, not the first piece, until we got to the last house. At that last house, a wonderful woman — her name was Ruby – gave us popcorn balls or caramel apples. Then we'd go back to the church and have some games while the adults counted the money. They always told us how much we raised for charity before we went home."

Nancy asked, "Well, would Joan ask the people of Chelsea to do the same thing? Will she ask them to have their change ready, all the money they would have spent buying candy, and just give to UNICEF? Then the Inn would be Ruby's house."

"That's a good idea, Mom. I hadn't thought it all the way through. I have the UNICEF boxes, but you're right. We need to really advertise what we're doing this year and hope everyone helps out."

"We're hoping the adults will stay at home for trick-or-treating, then come here to the Inn for the haunted house, or just to eat and have a good time."

"I think it's marvelous what you all do here. Sam, when we get home, we're going to have to tell folks how they do it in Chelsea."

Annie looked at the clock. They had been talking for nearly an hour and had not yet gone down to the basement. "Let's go downstairs, and then the creative folks will know what they have to work with. Hopefully you'll have some ideas by the time we gather at Frank's tonight."

Annie met Chris for a quick lunch at Sassy P's. She apologized to Felicity and Trudie for missing the lunch rush two days in a row, but she had to be at the Lighthouse for her volunteer shift by 1:00.

If she stopped at the Café, she would get sucked into a rush. She felt bad about not checking in with Tiger Lily but assumed the big girl would get over it.

Nancy planned to be at the Lighthouse by 1:30. Annie was scheduled to give a lecture for high school freshmen. She told her mother this would be a special treat.

"Pete will join me. I'll give the standard history of the town, what you would find in most history books but from the perspective of one family. Pete will put a different spin on it when he talks about his family."

Nancy and Pete arrived about the same time. Cyril came through the door with Pete and gave Annie a cheery lick hello. He dashed around the room, looking into corners. Finding nothing, he left to search the rest of the lighthouse.

"Where's he going?" asked Nancy.

"He's looking for the kids. If I'm here, someone else is supposed to be here, too. He's going to be disappointed."

Sure enough, Cyril came back with a 'hang dog' look.

Annie dug a dog treat out of her pocket, and he perked up a bit.

Annie noticed Pete was nervous. "What's up, Pete? Stage fright?"

"I'm not used to speaking to groups."

"You always speak to groups. You have a way with people."

"It's not quite that easy."

"You'll be fine. Busses are here."

Annie greeted the teachers and students and made sure everyone was standing or sitting where they could see and hear.

"You all know the Chief of Police, right? Pete and I will give you a history of the town, both from a different perspective. When we've finished, you'll have plenty of time to stay here and ask questions or tour inside and outside the lighthouse.

"I'm going to tell you about the history of the town from my family's perspective. My family's history mirrors the growth and changes of the town, so I'm just going to put some of those things into perspective for you by using buildings and places you can still see today.

"First of all, my family arrived in this area shortly after the Civil War ended. When did the Civil War end?"

Several voices said, "1865!"

"Right. So that gives you a date to hang onto for perspective. Chelsea is located on a deep water harbor. You all know it's known for recreational and tourist attractions, like boating, fishing, hunting and camping. We have a state park, which adds to the attraction. We didn't start out that way. We had a beginning, and this time in which we live is at some point along the middle of the time line. No one knows what our future will hold. But we know about the past.

"I'm not going to go back so far as the first known inhabitants, Native Americans, their tribes and their history. But learning that, learning what brought them here, what kept them here, and how they migrated away, forced and unforced, should be, I think, a standard in your education. I'm sure your teachers will or have already included that in your curriculum. If not, and if you can't figure out how to research that on your own at the public library, call me. I'll get you started.

"This area was involved in one of the first world wars. It's not discussed in our history books that way. In our history books, it's referred to as the French and Indian War. We basically study the conflict as it took place on North American soil. You can tell it was named by the victor, Great Britain. It sounds like it was 'us' against 'them;' 'us,' being British colonials against 'them,' some French people allied with all Native Americans to steal the land. Not so.

"French explorers passing through in the 1600s were the first to write this area into European American history. At that time, all of North America was colonized by Great Britain, France and Spain. This area was part of what was known as New France.

"In North America, the war was fought between the colonies of Great Britain and New France. Both sides were supported by military from their parent countries and both sides had Native American allies.

"The outbreak started here but escalated into an international conflict that came to include Spain. By the end of the war, there were many exchanges of colonial lands, placing this area into the hands of Great Britain.

"And the next war in which we were involved was called…"

"The American Revolution!"

"Right. So, moving on. We are now part of the United States of America, and this region was separated from a larger territory to become a state in the 1830s. The town itself grew around the home built by a trapper in the early 1840s. He found the area profitable, and after a couple of years, he built the house and brought his family here. Others joined them and a village grew around that first trapper's home. You know it as another tourist attraction, the Old Towne Village. The buildings there are either renovated originals or replicas of the original buildings. If you haven't taken the time to go, that's another thing to put on your local history bucket list.

"The county organized in 1860, about the time the Civil War was starting. By that time, logging operations were booming and the population was growing. The town incorporated in 1870. By then, my great-great grandfather was here. He was a lumber man. Sawmills were everywhere up and down the lakeshore and inland.

"Like all big businessmen, he needed operating capital to start. He was funded by friends from the east. He built a mansion to entertain and impress those friends.

"By the way, his mansion is the one of the few structures in town still maintained by the original family. The changes in its use mirror the changes made by the town through the years.

"So let's talk about how the town changed. Industry drives change. The lumber industry had great need of another industry, shipping. Other towns around the lake needed lumber, and sawmills needed products to survive.

"Local businessmen, like my great-great grandfather, saw the needs and filled them. They purchased shipping operations that used side-wheel steamers and soon had to add bigger ships to handle bulk freight.

"Several shipping companies nestled here in Chelsea and up and down the lakefront. In order to accommodate lumber shipping out, they needed a way to get the ships in. At that time, the harbor was too shallow to accommodate ships, so the town dredged it until it was sufficiently deep, and then dug a channel to connect the harbor to inland rivers.

"When you walk outside around the lighthouse, you'll see historical markers. They're signs that outline the history of this channel, when it was dug, how deep it is, and how it increased the capacity of the town to receive and send goods.

"The town also lobbied for and received federal and state funding to build a lighthouse and a lifeboat station. This lighthouse was a necessary safety feature for ships coming into port in the dark, or for ships just passing, to know how far away from shore they were.

"Another piece of history you may enjoy is the history of shipwrecks of the Great Lakes. Add it to your list. You'll thank me later.

"Back to the history of Chelsea, establishing lifeboat stations up and down the coastlines of the Great Lakes was the country's first effort at what is now known as the Coast Guard. You know where the Coast Guard station is now, but when it was first established, it was just across the channel from this lighthouse."

Annie pointed out a window and heads turned obediently. "When you walk around outside, look across there and imagine that area, in the late 1800s and into the early 1900s, as the place where volunteers gathered whenever news of a shipwreck or other water disaster was received. The Coast Guard is supported by volunteers today, but then, it was almost all volunteer effort.

"At that time, just as the lumber industry needed shipping, the shipping industry needed lumber. Ships were made of wood. Standards changed. By the 1890s the standard was steel. By that time, both the lumber and shipping industries in Chelsea were on the decline, and about that time, my great grandfather was taking over the family business from his father.

"Not only were his major businesses in decline, he had two long brick buildings filled with declining enterprises as well. The buildings that line Sunset Avenue, if you stand back and really look at them, were built as mirror images. Today, they look quite different from one another, but when my great-great grandfather built them, they were twins.

"They housed storefronts that supported both the shipping and lumber industries: a retail lumber store, hardware store, working man's diner, saloon, general store, laundry, and other supporting businesses. The apartments above were built so that managers could keep the stores open at all times. When ships came in, they needed to be open."

Annie stopped to make sure they were still paying attention. Most were. She went on. "The next generation, my great grandfather's generation, had a different social and economic landscape. With the lumber business fading and shipping of cargo all but over, he had to reinvent the family fortune.

"One growth industry was the transport of people from port to port. The tourist trade was beginning to take off. He moved his family to the third floor of the mansion and established The Grand Mack Hotel & Restaurant. This spearheaded a movement that made Chelsea a destination point for thousands of tourists.

"Steamships arrived with passengers from cities throughout the Great Lakes area. He reinvented his business buildings as well, filling them with shops that would support the tourist trade. There were clothing stores for men, women and children, a drug store with a soda fountain, a café with outside dining, an upscale tavern, a haberdashery, and a professional office with a doctor and a dentist. The town continued to thrive on this new industry as well, as hotels, restaurants and shops grew throughout.

"In the mid-1920s, shortly before the Great Depression, my grandfather, the third man to be in charge of the family fortune, sold the building on the other side of The Avenue. He knew it was wise to divest, but he did not know how bad it was going to get. He received full value for the building, while in a couple of years the new owner lost it to bankruptcy, beginning the downhill slide of that side of The Avenue.

"That was not the only building lost to bankruptcy during the Depression. The town suffered. But the town knew how to rebound. It took some years, but the town — and my family — reinvented themselves again.

"With my family, the reinvention came by closing the hotel. The family still lived on the third floor, and the restaurant survived, although not as grand as its name, The Grand Mack Café. The second floor was renovated into offices for professionals moving into town, attorneys and accountants. Even a private detective.

"The town survived the loss of many sons to World War I, then World War II, and all the while, social interests changed and the economy changed. By the 1950s, the town and my family were running businesses to support veterans and cater to their ever-growing families, the product of the Baby Boom generation.

"This carries us to the late 1960s and the 1970s, when tourist patterns were changing again. The town changed. My family changed. My family turned the former mansion into a bed and breakfast, remodeling the first and second floors once again to make the Grand Mack B&B. They changed the storefronts once again to handle the changes in tourist demand. And what happened to the town? Does anyone know how many bed and breakfasts there are in town?"

Heads around the room were shaking or nodding. Someone said, "Lots!"

"There are dozens, and they are all thriving. The shops up and down The Avenue and on Main Street all cater to a different kind of tourist trade now. Art shops, antique stores, restaurants of every kind. We don't have the industry; we don't have big jobs that keep our youth home. Unfortunately, many of you will leave when you graduate from high school, going on to college and starting a life somewhere else, but

Chelsea is still surviving, using the natural strengths of the area to continue to thrive."

Annie sat back. "I've been talking for way too long. I saw a few eyes glaze over, but I think a few of you are still with us. We're going to hear one of the more interesting parts of town history now, one you don't find so much in our history books. Pete?"

Pete began, a first a bit tenuous, then gaining confidence. "My family had a much different start in Chelsea. My ancestors arrived somewhat earlier than Annie's, starting with my great-great-great grandfather. He came by way of the railroad. The Underground Railroad."

Students whose interest had waned looked alert once again.

"This state became a free state in the 1840s. A lot of prominent abolitionists lived throughout the state, making it well known for its anti-slavery leaning. For a while, a runaway slave making it to this state could be free. Bounty hunters might come after them, but in most instances, townsfolk would protect the runaway. In 1850, the federal Fugitive Slave laws were passed, allowing for runaway slaves to be captured, wherever they were found, and returned to slavery. There were now lots of free African Americans living in the north who faced this indignity, and talk about industries on the rise, bounty hunting was now a growth industry.

"Canada had outlawed slavery in 1819. Many former slaves tried to make it to Canada, where American bounty hunters were not allowed. My ancestor was one of them. He made it, and he stayed in touch with his new friends from this great state.

"When the Civil War broke out, this state supported the Union. I've read history books that report nearly 25% of the men of this state served in the Union Army. This included African American soldiers, many of whom returned from Canada to enlist. My ancestor was one of them.

"He enlisted, he fought, he returned here, to Chelsea, picking up his family along the way. He got a job in the lumber industry, working in a sawmill. I don't know who owned the sawmill. It's possible my connection to Annie goes back that far. We don't know. He worked hard, became a foreman at the sawmill.

"As the generations came along, you heard Annie, the industry changed. My family worked at the sawmill for two generations. The next generation, my great-grandfather, made furniture. At first, he worked for a factory, then he started his own place. He put a special stamp to his work. It was quality work. Intricate, delicate, and sturdy. My grandfather continued that company, but my father did not have the skill required to do that kind of detail work with lumber.

"My father decided it was time for someone in the family to go to college. He did, and he returned to Chelsea, one of the first educated African Americans in the community. He got a job at the bank and rose to bank manager. When I came along, he told me that I could do anything, be anything I wanted to be. He also told me the family history, and impressed upon me the history of this great country.

"I decided to become a marine. I lived and worked in some of the world's most beautiful places and some of the world's most tragic places for twenty years, but I knew where home was. Chelsea. So here I am.

"Annie and I have histories that ebb and flow with the history of the town, the state and the nation. When you feel it, when you really feel the flow of the universe in your heart, then you know what it means to be home. You know that you will do anything to help your home grow and change with the times.

"Chelsea is filled with people who have many generations of attachment. Each one has his or her own story and his or her own interpretation of Chelsea. Hopefully, you will stay here, or you will come back after you graduate from college, and you can add your own rhythm to that of the town."

When the talking was over, the questions began, most of them directed to Pete, who was a little embarrassed about the attention. Annie and Pete got the kids started on their walks in and outside the building, and helped herd them back on the bus at the end of the afternoon.

Nancy said to Annie, "I'm glad to get a feel for your dad's connection to Chelsea. It makes certain things clear to me. Things regarding our relationship, and now, things regarding your life."

"History kind of does that. Puts things into perspective."

Annie and Nancy walked up to the Café, got Tiger Lily, then picked up the rest of the kids on their way back to the Inn. When they arrived, Henrie was settling in the last set of guests.

"Everyone is here, including the guests not connected with the cruise. I will meet with the mystery crew in, oh, it looks like a half hour. The crew is upstairs, but our four other guests are on the back porch enjoying refreshments."

"Where are the girls?"

"Upstairs. Kali is deciding with whom she shall fall in love, and Ko is trying to convince her that all men eat worms."

"Oh. I won't interrupt. I'll go say hello to our other guests."

Annie found the group of four sitting at the wicker table, sharing a bottle of red and a bottle of white wine. She sat down and introduced herself.

The perky young woman spoke first. "Hi! I'm Jessica. This is my brother, Alec, and Herb is our friend. We're the crazy ones staying in the carriage house."

Alec appeared to be the male equivalent to perky Jessica; Herb looked a bit sad.

Annie looked at the fourth guest who nodded pleasantly but said nothing. Looking around, including the other three in her smile, she said, "Do you have special plans? Do you need us to help you find anything or perhaps some special type of place?"

"Oh, no," said Alec. "Jess has been all over the website. She knows all about your places, and we plan to hit all of them, and we want to go to the flower and gift shop and the charity store at the church."

"And the cyber café. We used to have a place like that at home, but it closed up. I'm thinking we need another place like it, so I want to spend some time there and talk to the owner if I can," added Jessica.

"And Herb will spend a lot of time there, too. He's a gamer."

Herb said, "Well, it keeps my mind off things."

Annie said, "Well, all four of you should keep the mystery group in mind. With the exception of the tour director, who is also a character, they are here at the Inn now. They'll be in character the entire time, so please be polite and don't laugh when they introduce themselves to you."

Jessica laughed. "I went to one of those mystery dinners once. The names are so outlandish you can't help but remember them! I think that's why they do it, give out the funny names."

"I think it will be great fun for them and for those of us who are watching. And by the way, they start round one at Sassy P's Wine & Cheese tomorrow evening. It starts at 8:00, and we're making a party out of it. If you're interested, get there early. As soon as the chairs are filled, we close the door to anyone else getting in. Free food, free wine and a floor show."

"Can't beat that! Maybe we'll plan on getting there by 7:00. Do you think that will be early enough?"

"Surely it will be."

"Thanks!"

Annie turned to the last guest, who had to be Jeff Bennett. He, however, just nodded pleasantly, so she nodded in return and left the porch.

By the time Annie got upstairs, seven cats were gathered in the kitchen, meowing for fresh food and water.

Little Socks said to the others, *"We get to have our water without Tiger Lily's foot having been in it first. Yum!"*

Annie arrived early to the block party meeting. She presented Frank with the housewarming gift, and, as predicted, he loved it. He knew immediately where to place it. Annie helped while he hung it in the kitchen, next to the patio door, visible whenever he looked toward the lake.

Even Claire seemed to be impressed, standing back with the humans to admire the effect.

That evening, a rather robust group of friends enjoyed the sunset from Frank's deck. It was beautiful from that vantage point.

They laughed. They talked. They put some details together for the block party. Several watched discretely and with dismay as Frank and Mem seemed to argue for a while then keep their distance from one another.

On their way back to the Inn, Annie said to Chris, "What's up with that?"

"Don't know. I'm glad you didn't get the other charcoal for him."

"Me too."

Chapter 6: "I'm Spicy Pepper."

The next morning, Annie and the kids walked down to breakfast together. Well, with the exception of Kali and Ko, who are already at work, supervising Henrie's treatment of the new guests. And Uncle Honey Bear wasn't actually walking. He was moving down the steps like a slow slinky, herded gently by Annie's feet.

They came down with sound effects. Low growls from Honey Bear, snarls and hisses from five other cats who refused to get in front of him.

Annie introduced herself to the mystery crew, and they, one by one, introduced themselves to her in character, with much dramatic flair.

The woman who introduced herself as Mary Monroe asked, "Annie, do you have a Goodwill or Salvation Army clothing store in the area? We need to shop for a few clothing props for round one. We thought we would play it to the hilt on the first night, when we'll have an audience."

"Sure. Go back toward the interstate. Once you get past the town square, keep your eye open on the right. There are also some big box stores out there, if you don't find what you need at the Goodwill."

Ray arrived, his companion in tow, but as he walked toward the table he had to sidestep to the buffet. His companion, Jock, a Portuguese water dog, was suddenly covered in cat hair. Cat hair still connected to four cats. Kali and Ko held themselves above the fray. Uncle Honey Bear didn't even blink. Annie didn't see Tiger Lily.

Ray continued into the room. Annie held out her hand and said, "Annie Mack. I'm the owner of this establishment. And you are?"

"I'm Spicy Pepper."

The woman now called Mary Monroe howled in laughter, head bent back to her shoulder blades. When she recovered, she said, "I'm sorry. I thought I was over it. So pleased to meet you, Spicy. I'm Mary Monroe."

Spicy Pepper helped himself to a generous portion of scrambled eggs with chorizo and a couple of bacon, egg and cheese rolls. When he sat down, the introductions began, and the characters chatted amongst themselves as if they were, in fact, who they purported to be.

Annie sat back to watch, then said, "Good morning" to Jeff Bennett as he arrived for breakfast. He nodded to Annie, then nodded briefly to the table of characters. Before getting a plate, he took a cup of coffee to a side table, letting everyone know by his distancing to continue as if he were not there.

Annie decided she had better make an appearance at the Café this morning. She called to the kids and said, "Time to go!"

Little Socks, Mr. Bean, Sassy Pants and Mo came running. Tiger Lily was nowhere to be found. Where in the world could she be? thought Annie. She didn't even greet Jock.

"Tiger Lily! Tiger Lily! Let's go, girl!"

Sassy Pants looked at her siblings. *"Doesn't Mommy know Tiger Lily lefted when Ray comed in?"*

Mo gave a sad *"Trill."*

Sassy Pants continued, *"But what's wrong? Why is Tiger Lily hiding from Mommy?"*

Little Socks said, *"Her feelings have been hurt. She'll get over it, but she's going to make Mommy pay."*

Mr. Bean got in on the conversation. *"How much? How much will Mommy have to pay? Five cookies? Seven treats? Will Tiger Lily share?"*

Mo bopped Mr. Bean on the top of the head as they walked out the door.

When Annie arrived at the café, everyone dropped off except Mo, who was in tow, she noticed the fresh flower arrangement had a descriptive card. It read, *"You may notice this arrangement is somewhat different. 'Duckweed' has been added in honor of the murder mystery being held this weekend. Remember, you are all invited — 'all' being residents, campers and tourists — to join the first round of the mystery at Sassy P's Wine & Cheese. It starts at 8:00 on Thursday. First-come-first-served. When the chairs are filled, the doors will be closed, per Fire Marshal orders."*

Trudie noticed Annie reading the card and laughed. "Customers were looking at it like Clara had gone out of her mind, so all of us on The Avenue added this card. It keeps us from having to explain, and I think it's saving Clara a little embarrassment, even though she doesn't know she should be embarrassed."

Mo had run off to claim the women he thought to be the most attractive, and Annie looked around for Tiger Lily. Worried, she asked Trudie, "Is Tiger Lily here?"

"Yes. She was just there on the stand before you came in."

Annie looked around but couldn't see her. Pretty soon she heard a crash in the kitchen, and Tiger Lily ran out, coming to a halt as she saw Annie, then heading to the back dining room. The back room was empty. Annie went first to the kitchen. Felicity was picking up some dishes.

"Oh, Annie, I'm sorry. I didn't see the big girl. She was just standing there and I tripped over her. She hardly ever comes into the kitchen."

"Felicity, let me help you." Together, they cleaned up the mess, then Annie asked, "Has she seemed different to you?"

"You know, she does. She acts sad, somehow. Do you think she's sick or something?"

"I don't know. I'll go find her. She went to the back."

Annie looked and looked. Under things, behind things, up high. She couldn't find her. Cats were good at hiding if they didn't want to be found. Annie was worried now.

She was supposed to meet Joan of Chelsea at Mr. Bean's in a half hour. She picked up her cell phone, called and asked if they could meet at the Café instead.

Joan was pleased to meet in any of Annie's places. She knew Annie would pick up the tab, and the food and drinks were always delicious. Of course, she didn't say that. She said, "Certainly."

Annie got out the Café's notebook and sat at a table close to the back dining room. She faced the front of the Café and turned the notebook to face the back at an angle, so the camera was not impeded. She turned the camera on, hoping Tiger Lily had not yet caught up with the technology.

Mo jumped to the table. Annie had to move him out of the way of the camera every now and then. Mo noticed the monitor looked like the back dining room. He jumped down and walked into the room. He glanced over his shoulder to see that he, too, was now on the monitor.

Mo sat in the middle of the room and looked around to see what Annie was trying to see. He spied Tiger Lily and sat for a minute just watching her. Tiger Lily looked back at him but did not move.

He called to her, *"Trill!"* What he meant was, *"Mommy's watching you."*

Tiger Lily looked at Mo, not understanding. He soon became bored and left to find greener pastures.

In a few minutes, Annie saw Tiger Lily creep out from under a buffet. Tiger Lily watched Annie closely to make sure she was not looking. She walked quickly, stomach low to the floor. Once under a table, she selected a chair pushed up underneath, and with one last look back at Annie, she jumped to the seat.

What should I do now, thought Annie. Chris came in, saw Annie and came over. She gave him the universal sign for "be quiet," putting her finger to her lips. He quietly slid into the seat beside her and leaned over to look at the screen.

"Something's up with the big girl," she whispered, "and I don't know what. She's hiding from me. She could be sick. I don't think she's mad, but she could be sad. Her feelings get hurt. I missed two lunch rushes this week."

"Are you going to try to go back there and get her?"

"She'll run away from me. I don't know what to do."

"What if I try?"

"That might work. Taking a treat would help."

"I'll get something from Felicity, then go back. Give me a signal if she moves before I get back."

When Chris came back, she did not give a signal, so he went to the back room and slowly went straight to Tiger Lily's hiding place. He squatted down, held out the treat and said softly, "Come here, big girl."

Chris stayed there, quietly talking to her, holding out the treat, until she finally came to him. He softly petted her head, then gently slid his hand around her belly and picked her up.

She allowed him to cuddle her into his shoulder and neck, nuzzling him in the process and kneading his neck with her front paw.

Chris stood there rocking her side to side, while Annie came to join them. She stayed behind Chris, putting her hand on Tiger Lily's head and swaying in the same rhythm.

"Big girl, are you sad?"

"You hate me."

"I've ignored you, haven't I?"

"You don't love me anymore."

"You know I love you, darlin'."

Silence.

"I've not been in here during the lunch rushes, have I?"

"You hate me."

"It's not because I don't love you. I've had things to do. But you know what? I'm going to try my awful darndest to be here at the Café during lunch. Every day."

"Every day?"

"I love you, big girl."

"Well, maybe you don't hate me. You'll have to prove it, though."

They stood there for several minutes, a man, a woman and a cat. Swaying in time, side to side, side to side. Eventually, Chris handed Tiger Lily to Annie, and Annie cuddled her into her own shoulder and neck, continuing to sway. Eventually, Tiger Lily decided to forgive her Mommy. She brought her head up, pushed away and jumped down, trotting back to her hostess stand.

"I can't believe I did that," said Chris.

"I can't either. But thank you."

"You're welcome."

At that moment, Joan of Chelsea showed up. Chris said, "Well, once again…"

"I'll see you when I see you."

Trudie came to get the notebook out of the way and to get a drink order from Joan. As she returned to the coffee bar, Pete and Cyril came in. Pete noticed the notebook appeared to be showing the room behind Trudie.

"What's that?" he asked.

"Annie was using our Skype camera to take a look around the place. This is how we do a lot of our meetings now. Annie was using it to…oh…never mind…someone may be listening." Tiger Lily had turned to watch them talk, because Cyril was paying more attention to Pete and Trudie than to her.

Cyril was, in fact, looking at the notebook screen. Pete was, too. "You started doing this after that exciting little incident involving The Escape, right?"

"Yes. It's been working out really well."

"That's interesting. Do you have to get the permission of your customers?"

"No, the way I understand it, customers could be filmed with any number of security cameras, so they shouldn't expect privacy, except, of course, in the restrooms. We do have to let staff know when the cameras are pointed at areas they would be working. Just once if we're setting it up to stay, but since we move it around, we let them know each time." Her voice dropped to a whisper. "Annie was watching for…"

Her right hand came up to shield her left, which was pointing toward Tiger Lily. She continued to whisper, "She was hiding."

"Oh. So customers aren't the only ones that can't expect privacy."

Cyril finally broke free to chat with his friends. By now Mo, out of customers to love, sat beside Tiger Lily on the hostess stand.

Cyril said, *"You look sad, Tiger Lily."*

"My mommy ignored me for two days."

"Sometimes humans get busy."

"Does Pete ever ignore you?"

"Well, no, but he just has me, and I go with him everywhere. Your Mom has to go different places and she can't always take you."

"I guess so. I want to take some time to be sad, though."

"Okay, I guess. I think she was using that notebook to look at you."

"She was? Is that how she found me?"

Mo said, *"Trill!"*

Cyril said, *"Mo says yes."*

"I don't know how you understand everything he says! I have to guess!"

Cyril rolled his eyes as only an English setter can. *"You live with him. Figure it out! Anyway, Pete thinks that notebook is a neat thing."*

"It is. They have meetings on it. We can sit right here and see almost everyone on The Avenue. I like to sit behind Mommy, so they can see me too."

Mo agreed, with an excited *"Trill!"*

Pete had his coffee to go, and he gave Tiger Lily and Mo hugs on the way out the door. "Come, Cyril."

Joan was interested in the trick-or-treat for UNICEF concept. "We can make it an annual community event," she said. "I don't see any issue with putting out press releases and putting signs around the community. It would be a combination UNICEF announcement and an invitation to the block party."

"I was hoping you'd like it. We can publicize the trick-or-treat routes, and the people that live on the routes can give at home, then come in to the party. Everyone else who wants to come can just start out at the party. We'll have donation jars there for them to throw in their loose change."

Joan and Annie continued to make plans until they were interrupted – rudely – by Hank.

Hank was the Town Council member who tried to close Tiger Lily's Café down just a couple of short months ago. Hank's plan was discovered, and in the end he was embarrassed in the media and censured by the Town Council. He was not booted from the Town Council, but he was relieved of his role as President. Joan now held that position.

Hank had no use for either one of them. Seeing them together made his blood pressure rise. He continued to patronize the Café only because everyone else in town did. He usually didn't spend any money.

"So what kind of nonsense are the two of you planning?" he asked.

Joan, unconcerned, said, "Nothing sinister, Hank. We're talking about trick-or-treat hours for Halloween night, and coinciding them with the community block party. They're organizing a trick-or-treat for UNICEF event."

"There was a reason for that term, 'pinko commie,' and just to try to be politically correct, I won't use the third term."

"Thank you for that," murmured Joan.

"Why is the town getting involved in that? All that money just goes to Africa."

Annie stared at Hank. "Hank! Are you serious? UNICEF supports children worldwide. And what if the money only went to Africa? What would be wrong with that?"

Joan put her hand on Annie's arm. "Don't argue with him. Leave that to me."

Hank continued, "And anyway, there's another fundraiser going on that same evening. It's a high class affair. I'm going to ask the Town Council to support it, by advertising, attending and donating."

Annie said, "Another event? We have an established schedule of a community charitable event. The whole town knows about the last day of every other month. This will be the third year we've had our party on Halloween. Why in the world would you schedule something on the same evening? And another fundraiser. You're just going to split up attendees, and we'll both come up short."

"Your little Halloween party won't put a damper on ours. We might put a damper on yours, though."

"What's your charity?"

"What?"

"Your charity. For what purpose are you raising funds?"

"That's none of your business."

"I guess you're right. I won't think another thing about it."

She turned from Hank to Joan. "Joan, thank you for coming today, and thank you for asking the Town Council to support us."

Hank actually spit when he shouted, "Let me tell you, little lady, which event the Town Council is going to support. It's not going to be yours!"

Annie stood up, wiped her face of Hank's spit with a napkin, looked him squarely in the eyes, and started to say something. Joan stopped her with a touch of her hand.

"I'll see you later, Annie. Let me just talk to Hank for a minute."

As Annie left, Joan turned and started, "Now, Hank...."

In a few minutes, Annie and everyone else in the Café heard a loud, "Over my dead body!" And Hank stormed out.

Annie needed to move on. She stopped at the stand, leaned in to hold Tiger Lily close, and was pleased to find only minimal resistance before the big girl leaned into her as well. "Come on, Mo. It's time you got to the Tap, and I need to stop in at L'Socks'."

Pete's daughter, Ginger, was teaching the class as Annie entered. Annie liked Ginger. She was a hard worker, working here for both money and high school credit. Her dream was to go to school to study fashion design. While Pete and Janet supported her, they silently wished for a dream that would keep her closer to home.

Ginger threw herself into everything with vigor. The day before, she told Diana she wanted to make costumes for kids that couldn't afford it. Annie was here to talk about it. My goodness, she thought. The block party is just a few weeks away.

When Ginger was free, she came immediately to Annie. "So, what do you think?"

"It's a great idea, but do you have time?"

"I'll make time. Can someone get fabric and thread and some other things for me to use?"

"Sure. We'll have to get that now, in order for you to have time to make them. We'll just have to tell the kids, 'this is what we have' and go forward."

"That won't be a problem. How do we get the kids in to be measured and to know what they want?"

"I'll call the school right now and ask them to send a note home to parents this afternoon. They can come in tomorrow, Friday and Saturday to be measured. We can show them patterns and let them choose."

"Great! Can we get supplies today?"

"How about right now? We'll go to the fabric shop downtown."

Annie once again picked up her cell phone to make the call to the school as they walked to her car. At the fabric shop, patterns, fabric, thread and fillings chosen, Ginger quickly went down the notions aisle and picked up buttons, zippers, snaps and various decorations. The owner of the fabric shop was so supportive she gave a significant discount. Annie would turn this expense in to the committee, but they wanted as much as possible to go to charity, not to supplies.

Ginger was excited. There would be princesses, pirates, elves, witches, ghosts, goblins, angry birds, bad piggies, cats, dogs and little lady bugs. Time or resources were not available to provide the current super heroes or Disney characters, but Ginger thought the children would be pleased.

Kathleen Thompson

Annie assured Ginger that all she had to do was ask and help would come running. There were a few portable sewing machines on The Avenue, and those few belonged to talented seamstresses. Henrie had been known to turn a stitch or two himself!

Chapter 7: No One Looked Too Frazzled

Once again, Annie was running late to get to the Café for lunch rush; it had nearly ended. No one looked too frazzled or dazed, so it must have been an easy one. She went first to the hostess stand to lean in and get her lunchtime purr.

Tiger Lily said, *"Mommy, you didn't forget me today, but you're late again."*

"Did you have a busy lunch, big girl? Should I have gotten here earlier?"

"I did alright without you, but it scared me again."

"You're my little scaredy cat, aren't you?"

"Do the two of you really communicate?" This from Jeff Bennett. Annie had not heard him speak before.

"Oh, hello! Well, I think she knows what I'm saying, but I'm in the weeds, so to speak, when it comes to understanding her."

"It looks like everyone in town is going to be in the weeds for a few days. It looks like you're all going to have fun with this mystery cruise."

"We love doing them. Henrie is so good at coming up with the scripts."

"You and Jessica were right about those names. It does make it easy to remember them."

"I think you'll enjoy seeing round one. Do you plan on coming?"

"Can anything besides watching the mystery tempt me?"

"Free food and free wine. Free very good food and free very good wine."

"I'm in."

"You're here for lunch. Can I seat you?"

"Sure." Jeff looked around the room and saw the mystery crew sitting at a large table by the back window. I like window seating. Is that table in front of the mystery cast available?"

Sure. Have a seat and I'll have someone bring you a menu."

While Jeff walked to the table, Pete and Cyril came in for the second time that day.

"It's time for lunch!" said Pete.

"Yes, it is. I haven't eaten yet. Mind if I join you?"

"Please do."

Annie brought a coffee that Trudie had ready. "Here ya go, my friend. Do you need a menu?"

"Nope. I want the seared pork chop with pesto and mashed butternut squash."

"Good choice. Salad or soup with that?"

"Not today. I intend to dig in at Sassy P's tonight."

"Again, good choice. I'll take this to the kitchen."

Annie took his order and hers for butternut squash soup to the kitchen. On the way back to the table, she picked up a coffee for herself.

Pete drank his coffee and looked casually at the group of guests from the Inn.

"Guests of the Inn back in that corner?" he asked.

"Yes. The big table is the mystery crew. The table of one is a quiet guy, here, I think, on business, but I'm not sure what kind."

"Someone over there looks familiar."

"Familiar good or familiar bad?"

"Unfortunately, when I remember faces, it's usually for a bad reason. But I don't have a handle on it yet. Looks familiar, but...."

"Do you want their names?"

"Sure."

"The guy sitting alone is Jeff something." Annie tried to remember the crew members without turning to see in which order they were sitting. Unfortunately, she got hopelessly confused and could only remember their character names.

"I'm going to have to go home and look. I could give you their mystery names, but I don't have the others memorized. Which person do you think is familiar?"

"I don't want to influence you in how you treat your guests, Annie."

"Well...I think that ship has sailed."

"Sorry." After a bit, Pete said, "Hey, you know that Skype program you have?"

"Oh, no. What do you want me to do?"

"I'm just thinking. You have their names back at the Inn, right? How about setting up your notebook, point it where I can see them, and text or message me the names in order?"

"I could try that. If they happen to be in a place that it would be logical for me to do it. And you have to be able to receive it."

"Good point. I'll stop in at Mem's and see if she can set me up, without telling her why."

"Tell her I asked that you be added to our network, because we serve on so many committees together."

Tiger Lily went to the back of the room to greet the guests. They were, after all, guests at the Inn, so she needed to be polite. She first jumped up to greet Jeff Bennett. He was concentrating on his cell phone and started a bit when she jumped up. He quickly recovered, smiled and greeted her, giving her a pet from head to tail. Tiger Lily purred in response, then moved on to the next table.

She jumped up between a man and woman. The woman was pleased to see her, the man, not so much. The woman made up for it by saying to the table in general, "Look! This must be the famous Tiger Lily herself. The website said she would greet the guests, and it said sometimes she would recommend a meal for guests to order."

"Yeah, I saw her this morning at the Inn. She came downstairs with the group, then scooted out the door as 'Spicy Pepper' came in."

"Well, Tiger Lily, we're awfully pleased to meet you."

Tiger Lily purred, allowed herself to be petted some more and went back to her friend Cyril.

"They seem okay, but that one man was kind of mean."

"Not everyone likes cats."

"But they know we're here. Everyone who comes here looks at that website and it talks about us."

"Was anyone rude?"

"No, but I just got a weird feeling from that man."

Annie gave a call as she got inside the door. "Mom!"

"Yes, dear, are you ready?"

Annie and Nancy left to see Mem, to tell her what kind of computer Nancy had purchased. Annie hoped to hear about

Frank and what might be going on between the two of them, but she didn't want to ask.

Mem was in the back of the room, settling Annie's guest into a gaming chair. Annie pointed him out to Nancy. "That's Herb. He's one of the three staying in the carriage house. I'm not sure about his story, but he seems sad, somehow."

"Oh, yes, I talked with him this morning after you left. He recently lost his significant other. That's the way he said it. He still wears a wedding ring, so apparently he's having a very hard time getting over it."

"And what else did you find out?" Annie had a smile on her face. Her mother was very good at getting information from people.

"Well, Alec and Jessica, they're twins, did you know that? Herb has been a best friend to both of them since grade school. They decided it was time for him to try to get back into the world, so they brought him here, figuring a small tourist town would be just the thing. They are forcing him to do some things with them, but allowing him time to do his gaming or just wander on his own, too."

"And did they tell you this in front of him?"

"Oh, goodness no! Jessica shared that with me after the gentlemen got up from the breakfast table."

"Mom, how do you do it?"

"I don't know. I'm very good at this with everyone but you, dear."

"Well, maybe you can find out what's going on between Mem and Frank."

The three women sat down at a table already set with a carafe of hot water and a basket with a variety of teas. "Let's relax before talking about that computer," said Mem. She continued, "Annie, I'll have Pete set up by 4:00. It's a good idea to add him."

The women chatted for several minutes, then Annie watched her mother do her magic. Little by little, Nancy worked the conversation around to Frank, and then the floodgates opened.

"I just don't understand it! Annie, you know how hard it was for Frank, when he was still a guest at the Inn. You were so good to him; we all were. We helped him through a very bad period of time, and helped him find a building, and supported him in every way. And now! Now, he's going to that fancy dancy black tie ball on the same day as our block party, and he's going as Geraldine's date!"

Annie sat back in her chair. Hard. "Geraldine's date? Geraldine? Date? Since when are the two of you 'seeing others'? And Geraldine?"

"Well, apparently, we've never been exclusive. At least, that's what I've recently been told. And yes. Geraldine."

"I don't know what to feel first. Angry because of the way he's treating you, sad because he won't be involved with our party, or maybe confused about the Geraldine part."

"I won't mind if you feel angry for me first."

"Okay, then."

Nancy said, "I've heard that name before. Geraldine. Remind me who she is."

Annie and Mem laughed. It was good to see Mem laugh about something, Annie thought. Between the two of them, they told Nancy about Geraldine.

Geraldine had been all the rage in high school. She was the cheerleader that nabbed the football star. They married right after high school and their dreams…well, their dreams never did get off the ground.

They lived in a beautiful house purchased by Geraldine's parents, and through the years they held and lost a number of jobs. Most recently, Geraldine opened a rival restaurant to Tiger Lily's Café.

Called Chelsea Diner and located in the building now housing Frank's antique shop, she modeled it extensively after the Café. It had the same color scheme, layout and menu, and Geraldine tried to give it the same cheery ambiance.

In league with the President of the Town Council, a baboon named Hank, she intended to force the closure of the Café while the Diner seamlessly took over as the town's unofficial headquarters. Not only did her plan fail, so did the Diner.

Geraldine was arrested and charged with a number of criminal offenses. Now she was out on bail, and it looked as if she would be able to buy her way out of the charges.

Mem brought the conversation back to the present day. "Let's talk about that fancy ball she's going to have. Hank is helping her, you know. They don't even have a charity picked out yet! They just wanted to do a black tie event to keep the big money away from us!"

"To be honest, most of the big money folks don't come to our parties anyway, but some do."

"They sent special invitations to a lot of the people that do come to ours. The superintendent of schools, and all of the principals and counselors. All of the attorneys, realtors and accountants in town." Here, Mem paused.

"Business owners, except, apparently, any of the owners of businesses on The Avenue," she added ruefully.

Annie added what she learned from the confrontation between Joan and Hank. "I think Joan will swing the Town Council our way, at least in terms of town support, and perhaps some advertising money."

"Oh, Geraldine's invited all of the elected officials as well, town, county and state, probably even federal."

"How is she going to get them there, if she hasn't specified a charity?"

"She's counting on the 'black tie' to bring them in."

"Where's she having it?"

"Can you believe this, she was going to ask Felicity if she could use the catering hall at the Café. But someone stopped her before she really put her foot in it. They're having it in the community building at the town park."

"Is that even heated?"

"Well, now you say that, I don't know. It's not open for events in the winter."

"There can be snow on Halloween. It can get cold."

"I'll be watching the weather forecast and praying for a polar vortex."

When Annie arrived home, five cats in tow, Sam was in the kitchen. He had a few pieces of driftwood art for her to see.

"Oh, Sam! I didn't know you were so talented!"

"Well, I'm not, really. Greg has been very helpful. I take a few pieces over at a time and use the workshop in his garage. He has tools, and I picked up some art supplies."

Annie picked up a fish made with several small pieces of wood held together with a piece of wire down the middle. Sam started with a piece of wood in the shape of a mouth, a button eye, and pieces that moved from small to large to small again, and two pieces glued together to make a tailfin.

She picked up a birdhouse. Several pieces of wood of a similar shape and size were nailed around a base. A cone-shaped top and some unique, curved pieces that went from bottom to top, like thick branches of ivy, finished the piece. Holes were cut for birds to get in. Annie looked inside and saw three perches as well.

The last item was a whimsical dancing girl. One cone-shaped piece of wood served as the body; two long, thin pieces served as legs; one long, thin piece served as two arms; and it didn't matter that the head was a lumpish piece that didn't exactly look like a head. Together, it was perfect.

"I can't believe it. You're a natural."

"I've found a new hobby, that's for sure. This will give us an excuse to come here a couple of times a year, Annie!"

Annie went upstairs to make sure the kids had a good supper. They would join her at the mystery party that evening.

Tiger Lily followed her up and went straight to the water bowl, put her right foot in the middle of it and took a very long drink.

"Disgusting," spat Little Socks.

Chapter 8: Honey Bear Now Claimed The Porch

Around 4:30, Annie was back downstairs. She noticed Honey Bear now claimed the back porch as his own. He napped on the most comfortable chair, a love seat that could actually fit two people, or one person and a big cat, except Honey Bear was stretched over both seats.

The mystery crew had a large plate to share Bing cherries, chocolate covered strawberries and finger sandwiches. Jeff had a plate but sat by himself. Annie said hello as she set her notebook up in the corner.

She had her back to the group as she got into her instant messaging account. She sent a quick note to Pete and set up the camera. As the camera focused on the group, she saw Pete was on and taking a look. She quickly typed in the names, starting with, "Man at 12:00, Hirsch Stone…."

She didn't know Pete had taken a few screen shots, but then, she didn't need to know. She was just helping a friend, after all.

After a few minutes, she signed off. As she left the porch, she said, "I can't wait for the fun to begin. I'll see you at Sassy P's!"

Annie called up the stairs, "Come on, kids. Time to go. You too, Kali and Ko." Everyone trotted downstairs, looking around corners to make sure the dreaded Uncle Honey Bear wasn't lurking around. Annie opened the big door for them, and they all went out into the crisp fall evening, excited about "something new" that was about to happen.

At Sassy P's, Annie noticed Jesus had closed the back room to guests with a rope and a standing sign that read,

"Welcome to the One Year Anniversary of Duckweed Spirits! Doors will open at 7:00."

Annie gave final instructions to the kids. "You are going to stay in this back dining room tonight. I don't care who sits at that bar in the main room, you stay here. I've got some special seats for you. They're back here on the wall, away from the feet of people who might have too much to drink. There are nice, soft cushions, and they're too tall for humans. They are for you."

Annie turned to leave, then turned back to say, "And there's a bowl of water, because we're going to be here a while. You might get thirsty. Now listen to me. When people start coming in, you stay back here."

Seven cats looked obediently at their Mommy. Two cats thought to themselves, *"Thank goodness!"* Five cats thought to themselves, *"Yeah, right."*

Kali and Ko obliged immediately, taking the cushions in the middle. The best ones.

The other five decided they had work to do. First of all, they had to help Mommy, Felicity and Trudie set out the food. Yum! The humans were in and out of the kitchen area. Every time they came back, something else delicious was in hand.

Tiger Lily's nose was honed to all kinds of ingredients and spices. She explained the food items to her siblings.

There was brie, baked with brown sugar, brandy and pecans. Slices of apple and pear and several different kinds of crackers were piled near.

Rosemary flatbread was topped with bleu cheese, grapes and honey.

There were wontons made with butternut squash and sage.

115

Butternut squash was also included in another dish, with Portobello mushrooms and gruyere, wrapped in phyllo dough.

Individual servings of spanakopita were also present, with the phyllo dough serving as a wrap.

There were sesame chicken wings, crabmeat stuffed mushroom caps, crab Rangoon and mini vegetable spring rolls.

There were dishes with deep fried tortellini, parmesan garlic bread, and fried feta ravioli.

Tiger Lily didn't get the finer point, that everything was prepared to be finger food, no utensils required.

Jesus and Minnie moved tables so they would have a theater in the round. A large table to seat seven was placed in the middle of the room. One table was closer than the others, but all of the tables were spaced so that this table stood out. A remote wireless microphone was in the center of the table.

Bottles of dry red wine and chillers with bottles of crisp dry white wine were set on every table, with as many glasses as there were chairs.

By 6:00, Ray and Chris arrived with Jock in tow. The humans got busy with set-up. Jock sat next to the food table, hoping someone would drop something on the floor.

Ray and Chris put the basket with mystery booklets on the table in the middle of the room and put the basket with investigator questions on the table that stood closest to it.

They hung banners, balloons and streamers around the room. This was a celebration, after all. The banners said, *"Happy Anniversary!" "One Year Of Success, A Century To Go!" "Congratulations On Two New Products!" "Duckweed Spirits, A Miracle Company!"* and *"To Many More Years!"*

One large sign was hung over the large table. It read, *"In The Weeds, A Murder Mystery."*

Mr. Bean and Mo helped Ray and Chris by getting underfoot. Actually, they were saying things like, *"Put balloons here, Ray,"* and *"We need more streamers in this corner."* Of course, neither Ray nor Chris could understand them. And Mr. Bean couldn't understand Mo.

Tiger Lily, swooning with the smells, sat under the buffet table and wouldn't move.

Little Socks found Ray's jacket and curled up for a nap.

Sassy Pants followed Jesus and Minnie, jumping on tables and proffering her stomach for tickles. Sometimes, they obliged. Often, not. They obliged on occasion, though, which gave her the hope she needed to carry on.

Candice came in shortly after Ray and Chris. She would act as server for the evening while George handled Mo's Tap without her.

At 6:30, Carlos and Jerry arrived. Jerry brought in tiered serving platters filled with pumpkin truffles, sea salt caramel truffles and other best sellers from the Confectionary.

Carlos had mini muffin servings of orange bread with nuts and dates, cranberry nut bread, and dark chocolate cake with cream cheese.

They left and returned with two large platters of apples, cored and sliced into individual servings. They were covered with caramel or dark, milk or white chocolate, nuts, candies and sprinkles.

At 6:55, they stood back to survey their work.

Perfect.

At 7:00, Jesus removed the rope barrier and invited guests to come in.

It seemed the entire town had arrived. The cats were actually scared at first. Little Socks and Sassy Pants joined Tiger Lily and Jock under the buffet table. They soon realized they could be trampled by people pushing to get the food. They saw the wisdom in Mommy's madness and rushed to the seats she had prepared for them. Jock followed and was happy to find a couple of dog-sized cushions as well.

Mo tried at first to find some women to love, but realized quickly that no one paid attention to him. They wanted to claim seats with coats and purses and then help themselves to food. He, too, quickly found his way to the cushions.

Soon, Mr. Bean was the only kitty without a cushion. The little guy found himself stranded on the wrong side of the dining room. He looked with terror at the crowd and cowered behind a potted plant. Thank goodness Chris saw him. Before Mr. Bean knew it, a strong, steady hand picked him up. Chris held him close as he carried him across the room to the cushions in the back. Mr. Bean scurried behind Tiger Lily and peeked out from behind her tail. She allowed him to stay. After all, she was the big sister.

By the time Mr. Bean was safely placed in the back, they had been joined by Cyril as well. Tiger Lily silently prayed that neither Uncle Honey Bear or that dreaded Claire would come. They didn't usually come, but this wasn't a typical night.

Jesus and Minnie counted heads as people entered. Not counting the mystery crew, they could seat 88. When they thought they hit 70, they closed the rope again and announced to the room, "We need you to take a seat, please, so we can assure there is still seating left."

The crowd was in a good mood and everyone obliged. The mystery crew and investigators sat down as well. Annie was pleased to see Jeff Bennett at that table, with Chris, Clara and Holly.

Annie, Candice and Felicity walked around the room to do a quick count and realized they were right to stop letting people in. There were only four seats left.

Annie went to the rope line and said, "You can let four more people in, then we're full." She noticed out of the corner of her eye that Geraldine and Hank were in line, but they were not included in the first four. She smiled to herself.

As Annie moved around the room, greeting everyone that she could, she was happy to see all of her friends from The Avenue had been on time. Laila, Teresa, Jennifer and Marie were at a table. Jolly and Frank sat with Pete and Janet. On the other side of the room, she saw Henrie, Mem, Diana and Cheryl, Ray's wife. Greg and his wife sat with Nancy and Sam. Annie was pleased to see her other guests, Jessica, Alec and Herb, had come in time. They conveniently found one of the few tables that sat only three people on higher café chairs.

As she moved through the room, she could hear a high-pitched voice, "Don't you know who I am? I demand to be seated!" and a loud roar, "She did this on purpose! She counted the number of people in front of me and cut the line there for spite!"

Annie could tell that Jesus was responding in a calm, quiet and firm voice, but he wasn't making any headway. Pete walked through the room, stood behind Jesus and asked, "What's the problem, Jesus?"

Hank knew better than to argue with Pete in front of an audience. He tried it before with disastrous results. Geraldine had not witnessed that event, but she heard all about it. The two of them decided to find a seat at the bar in the tasting room.

Chapter 9: In The Weeds, Round One

With the seating situation clarified, guests were invited to help themselves to food again. Jesus and Minnie walked the room, making sure each table had enough wine. Felicity, Trudie, Carlos and Jerry kept the buffet table filled. Candice and Annie made sure tables were clean and everyone had a glass.

Ray, acting his part as the Mystery Cruise Director, gave each character a booklet and each investigator a set of questions.

"The main characters have already read the first page. They will be introducing themselves using that. Characters, you are not to turn to page two until you've been instructed.

"Page two includes the murder. Each of you have instructions that will lead up to the murder.

"Following the murder, the investigators start to do their job, and characters, you have instructions and scripts to follow as well, starting on page three.

"Investigators, you need to be familiar with the questions in your envelopes. It's important that you ask your questions in order. You all have cues to guide you. After the first question, one of the characters will recognize the cue and will speak again. That will cue the next question.

"Do not look further than page one until instructed. Then do not move past page two until instructed. And under no circumstances are you to look beyond page three tonight. We'll start with page four tomorrow.

"We'll start our play at 8:00. That will give everyone here time to eat, drink and be merry."

Ray looked at Jeff. "Jeff, have you introduced yourself to the other investigators?" He nodded that he had. "I want to thank you again, for being willing to take a part in a silly little play."

"I think it will be fun. Thanks for asking."

At 8:00, Ray called the room to attention and announced, "Welcome to In The Weeds, a murder mystery. This is the first round, and unfortunately, we are not going to solve the mystery tonight. The mystery will be concluded over the course of two more nights, but the setting will not be in Chelsea.

"I'll have to ask you to pay attention to the action this evening. There is a microphone at this table, as you can tell, but there will be other things to observe, acts on the part of the characters, that will be important to solving the crime.

"This is a murder mystery. One of the seven major characters will die tonight. We will not know who that is until we reach that part of the script.

"One of the remaining characters will be the murderer. We will not know who that is until some point of round three. The murderer him or herself will not even know the truth until that point.

"We want to thank all of you for being here, to help us, to enjoy an evening with friends, and hopefully to tell all your friends and enemies what fun you had here tonight."

With that, Ray sat down and signaled the first character to begin.

The first character was dressed for the part. He looked like a rich playboy from the 1970s, dress shirt unbuttoned to the bottom of his chest, sleeves rolled to mid-forearm. Gold chains reached from neck to naval, and a jaunty scarf was tied around his neck. Several rings adorned his fingers. He stood up and with dramatic flair said, "I'm Brad Spit." He had to pause a bit for the laughter to die down.

"I have a lot of connections, if you know what I mean. I live here in Chelsea, in the family mansion built in the 1800s. To be honest, it's a bit run down now.

"The Spit family got rich from a large farm on a remote island in the north, actually in Canada. We import crops into the United States through Chelsea's port. You've probably never heard of the island. We call it Spit City." There was more laughter, so George paused once again.

"It has another name, but let's not mess with that. Anyway, we were rich back then, but a long line of...well, let's just say a long line of party boys pretty much used up the family fortune. Unfortunately – that's me without a fortune – I take after those Spits."

He paused for a second. "No one got that joke. Oh, well. I'll move on.

"A weed grows wild there on the island. We never paid any attention to it; it was basically a nuisance. The ducks love to nest in it, so we call it duckweed."

At this point, Brad spoke from the cuff rather than from the written script. "I've noticed your local florist seems to like it also. I've seen it in fresh flower arrangements all over town." The crowd howled and several called for Clara to stand up and take a bow. She did.

After the laughter died down, Brad continued. "I digressed. Back to my introduction. My sister still lives on the island and manages the family farm. She has no problem whatsoever supporting me. Well, she might have a little problem supporting me. She does, every now and then, tell me to get a job. But really, I'm sure she doesn't mean it. She did stop sending money to fix the mansion. I'm sure if she knew how badly that rundown rat trap is affecting our local reputation, she would step right up. Oh, did I get off track again?" Laughter rippled around the room.

"Ahem. A large corporation – I won't name them – recently started dumping nuclear waste on the island."

Brad had to pause again while the audience yelled out the name of a regional nuclear facility.

"I cannot confirm that. But you know what you're talking about, I'm sure. Anyway, my sister was going to report this company, but then she noticed the duckweed had become a little strange. She sent some of that weed and said I should use some of my underhanded connections – she really said that – to make us some money.

"I realized she's not a complete idiot. There did appear to be some commercial potential in this weed. I sent samples to a famous scientist, Dr. Mortimer Bong." Once again, laughter played around the room.

"Long story short, my sister and I are now quite rich. Duckweed Spirits has an exclusive contract with us, and they pay us very well."

As Brad sat down to tremendous applause, the second character stood up.

He had on a bright blue bow tie and a ratty-looking jacket with patches sewn on the elbows. His glasses were large and kept slipping down his nose, which looked to have a permanent upturn. He began. "I am Dr. Mortimer Bong." Laughter again.

"I am – well, as Mr. Spit said, I am, in fact, a famous scientist. A very famous scientist. If you have not heard of me, you need to broaden your horizons.

"I have a degree from Cheerio University." He paused while the crowd once again was wild with laughter. He looked around and said, "Some of you are looking at me as if my degree came out of a box! Egad! You may not have heard of it, but it is famous in some circles. Very small circles." He mimicked a circle the size of a Cheerio to the laughing crowd.

"My doctoral thesis connected plants with the significant growth in the alternative lighting industry. This industry will continue to experience significant growth as our infrastructure grows ever more unreliable.

"My favorite plant is already used in the alternative lighting industry; oil for burning in any ordinary oil lamp can be extracted from its seeds. You may have heard of it. Cannabis sativa, or hemp." This time there was not only laughter, but some people stood to clap their approval.

"So far, my ideas are far ahead of those in the industry. I'm still working on making inroads. I believe I'm making significant progress.

"Mr. Spit delivered duckweed to me for experimentation. I was astounded by the results. I have used it to produce a wide range of products, all with great commercial potential. Again, some of those products are ahead of their time. I'm still working on making inroads.

"Hmmm. It sounds like I'm repeating myself."

Clearing his throat, he continued. "I'm not a business man. My skills are in research. I asked my great friend, Spicy Pepper, to help me set up a business. My goal is to take the alternative lighting industry by storm, but first, we've had to market a few other products to get off the ground."

Dr. Bong sat down to applause and Ray stood. He hadn't dressed up. He looked like Ray, but with the flippant air of a playboy, he said, "I am Spicy Pepper." The room was filled with laughter, and some folks called to Cheryl, "How spicy is he?" Cheryl, red-faced, put her head on the table.

Ray continued. "I'm rich; I love cars and women love me. Well, I love women too, but I don't have to work at it. They fall all over themselves to get to me. And I've got the Midas touch in business. Everything I touch turns to gold.

"My very good friend, Dr. Mortimer Bong, asked for my help in setting up a business. He demonstrated products he had in development and I saw the potential immediately. Between the two of us, though, we didn't have enough capital to make it work.

"Fortunately there are several rich women in my stable. One society hag – excuse me – beauty, is Mary Monroe." Claps and laughter rolled around the room again.

"Ms. Monroe is quite wealthy. She handed over the cash we needed without question. I enticed her to give 48% of the shares to Dr. Bong and myself."

As Ray sat down to much applause, the next character rose. She took off her coat to reveal a tight fitting dress, red, with sequins and cheap jewels from shoulder to hem. The hem came to mid-thigh. Annie remembered her as she looked the other times she'd seen her and realized she had purchased a much larger bra than needed and stuffed it with something that rounded and firmed her breasts. From some bin at the Goodwill store she must have found a gold wig with piles of curls. It looked to Annie as if she had padded her hips as well. Her shoes were retro 1990s, colorful and high heeled.

With a touch of her hand to her hair, a little wiggle of her hips and a shake of her healthy bosom, she simpered, "I am

Mary Monroe." Applause rippled, and some men shouted, "You've still got it!"

"I'm wealthy, and as you can tell, I'm quite lovely. I am not prepared to reveal my true age. It is sufficient to say that I am 'mature,' but with sufficient application of make-up, I look to be a model in my thirties. At least from a distance. I am always looking for ways to, shall we say, recapture my natural youthful beauty.

"I have a mansion just outside the town of Marsh Haven. This mansion is the perfect place for the little 'visits' I have with young men. These young men amuse me greatly, but recently I fell in love with one of them, Spicy Pepper.

"When he asked for money for his little venture, I thought handing over the cash would win his heart. I'm still working on that part, but for now, I am the Chair of the company. I own more than half of the shares. Being Chair isn't hard, really. I attend a few meetings and sign thingies prepared by the secretary, Alabaster Pearl."

Mary wiggled into her seat to rousing applause and more wolf whistles.

Alabaster rose. She was dressed very simply in a black business suit with a gray blouse, ruffled at the neck. Her hem fell somewhere below the knees and above her calves. Her hair was an unsightly mess of straight areas and curls. Annie thought she must have worked for hours to achieve the look.

Alabaster looked nervously at the table, then up at the crowd, then back down. Finally, with eyes directed somewhere toward the ceiling, she said, "I am Alabaster Pearl. Recently, I took employment as secretary to the directors of Duckweed Spirits. I must appear quite dull to you, but I'm actually extremely efficient and intelligent.

"I am impressed by strong business women, like Sparkle Shine. She owns the marketing agency we use. She's high-powered, seductive, and very successful. I hope to emulate her someday."

Alabaster sat quickly to cede the floor to Sparkle. Her exit from the stage was so sudden, and Sparkle's rise so dynamic, the applause for Alabaster was muted and brief.

Sparkle was dressed to kill in a tight fitting business suit. The skirt, hitting at mid-thigh, hugged every curve. The tank top under her jacket revealed a few inches of stomach, and the jacket itself curved like the skirt, hugging every inch of arm, back and hips. Her shoes were 21st century stilettoes.

With sexy-professional flair, Sparkle pronounced, "I am Sparkle Shine. I am more successful than anyone expected me to be. I have a marketing degree from the Wharton School of Business. I've worked for several multi-national companies, but I just wasn't satisfied until I started my own business, called – this is so catchy – Sparkle!

"We conduct marketing campaigns to give some sizzle to mundane products. I was called in to help Duckweed Spirits launch their two latest products, Duckweed Diet Pills and Duckweed Drawing Paper. I mean, really! Two products screaming for sizzle!

"At great expense I pulled off a coup and convinced super sexy Onstair Royds to become the face of Duckweed Spirits!"

The crowd laughed and applauded Sparkle as she sat, looking radiantly at Onstair Royds as he stood.

He began with a sexy swagger. "I am Onstair Royds." The audience exploded with applause. Annie laughed as she took in his clothing. His jacket was padded to produce the effect of bulging muscles on his shoulders, arms and back. The tight pants were padded with leg muscles and what looked like a large sausage. He wore a wig as well, a 1970s style brown wig covered with, the only way Annie could describe it was "man curls."

"As you can tell, I can turn the eye of any lady. I'm built, you might say. I'm also a triathlete.

"A couple of years ago I took gold in the World games. Unfortunately, I tested positive for drugs. Someone rigged the test. No matter how I protested, they took the gold away from me.

"Finally, I was able to convince the authorities of my innocence. The ruling was overturned and now I'm training for the Olympics.

"When Sparkle asked me to join her ad campaign, I said yes. The company and the products sound boring, but I need to improve my marketing potential. And now that I'm working with the folks at Duckweed, I'm actually impressed."

Onstair sat back down to much applause. Women in the audience stood and shouted, "Take it off! Take it off!" until Onstair rose to quiet them with his hands, acknowledging the accolades with a sexy smile and kisses blown around the room.

Onstair Royds was the last character to be introduced. Ray quietly asked the characters to turn to page two.

Following the script from the booklet, Dr. Mortimer Bong stood to propose a toast. "I would like to thank you all for coming here tonight. One year ago, Spicy Pepper and I opened the doors to Duckweed Spirits…with the help of Mary Monroe, of course," this last was said grudgingly. "Due almost completely to my intelligence, we have had astonishing success. We can look forward to a very exciting future! Please stand with me while I propose a toast."

Everyone stood, and Dr. Bong allowed a few seconds to pass while some refilled their own glasses and others helped their tablemates to do so. He then proclaimed to the room, glass raised, "Ladies and gentlemen, to the glorious future of Duckweed Spirits!"

Glasses were raised, a chorus of "Duckweed Spirits!" could be heard around the room, and soon people were sitting down, placing their glasses back on the tables.

The microphone on the table allowed the characters to be heard above the noise of everyone settling back down.

Three things happened simultaneously.

Alabaster Pearl, before sitting down, put her hands to her breasts, heaved her bosom and declared, "Oh, my. Now that's a nice little rush!" She sat, looking a bit confused.

Onstair Royds grabbed his throat, appeared to choke, quickly caught his breath and sat down suddenly with a dazed expression.

Spicy Pepper grabbed his throat as well, made loud choking noises and collapsed in his chair, head slumped to the side.

The crowd gave a collective, "Oh no!" After several seconds, Spicy stood up to announce, "Friends and colleagues, Spicy Pepper is dead. It looks like murder. We are going to have to call in the police, but first I will remove his body."

Everyone was silent, even the audience. Perhaps they were shocked to see a resident of Chelsea murdered in front of their eyes.

Spicy walked out of the garden area and around the rope, waited a few seconds and then announced from the other room, "The police are here."

The former Spicy Pepper walked back into the room. "Good evening. I'm Detective Brown of the State Police."

The audience roared its approval of Ray's resurrection.

Ray acknowledged the applause and continued, in dramatic fashion, "I will conduct the investigation into Spicy Pepper's death. I'm the best detective in the State, so you can be assured I will find the guilty party.

"I will ask questions and demand answers. As part of my brilliant plan, I impounded this panel of employees and associates of Duckweed Spirits to assist in the investigation." Ray gestured to the table of four as he spoke.

Three investigators stood and bowed to the audience while Holly waved, acknowledging their applause. They drew their chairs around the large table, so their voices would be picked up by the microphone. From here on, the characters would remain seated as they spoke.

Ray instructed the characters to turn to page three.

Jeff said. "Detective Brown, I have just received confirmation of the cause and manner of death. Spicy Pepper was poisoned with one of his own products, Duckweed Sewage Cleaner. He was murdered."

The characters reacted with shocked gasps as they looked around the table at one another accusingly.

Chris, allowing a few seconds of outrage and dismay to pass, looked at Onstair and said, "Onstair, I noticed you had a reaction very similar to Spicy's after the toast. Are you ill?"

"I'm not sure what happened. My throat got really tight so I couldn't breathe, then it just loosened up. I must be allergic to something. I dumped out the red wine and switched to the white."

Clara stepped in with a question. "Alabaster, you seem to be very competent. Surely you could be working somewhere more prestigious. Are you happy at Duckweed Spirits?"

"Well, as it happens, I am very competent. I've had high profile jobs in the past. Very high profile jobs. For example, I worked for Barry Goldfinger and also for Mitt Downey, Jr. But I don't do well in the public eye. I decided to take a quieter position. Spicy Pepper was impressed with my references, and he hired me to be the secretary for the board."

Jeff stepped in again with a question for Sparkle Shine. "Sparkle, earlier this evening you handed Spicy Pepper a container of some sort. He put it in his pocket. Can you tell me what it was?"

"Spicy said he had a headache. He's been having dizzy spells and sometimes he sees flashing lights. I had some extra strength liquid pain killer with me and I gave it to him. He said he'd take it later if he didn't start to feel better."

Holly had questions for Dr. Mortimer Bong. "Dr. Bong, I'm sure rival companies want to get their hands on duckweed and on your product recipes. How do you secure the recipes, and how do you keep products secure?"

"Security is very tight. As a safety measure, recipes are named for cigarettes, like Lark and Kent. Nothing is on paper. Everything is stored online. A separate password is required for each recipe, and I am the only person who knows them. I keep a written copy just in case I have a memory lapse. That list is in a very safe place.

"Product samples are in the lab, but they are locked in refrigerated storage secured with a combination lock. I'm the only person with the combination. I keep that with the list of passwords, but again, in a very safe place."

Detective Brown challenged Dr. Bong. "The recipes are not as secure as you think. I searched Spicy Pepper's body before coming in. A letter was in his jacket pocket. Let me share it with you. I present Clue #1!"

Detective Brown held two pieces of paper which he waved at the characters. "This is a letter addressed to Spicy Pepper from a computer security company. The secret recipes were hacked by someone working out of Marsh Haven. In addition to the letter, the company sent a printout of passwords they were able to discover, showing the possibility that others could easily find them."

Dr. Bong sputtered his protest, but he was silenced by Holly, who turned to Mary Monroe. "Ms. Monroe, the hacker was in Marsh Haven. Isn't that where you live?"

"I am shocked – shocked, I tell you. It is ridiculous to suggest that I, or that any of my friends, had a hand in it."

Jeff asked another question. "Sparkle, is your marketing agency really a success? Do you have other contracts?"

"Sparkle is a great success. We have the Duckweed contract and a contract with Manly Men. They make luxury man purses. They gave two of them to me, and I gave one to Dr. Bong and one to Onstair Royds. They can tell you what an outstanding company it is."

Jeff looked at both men. "Is she telling the truth?"

Dr. Bong confirmed Sparkle's statement. "Sparkle did give me a Manly Man Purse. I have it here. See how detailed the pattern is."

Onstair agreed. "Here's mine. It is definitely made for us manly men."

While Onstair spoke, Alabaster stood up and walked behind him. She put her arms on his shoulders and leaned over to – apparently – smell his hair. She gave him a sexy little smile as she walked around him and back to her seat.

Sparkle Shine, watching this little display, started the conversation again. She had a question of her own. "Before coming here tonight, a group of us met at Mo's Tap. Spicy and I arrived early to have a drink and a…a little meeting. We didn't want anyone to…get the wrong idea, you see. We went to the parking lot to pretend we had just arrived, but as we walked out, we were almost run over by Brad Spit, driving like a bat out of Cleveland. Spicy thought he was trying to kill us, but I believed you, Brad, when you said you didn't see us. What really happened?"

"I thought I was running late, and I was driving fast. You fools stepped right in front of me. I was fortunate to miss you."

Brad, having the floor, turned to Mary Monroe. "Mary, you don't care much for Sparkle, do you?"

"You're right. I don't care for her. If you must know, I am heartbroken Spicy Pepper is gone. I love him so much, I made a new will naming him my sole heir. Sparkle was trying to seduce him away from me. She is shameless! Her skirts! They barely cover her essentials! I'll bet their meeting tonight was not about business at all." She turned and said, "Sparkle, I demand to know what your meeting was about!"

Sparkle bristled with indignation. "Spicy and I were not having an affair. I'll do whatever is necessary to make my business a success. Spicy was attracted to me, so I used it to my advantage. And anyway, he's not my type. I prefer an athletic man." With this, she cast a glance at Onstair Royds.

She turned back to Mary and continued. "This evening, I tried to persuade Spicy to spend more money on marketing, but he refused. I even wore my shortest skirt and sat in a very…well, in a very flattering position!"

Mary starred daggers at Sparkle, then looked quickly away.

Clara had another question. "Mary and Dr. Bong, I was outside the boardroom during your last meeting. You were actually yelling at one another. What was that about?"

Mary was the first to respond. "We, the board, discussed which product to promote next. I insisted on Duckweed Risqué Lingerie. Dr. Bong argued for some stupid candlewick. I'm majority shareholder, so of course I got my way." Even though she had answered the question, Mary appeared a bit distracted.

Dr. Bong answered as Mary's attention waned. "I believe Duckweed Candlewicks is the product to take us to the next level. Of course, Mary refused. She is going to bankrupt the company!"

Mary, still distracted and appearing somewhat confused, stood up to go to Onstair Royds. She leaned in to smell his hair and gave him a timid smile. Looking even more confused, she returned to her seat.

Around the room, people looked at one another, also confused. Holly, seeming unconcerned, had a question for Brad Spit. "Brad, just before the toast, I saw you take a small bottle out of your pocket. When Alabaster wasn't looking, you poured something into her wine. What were you up to?"

Brad looked smug. "I've taken her out few times. She's very interested me, but she claims to be interested in the import business. Of course, because I import duckweed, I can give her some pointers. I know how to play along. Alabaster is very prim. She's probably scared of the action she would get from me. I wanted to liven her up a little. I keep vodka in the bottle, and I was hoping to, you know, shake her loose. I planned to offer her a ride home, and, well, you know what I expected."

Jeff had another question. "Onstair and Alabaster, the other day I saw the two of you talking. It looked like you were making advances, Onstair, and that you, Alabaster, were uncomfortable with it. What was going on?"

Alabaster was the first to respond. "Onstair came in for a look around the office. He flirted with me, but he's not my type. I prefer a more mature man, like Brad." She looked shyly in Brad's direction and continued, for Brad's benefit, "I probably don't need to be loosened up at this point." She turned back to Jeff and said, "Anyway, I told Onstair I wasn't interested."

Onstair, with a look of disgust, said. "I did flirt with Alabaster. She's actually quite sexy underneath that efficient exterior. I'm no longer interested, though. I'm not used to being turned down."

Detective Brown addressed the group. We've made a great deal of progress tonight, but we still have a long way to go. We're going to stop our investigation for the moment, and we'll pick it up tomorrow night at the time and place previously scheduled.

The play had been so much fun that Sassy P's did not close for another hour. Jesus stopped the free flow of wine, however, and guests eventually left. Most of the food was gone before the play began, and only a few crumbs remained by the end of the evening.

The cats stayed back on the high cushions until almost all of the guests were gone.

Tiger Lily said, *"Well, that was confusing."*

"What was?" asked Sassy Pants.

"The whole thing. I guess that's why people were laughing. It just didn't make sense to me."

Little Socks, stirring from a nap, said, *"Why did it have to make sense? Humans are silly sometimes."*

Tiger Lily persisted, *"But there's something not right about them."*

Cyril agreed. *"Pete knows one of them. I'm not sure which one, but I think it's that big guy. The one with the funny name."*

Kali and Ko said together, *"They all have funny names." "I can't tell which one is funniest."*

"Trill!"

Jock looked at Kali and Ko. *"What do you think about them? They're staying at the Inn."*

Kali, the man lover, looked dreamily at the Onstair Royds character. *"The big one is so handsome."*

Ko, ever the man hater, rolled her eyes. *"He's a big galoot. And his wife, she's mean."*

"Then he needs someone to love him. I can do that. He gives good pets."

Tiger Lily thought to herself, *Why do I have to put up with this?* She tried to get the group back on track. *"Kali, Ko, straighten up. What are they like?"*

Ko said, *"Well, that older man, the Spit guy, he doesn't like us. He doesn't like cats or dogs, and he's really kind of mad that they're staying in a place that has us all over."*

Mr. Bean cried, *"Oh no! Not again! We can't have people here that don't like us!"*

"But that Hank doesn't like us, and he still comes in here. He's out there in the bar," added Sassy Pants.

Mo, upset, gave several trills in a row.

"What did he say?" asked Tiger Lily.

Cyril answered before Kali and Ko. *"He said we shouldn't get sidetracked. They were all in at Mo's Tap earlier today, and the big guy and his mousy wife were fighting. And the others are getting tired of it and said this would probably be their last trip together."*

All of the cats and Jock stared at Cyril. *"You understood him?"*

"Oh, for crying out loud! You guys live together! Learn the language!"

"He could learn ours!"

"He can't. He had a terrible trauma as a kitten, and he can't fix it. He'll always speak in that secret language, but you can learn it."

Hopelessly sidetracked by now, they didn't talk about the guests at the Inn after that. Now that fewer human feet were in the room, they ventured out to look for anything tasty that might have fallen on the floor.

Chapter 10: Tired Humans Sat, Feet Throbbing

By the time the last of the guests were gone, Sassy P's was cleaned and ready to go for the next day. Tired humans sat at tables, feet throbbing, legs aching, but overall, happy for the good turnout and the great time.

Candice said, "Mo's is still open."

"Yes, it is," came some tired responses.

"Does anyone really want to go home?" This from Chris, who was tired, but beginning to perk up.

Suddenly, everyone began to perk up. "No!"

"Let's go for a drink and talk about how this went. This is much better than the first one we tried to do. I think we might be onto something now."

Ray summed it up. "Let's go. Beer, nuts and debriefing!"

Henrie, always the first one up at the Inn, said, "I'm going to call it a night. Which of you lovely ones are coming home with me?"

He stood up to go, and five cats went to the door. "It looks like Mo and Mr. Bean are going with you, Annie."

"Perfect."

Chris and Annie, carrying Mo and Mr. Bean, Ray, Cheryl and Jock, Candice, Felicity, Trudie, Carlos and Jerry set off for Mo's. Minnie and Jesus would join the group after locking Sassy P's.

Once settled, everyone started talking at once, mini-conversations floating around the table. Mo and Mr. Bean sat on a chair at the end of the table, Jock on the floor beside them.

Mr. Bean said, *"Hey, look around the room. All of the Inn people are here."*

"There are more than those play people?" asked Jock.

"Yeah. You see that guy sitting alone, kind of close to the play guys? He's there. He's always by himself."

"Are there others?"

"Those three at the back of the room. They stay in the big room in the carriage house. Sometimes they're all together and sometimes that sad looking guy is by himself."

"I want to go around and take a look. After that last big group, I'm extra careful about who gets on the boat."

"Do you want us to come with you?"

"Yeah. Come with me, and do your little lovey-dovey stuff, both of you. Let's see how people react."

Jock went first to the table with the mystery crew. He know the Brad Spit character was supposed to dislike dogs, so he started there, sticking his nose in between the chairs of the Spit guy and the woman he was with. She was the woman with the big bosom, but it looked fake to Jock. Just as predicted, the man said, "What in the world! Get away from the table." He also put his hand on Jock's head and pushed.

"Hirsh!" exclaimed the woman. "Don't do that! Come here pretty doggy. What's your name? Aren't you pretty?"

"Linda, don't encourage him. Get him out of here. You know how allergic I am."

"Oh, all right. You'd better go somewhere else, boy."

Just as she said that, there was a howl from Hirsch. "Cats! Get them out of here!"

Two cats, shocked at the rude behavior of the man, jumped down and ran to cower by the wall and wait for Jock to finish.

Jock went next to the big guy and mousy woman. He didn't say there. He didn't like the smell of either of them.

Next, Jock visited the funny looking guy with the fake glasses and his hotty totty wife. They were both reasonably friendly. They didn't talk to him like the other woman did, but they both petted his head and shoulders while thy continued to talk with their friends.

The table appeared to be having a good time, all in all. The only rude person in the bunch was the Brad Spit guy. But Jock didn't like those other two.

Next, the three friends visited the lone man. He welcomed their company. "Hey there. Nice to see some friendly faces. That guy was pretty rude, wasn't he." He was doing a very good job keeping up a petting sensation with two cats and a dog, being human and having only two hands. Jock often wondered why humans couldn't develop what they called feet to be more considerate to their companions. Perhaps if they didn't cover them with cow skin….

Mr. Bean said, *"Those three are leaving, Jock. Let's go over now."*

They quickly left the nice man, who frankly wondered what he had done wrong. Jock stuck his nose in the crotch of the man who had just risen from his chair. "Oh! Well look at you!"

Jock, tail wagging, accepted several pets from the standing man and had a hard time being "polite," as Ray called it, by keeping all four feet on the floor. Mr. Bean and Mo jumped to the table to get some much needed attention from the other man and woman. They seemed nice enough, but they were on their way out, so the petting and animal talk didn't last long.

Back at the table with their own humans, Mr. Bean asked Jock, *"Did you learn anything?"*

"Not really. But at least I have some first impressions. I kind of know what Tiger Lily was talking about, though. There's something a little off about them. Maybe not all of them. Maybe not even the guy that doesn't like us. At least he's honest. But there's a certain smell in the air."

Annie was tired. It had been a great evening, and everyone had worked hard, but she was more tired than could be explained by hard work. Maybe it was having company for the last few weeks. Maybe she needed to get more sleep. Maybe she needed a vacation.

Instead of joining in the conversations going around the table, she sat back and did some people watching.

She saw the interactions between the companions and her guests at the Inn and wondered why they had picked those tables to visit. She saw Brad Spit – she was going to have to just use the character names for them or she would be completely lost – push at Jock and yell at the two boys. She tensed immediately and almost got up but saw the boys extricate themselves from the situation. Jock was okay and continued to visit around the table.

What was it about the cats and the dog. It almost seemed as if they were investigating the guests. Oh, for the love of all that's holy, she thought to herself. I really do go 'round the bend sometimes.

Annie closed her eyes and shook her head. She decided to watch real people for a while.

Looking around the table, she saw a private conversation between Minnie and Jesus. They had been a private couple for several months now. Annie loved the way they worked together and the way they seemed to read one another's minds. She worried for a second about having the fate of Sassy P's in the hands of two people who were developing what looked to be a life-long commitment. It would be great if the commitment turned out to be life-long. Not so great if something happened to derail it. She decided not to worry.

Then she looked at Candice, laughing at something Carlos said. Her head was thrown back, her great mane of hair falling down the back of the chair. Something made Annie look at the bar. Brad stared at Candice, something sullen in his eyes. Well, there was one relationship that had been derailed, and so far, no damage had been done to Mo's Tap.

Annie realized with a start that Mo had been on top of tables with candles. She looked around at him quickly, now safely back in the chair at the end of their table. All of his hair seemed to be intact, and she couldn't smell anything burning. The candles at this table had been extinguished long ago.

Soon, the companions fell asleep, Mr. Bean on top of Mo in the chair and Jock on the floor. Annie was getting ready to fall asleep, too, until Chris said, "Let me walk you and the boys home." And she did. She carried Mo, who was grateful to be held in his favorite position while Chris carried Mr. Bean. Normally, Mr. Bean wanted to walk on his own, but he was tired, and he was grateful to Chris for saving him earlier. So, okay, carrying was going to be alright. *For tonight only,* he thought as he fell asleep on a very comfortable shoulder.

Chapter 11: Mo And Mr. Bean Were Rudely Awakened

Mo and Mr. Bean were rudely awakened when they got back to the Inn. Annie and Chris noticed the front door was open, and no one was on the porch or anywhere near the entryway.

"Someone must have forgotten to close the door," said Annie. "I hope Honey Bear didn't get out. I'll have to check on him."

They walked upstairs with the boys still on their shoulders, still sound asleep, until reaching the second floor landing. Annie happened to glance down the hallway, and she saw two of the guestroom doors standing open.

"That's not right. They were still at Mo's when we left."

They walked around the second floor and discovered all the guest doors were open.

"Chris, please take the boys to the apartment, check on the rest of the kids and lock the cat door. I'll check on Mom, Sam and Henry."

"I'll call Pete," Chris said, as he scooped Mo from Annie's shoulder. Mo and Mr. Bean struggled in protest, but Chris held them firmly as he ran up the stairs.

Annie ran downstairs and to the back room. "Mom!" she yelled as she knocked on the door with a flat hand.

Nancy came to the door and said, "Annie, what in the world…"

"Are you okay?"

"I'm fine, dear. What's wrong?"

"I think the guest rooms were burglarized. Is Honey Bear in here? The front door was open when I got home."

"I don't think so, I'll look around to make sure."

"I'm going to check on Henrie."

Annie rushed next to the kitchen, where the door to Henrie's suite was located. She didn't make it to the door. Henrie was lying on the kitchen floor, face down.

"Chris! Chris! I need you down here!"

Chris was already on his way, cell phone in hand. Pete was on the other end. "Pete, get an ambulance here. Henrie's been hurt. We're in the kitchen." Chris hung up and said to Annie, "Does he have a pulse?"

"Yes. It's strong. Looks like he was hit on the head."

"I'm sorry to have to do this, but back away. Let me take some pictures with my phone."

After snapping some quick photos from various angles, Chris motioned that Annie could get back down with Henrie. "Don't move him. We don't know how badly he's injured."

As he said this, they could hear the sirens headed in their direction.

"Chris, let me stay here with Henrie. I need you to check on the guests in the carriage house. Oh, are all the kids okay?"

"Yes. I counted seven heads. And a couple raised a stink when I locked the door. Are your folks okay?"

"Yes. Mom is looking for Honey Bear now."

"Okay. I'll keep an eye out for him on my way out, and also while I'm outside, just in case. What do you want me to do if the guests are in the room?"

"I guess ask them to stay there until the police come around. They will probably want to question them. Make sure they have some coffee or something. I don't want them coming over here until the police are finished."

Two EMTs were at the kitchen door by now. Chris let them in on his way out.

Henrie opened his eyes just as the EMTs moved Annie out of the way. He gave a weak smile and then closed his eyes again.

Annie refused to leave the kitchen until one of the EMTs turned and said to her, "It looks like a good knock to the head; he probably has a concussion. We'll need to take him in and get him checked out."

"I'll follow you to the hospital as soon as I can. I need to take care of the guests first, then I'll come right away."

Pete and Cyril finally arrived. Pete and Janet had not joined the friends at Mo's and they were already asleep when the call came through. Cyril rushed into the house ahead of him and went straight to Annie.

"Hey, big boy. Thanks for coming. The kids are all okay. They're locked in the apartment right now, so you can't see them, but they're fine."

Cyril seemed to nod his approval, then trotted off to smell everything.

"Cyril! You're messing up my crime scene!" yelled Pete. But he didn't stop. Cyril went through every downstairs room, up the stairs, through the hallway and a step into each of the second floor rooms, up to the third floor, where he sniffed all around, and then, as Pete finally caught up to him, he jumped to press the elevator door. As it opened, he ran inside to smell it as well.

Finally, satisfied, he allowed Pete to lead him downstairs and outside to the porch. Realizing he had missed a sniff, Cyril took a good whiff of the front door and the porch as well.

Pete and Annie, both on the porch now, looked at one another and shook their heads.

The mystery crew and the mysterious Jeff Bennett were headed to the Inn as fast as they could come. The women were still wearing those ridiculous shoes. Apparently, they heard the sirens and realized something had happened at the Inn.

Chris came around the corner to the porch. He said to Annie and Pete together, "They're all in there. They were in bed, but they're getting dressed and they'll be ready if anyone needs to question them."

In a low tone, Annie said to Pete, "I'm not sure when this happened, but the folks headed this way are all of the guests staying in the rooms on the second floor. They have been in our line of sight from the time they got to Sassy P's until just a few minutes ago. I'm pretty sure none of them had time to get back here and do this."

Annie moved forward to greet the guests. "I'm sorry to tell you that it looks as if someone went through your rooms. I'm going to have to ask you to wait here until the police have finished looking around – unless, Pete, we can go to the library?"

"I'll take a look in the library myself, then you can all go in and sit down."

"Chris, could you please stay with them, while I go to the hospital to be with Henrie?"

"Sure."

There were choruses of, "Henrie?" "What happened to Henrie?" "Is he okay?"

Pete stepped up while Annie moved away. "It looks like he was knocked on the head, but it is probably not a serious injury."

The sound of his voice trailed away as Annie went back in to check on her mother. Nancy was on the enclosed porch. She had been in every room but the kitchen; the EMTs and police would not allow her to enter that room.

When she saw Annie, she said, "How is Henrie? What happened?"

"It looks like he was hit on the head. I'm not sure who it was, but someone went through all the second floor rooms. I don't think they were on the third floor. Did you find Honey Bear?"

"Not yet. I just don't know what to think. You know him. He'll just sit somewhere and not come if he's called. He could have wandered outside, or he could be hiding anywhere in this huge house."

"I wish I could help you look, Mom, but I have to go to the hospital."

"Certainly. As soon as they let me into the kitchen, I'll make some coffee and get out something for your guests to eat. I'm sure they've already had plenty to drink for the evening, and they may be in need of something to take off the fuzziness."

On her way to the car, Annie dialed Carlos. He was the manager Annie used as her "second" in the loose-knit group of managers. She apologized for the late call, informed him of the incident and asked that he call around and make sure someone could stand in for Henrie in the morning. Annie sent up a silent prayer of thanks for the camaraderie of the group. She had nothing to worry about at the Inn. At least, she didn't have to worry about breakfast.

A couple of hours later, Annie returned home, tired, angry and a little scared. Chris and Nancy waited for her in the dining room. The guests were settled back into their rooms and the police were gone, with the exception of Pete and Cyril. Chris had relented once the police were gone; he went to the third floor and unlocked the cat door. Later, he told Annie he had to stand back while they stampeded out the door and down the stairs.

Annie could see most of the kids in the entryway with Cyril. Kali and Ko wandered from dining room to kitchen and back again, over and over, with worried faces. They could not or would not stop meowing.

Annie picked Kali up to cuddle with her and whispered that Henrie would be fine, and he would be home tomorrow afternoon. She did the same with Ko. They stopped pacing but stayed in the dining room, worried expressions on their pretty dilute calico faces.

Annie updated the humans with Henrie's condition; he had a concussion but that appeared to be all. "Pete, I know I shouldn't be questioning him, but I did ask if he saw who did it. He said he didn't. There are always people walking around the Inn at night, especially when we have a full house, so he didn't pay any attention when he heard someone coming down the stairs. He was reaching up to get some pans down for tomorrow morning. Well, I guess I mean this morning. He had his back to the door. Next thing he knew, he was on the floor surrounded by people. Did you learn anything?"

"Not really. We took a look at all the rooms. They had all been tossed, as if someone was looking for something specific. After we looked around, we took your guests up, one at a time – or one couple at a time – and asked them to look around to see if anything was missing. The Stones were missing some jewelry, but that's about it. I don't think anyone else had valuables with them."

"Did you find out who the guy was you thought you recognized?"

"No. I know I've seen him, but I can't come up with the name. I know I would know the name if I saw or heard it."

Chris said, "Is it one of the mystery crew, Pete? You know, Ray and I are going to be out on the lake with them two nights in a row. You know what can happen when a crook gets in a boat."

They all knew, only too well. Ray had come close to being killed on his boat just a couple of months before, taking a crew on a fishing trip. The crew had crime in mind and did not want to leave messy witnesses around.

"I'm sure you don't have anything to worry about. If there were a violent history, I'd have that name at the front of my mind."

"And you're not talking about our mysterious Jeff Bennett?"

"You keep trying to get me to tell you what I can't tell you. Something may have been missing from his room, though. I just have a feeling. He gave a little bit of a start when he looked through one drawer, but he recovered quickly and said nothing was missing."

Annie got serious. "Pete, why the Inn, and why those four rooms? Why not the rest of the house. There are lots of expensive electronics all through the house, and anyone who came in was probably aware I wasn't on the third floor. Why didn't they go there?"

"It was probably a crime committed without any forethought by someone who saw all of you at Mo's. They probably thought the tourists would have valuables in their rooms."

In the other room, five cats and a dog discussed the events of the evening. Cyril explained his findings to them.

"No one was here that wasn't supposed to be here. I have the scent of all of the guests, and there were no other scents in the house. One of the people staying here did this."

Mo said *"Trill!"*

"I know. I heard Annie say that all of the people staying on the second floor were away all evening. But the other three, the ones that are staying in the carriage house, their scent is all over the building too. It's probably normal for them to be everywhere on the ground floor, and maybe even on the landing upstairs. But I smelled them in the second floor hallway and inside the rooms too. All three of them."

Sassy Pants was confused. *"Their stuff isn't in these rooms in here. Their stuff is in that room out there. Why would they go in the rooms?"*

Little Socks rolled her eyes and said, *"They were stealing things, you dimwit!"*

"I's not a dimwit!"

"You are too!"

"I's not!"

"You don't even grasp the English language! How can we expect you to understand this? Let me speak sssllllooowwwlllyyy to you...."

Tiger Lily whacked Little Socks on the ear. *"Shut up. You aren't helping."*

"Hiss!"

Mr. Bean said, *"How about you be a cat burglar again, Little Socks? How about you go find stuff in their room?"*

Little Socks looked at Mr. Bean with disgust. *"And what do you suggest I burgle? What do you think they have that I could find? And how do you think I could tell Mommy if I did find something?"*

Tiger Lily was thoughtful. *"Last time it worked out. You didn't know what you were looking for, but you found something, and it turned out to be important."*

"Yeah, and now Mommy thinks I'm a thief."

"No, she doesn't."

"She does too. She called me 'a little thief of a cat.'"

"I'm sure she meant it in the kindest possible way..."

Cyril jumped back in. *"There's nothing we can do now but keep our eyes open. We all need to watch them. See what they do. Listen to what everyone says. That's how we'll find a clue."*

All of a sudden, Uncle Honey Bear came into the room, a calm swish to his hips. The cats were too surprised to hiss.

"Everyone was looking for you," said Tiger Lily.

"I know."

"Well?"

"Well, what?"

"Didn't you care? Did you mean to scare Grandmommy like that?"

Honey Bear couldn't be bothered.

Cyril gave a low growl and followed it with, *"Did you see or hear anything, and are you going to help us or not?"*

"What will you do for me if I help you?"

"I won't bite your fool head off," growled Cyril.

"Oh, for goodness sakes. Such drama. Well, if you must know, all three of those idiots were here. They were rushing, because they didn't know how long everyone would be at that Tap place, whatever it is."

Cyril pushed on. *"What were they looking for?"*

"Oh, goodness, I don't know. I know they didn't find it."

"How do you know that?"

"Because they said, you numbskull of a big bad dog, that they didn't find it!"

"But did they say what it was?"

"They did not. Certainly, if they were all looking for the same thing, they didn't need to discuss it."

Cyril looked at "his" five cats and said, *"You have my complete and total sympathy for having to put up with this."*

Honey Bear, not moving an inch, said, *"But do you want to know the really big news that I have, you thick-witted dunderhead?"*

Cyril looked at him and growled again. Through his teeth came, *"What?"*

"They found a police officer's badge in the front room. The room that looks over The Avenue."

Cyril's mouth dropped open and his tongue came out.

Tiger Lily said, *"That's Jeff Bennett's room!"*

"That's what I said."

Mr. Bean said, *"He's a Pete?"*

Sassy Pants said, *"Did it come from a box of Crackly Jacks?"*

Little Socks, rolling her eyes, said *"Cracker Jacks!"*

Sassy Pants, excited, said, *"I was right? It comed from a box?"*

"No, no, no! I was telling you to pronounce it correctly!"

"Box. How else to you pronounce it?"

Tiger Lily, no longer thinking to herself, said, *"Why do I have to put up with this? Quiet! All of you!"*

She turned to Uncle Honey Bear. *"You're sure? A police badge?"*

Honey Bear nodded, then said, *"And they wanted to leave the rooms a mess so someone would know they were looking."*

"So who would know?"

"I don't have any idea, you idiots. I'll leave you all to your precious little detecting. Just remember, you wouldn't be this far along without me."

Honey Bear stood and sashayed into the dining room, where they heard Nancy cry, "Honey Bear!" at the same time Kali and Ko came back to life, hissing and snarling, no longer worried about Henrie.

Tiger Lily turned to Cyril. *"I wonder why it was in his drawer."*

"Because he didn't want anyone to know he was working. And now, he's in danger."

Chapter 12: A Cacophony Of Hisses And Spits

Ray was at the breakfast table the next morning when Annie came down, once again herding Uncle Honey Bear between her feet to a cacophony of growls, hisses and spits.

Felicity had a hot egg dish in one hand and pastries in another. As Annie entered the dining room, Felicity said, "I called the cleaning company that my mom uses to come over and get rid of the crime scene stuff. You know, fingerprint powder and things like that."

"Thank you, Felicity, and thank you for taking care of breakfast here. What's the Café doing without you?"

"Trudie was going to take care of it. I didn't have time to stick around, so, frankly, I'm not sure! Maybe Tiger Lily will be cooking!"

Ray said, "Felicity brought me up to date. I saw the police vehicles last night when we went home, but you were all standing out on the porch, so I knew you were okay. It was tough waiting until this morning to get the news, though. Cheryl said I have to call and let her know what happened."

Nancy and Sam were up and at the table as well. Sam was just putting the pieces together; he had not awakened from his typical deep sleep while all the activity was going on.

Kali and Ko had taken up shelter from Uncle Honey Bear behind calm Jock. The other cats slipped sullenly under the buffet, getting as close to Jock as they could. Honey Bear walked calmly through to the kitchen to see if any tasty morsels were on the floor.

While the humans had their conversation, the companions filled Jock in on "the rest of the story," the part the humans weren't bright enough to know. They hated to tell him the part Uncle Honey Bear played, but were happy to let him know Cyril was on top of everything.

Annie looked at the papers in front of Ray and said, "What do you have there, Ray?"

"This is the scavenger hunt."

"The what?"

"Henrie and I decided to add a scavenger hunt for the day. We thought it would be a fun diversion, and I guess we all need one of those today. It will get them walking all over The Avenue. It's a pretty day for it. Crisp, clouds building up on the far side of the lake, but sunny here."

"Are they expecting this?"

"Kind of. They knew we would have something for them to do and that it would be optional."

"So what will they be trying to find?"

"Duckweed Spirits products. We've fixed up some cheap items and tucked them around The Avenue, down at The Marina and at Antiques On Main. They won't have to pay for anything, but they'll have to go 'shopping,' and somehow find them on the shelves. The businesses themselves have been instructed to be particularly unhelpful if they ask where to find them."

"What do they do with them?"

"Nothing. You might find all of it in your trash when they're gone. It will be a nice diversion for everyone, and maybe they'll spend a little money in the process."

Nancy, getting Annie's attention, said, "Honey, will you have dinner with Sam and me tonight? You know it's our anniversary."

"Oh, well, Mom, um, I forgot about that and I made plans with Chris."

"I thought Chris would be with Ray on The Escape?"

"Oh, did I say Chris? I meant Laila. Laila and I have plans tonight. We're going to spend the evening with her kids and mine."

Nancy, looking confused and a little hurt, said, "Oh. Alright. I had just hoped…."

"I know, Mom, I'm sorry. I just didn't think." Annie cut a sly look at Sam, who kept his eyes firmly on the oatmeal. No help from that corner.

To keep from making a bad situation worse, Annie said, "It's late. Let's go, kids. I've got to get to the hospital to see Henrie."

Annie dropped the kids off, one by one, leaving Mo at Sassy P's Wine & Cheese.

At the Café, she checked in with Trudie to see if she needed to stay, since Felicity was at the Inn.

"No, we're fine. As a matter of fact, Candice is back there and Cookie is with her. He was happy to help."

"So, did I notice a little tension between Candice and George last night?"

"Probably. They've decided to see other people. Or, rather, George decided to see other people after some pretty redhead came in last week, wearing a dress with a plunge down to here and a slit up to there."

"I hoped he was going to settle a little."

"We all did. Anyway, that fling lasted all of one date, and he wants everything to go back to the way it used to be. Candice isn't having any of that. She had a date last weekend with the biology teacher. He just moved here this year, and he doesn't know many people. He's been going to the Tap and Sassy P's just to get to know some folks his own age, and she offered to show him some other places to go, here in Chelsea and up and down the coast. Then he asked her out on a 'real' date. They went to that restaurant in Marsh Haven, and she's planning on going out with him again. George doesn't know whether to be angry, sad, jealous, nonchalant, you name it. This is new territory for him."

Annie laughed. "Let's hope he learns something. I'm going to go check in with her, thank her for stepping up, and then I'm headed to the hospital."

"Tell Henrie how much we're thinking of him."

In the kitchen, Annie thanked Candice and Cookie. Normally reticent, he said, "I'm happy to get the experience in the kitchen here. Thank you for letting me come."

Annie stopped on her way out to give Tiger Lily a hug. She saw Nancy walking up the sidewalk. "Oh, no," she thought.

Nancy walked in. "Hi, Mom. Out for a walk?"

"No, I thought I'd go to the hospital with you, if that's alright."

"Sure. Henrie would love to see you."

As they walked back to the Inn to get Annie's car, Nancy asked, "Annie, have we overstayed our welcome?"

"What? No! Why do you ask?"

"You are not a good liar, Annie, and you made it clear to me you did not want to spend the evening with us."

"Well, um, let's talk about it in the car."

When they were on the way, Annie said, "Mom, Sam wants to spend a romantic evening with you tonight. He asked me not to plan anything with you."

"Well, why didn't you just say so this morning?"

"He wants it to be a surprise."

"He knows I hate surprises."

"I know, I know. But there it is. Will you please be surprised?"

"Well, okay, but how should I dress for this surprise?"

"Swanky."

"Ooo. I think I'll like this surprise."

Henrie was anxious to get back to the Inn. When they walked into his room, he was arguing with a nurse who insisted he stay in bed.

Annie said, "Henrie, we don't want you to get up too soon. Felicity served breakfast; Mom and I will do laundry and clean the rooms today. Everyone will understand if service isn't quite up to snuff."

"But we cannot have that. Things must be 'up to snuff' as you say if we want to keep our approval ratings high."

"Henrie, don't worry about it."

"What did Felicity serve this morning?"

Annie paid no attention before leaving for the Café, but Nancy was able to tell him everything. "And it was all very nice, Henrie, just not as nice as you would have done."

Assuring Henrie they would return at 3:00 to pick him up, unless the doctor refused to release him, Annie and Nancy went back to The Avenue. They stopped in to see Mem and have a cup of tea.

Annie was surprised to see Tiger Lily keeping Mem company. She threw a questioning look at Mem, who said, "She came in a few minutes ago. She's been sitting in the window, watching people walk by."

Geraldine spied Annie, Nancy and Mem through the window and came in. "Annie, I'm certain you didn't realize Hank and I were not allowed into your little mystery dinner last night. You were so busy, I'm sure you can't attend to all the details."

"I'm sorry you weren't further up in the line, Geraldine. I did see you, but we had a limited number of seats, and it was first-come-first-served."

"Well, you know, that hardly applies to a woman of my stature. Women like me do not stand in line."

"Oh, well, I'm sorry you don't. You missed a great time."

"And you're going to miss an even more delightful evening. My fundraiser is literally the talk of the town. You know, it's a black tie event. By invitation only. And of course, I'm looking forward to my date with Frank."

Geraldine purred his name just a little as she slid a glance in Mem's direction.

Nancy, who did not live in Chelsea and consequently cared little for the opinions of others, brought out her sugar sweet voice. Annie knew this voice well. It was the voice of a viper coiling to meet its next victim.

"Geraldine, I don't know that we've been introduced. I'm Nancy, Annie's mother. And Mem's new friend, I might add. I have to ask, what do you hope to gain by coming in here, talking about your date?"

Geraldine looked, for once, a little flustered.

"And might I add, since we're being familiar, how very nice you look today. I saw a photo of you in the newspaper. It was a clipping from a few months ago, when you opened your diner. I hear it was a lovely place. I'm so sorry it closed under, should I say, unsavory circumstances. Well, anyway, I must say that since that time you've grown a couple of bra sizes. That's such an accomplishment for women of our age, don't you agree, Mem?"

Nancy turned to Mem, who got up to help a couple – they were guests of the Inn – looking around and apparently not finding what they needed. Of course, Mem knew she was not supposed to help them, but she had to get away from that woman.

Geraldine, nose upturned, left without another word.

Ray waited at the Inn until the mystery crew arrived for breakfast. Jeff seated himself at the side table again. The trio was next to appear. They introduced themselves to Ray and told him how much they enjoyed the play.

The mystery crew finally straggled in, a couple at a time. After they helped themselves to eggs and cinnamon rolls, Ray told the group about the scavenger hunt.

One couple opted out of participating. Jessica and Alec talked quietly to Herb. Alec then said to Ray, "Hey, do you mind if Jess and I play along? Herb doesn't want to, but the two of us think it sounds like fun."

"Sure. We put six of each of the products out, and we now have two left over."

"Great! What do we do?"

Ray turned to Jeff. "Do you want to get in on it?"

Jeff shook his head in a pleasant refusal.

Ray handed six sheets of paper around the table. "You'll go into each of these businesses, and somewhere on the shelves you're going to find these products. Now you might think, by looking at the name of the products, that a particular store might have it. Not necessarily so. If that were the case, most of the items would be at The Drug Store."

Business	*Product*
Antiques On Main	Duckweed Candlewicks
Babar Foods	Duckweed Desire
Bloomin' Crazy	Duckweed Diet Pills
CyberHealth	Duckweed Drawing Paper
DoubleGood	Duckweed Endurance
Soul's Harbor Gift Shop	Duckweed Risqué Lingerie
The Drug Store	Duckweed Sewage Cleaner
The Marina	Lily Spit

Ray gave them a moment to look over the list. He continued, "Wherever you find the first of the products, you will be given a shopping bag large enough to carry all of the items. I think you'll find everyone in town wants to have fun with this."

"How long do we have to do this?" asked Jessica.

"Until about 2:30 in the afternoon. Once the kids get out of school, we want the racier items off the shelves."

Brad and Mary told their friends they were going to take a ride up and down the coast for the day, looking for antique stores.

Herb, looking at Alec, said, "That sounds like a great idea. Would you mind if I took the car to do some poking around?"

Alec and Jessica looked at one another, and Jessica said, "Great. It'll get your nose out of those online games."

The others talked among themselves, deciding to split into couples and start at different points. They agreed that if one couple saw another couple in a store already, they would back out so as not to spoil any surprise.

Jock looked at Kali and Ko. *"One of you is going to have to go up to the Café to tell Tiger Lily. Maybe she can get some of the other kids to follow them around."*

Kali and Ko said together, *"Can't you go?" "We can't leave by ourselves."*

"One or both of you is going to have to go. When we leave, we're going back to The Marina. Ray doesn't like it when I run up The Avenue without him."

"Can't you do it just this once? Please?"

Two sets of pleading eyes looked at Jock.

"Oh, alright. I'll go right now. Maybe I'll be back before he notices I'm gone."

"How are you going to get out?"

"I'll go into the kitchen and act like I have to do some business. You know. Felicity will let me out."

"Good idea. Go now."

Luckily for Jock, Ray got up to pour himself another cup of coffee and grab another cinnamon roll. He enjoyed talking to Sam, and he settled in for a relaxed chat before starting a busy day. By the time he got up to go, Jock was barking at the kitchen door, asking to come back in.

Sam helped Felicity clean up the dining room and kitchen. They decided to leave the coffee, cinnamon rolls and fresh fruit parfaits out while they cleaned everything else from the dining room. All of the Inn's guests seemed to be in no particular hurry to get going this morning. Even Jeff was hanging around. Sam could swear he had read the same page of the paper three times already. In the kitchen, he said to Felicity, "That poor man must have one heck of a learning disability."

The Stones left around 10:00 and Herb told his friends that he should probably get on his way as well.

It was nearly 10:30 before the rest of the guests left the Inn to start their scavenger hunt. Even though Alec and Jessica were not part of the original mystery crew, for this event, they seemed an integral part of the group. They agreed to try to finish at least three stores each and meet at Mr. Bean's for a late lunch at 1:00.

Tiger Lily followed Jock out of the Café and stopped at each of her siblings' places of business to give them instructions. Jock, of course, was going to stick as close to The Marina as he could to watch and listen.

Tiger Lily sent Little Socks to Bloomin' Crazy, because for some reason, Clara was bloomin' crazy about that cat.

She sent Mo to DoubleGood. Holly and Jolly would enjoy having him there; he could sit on the counter and entice guests into the store.

Mr. Bean was sent to Babar Foods. She thought about sending him to Soul's Harbor, but she didn't want him that far up on The Avenue. He was still a kitten, after all. She knew Laila would watch over him.

Sassy Pants drew Soul's Harbor Gift Shop. That would give her the opportunity to spend some time with Teresa. She loved Teresa.

Tiger Lily's last stop was back at the Inn. She couldn't get in, because the doors were locked. *That blasted Uncle Honey Bear! He has ruined us!* She settled for meowing, screeching and generally setting up a racket outside the kitchen door. Sam finally heard her and opened the door to her. Tiger Lily nodded her thanks and ran in to find Kali and Ko.

She found them in the library, sleeping underneath the television table.

"You have to go to The Drug Store and watch and listen."

"What?" "No!"

"Yes. You're part of this family, just like all of us. You have to go."

"We won't be able to get out!" "We won't be able to get in!"

"I'll get Sam to let us all out, and you can come to the Café when you think you've done all you can for the morning. We're going to meet there and compare notes."

"Can't we just not and pretend we did?"

Tiger Lily cuffed each of them on the ear. They drug themselves out from under the table and walked slowly behind Tiger Lily to the kitchen and certain doom.

Sam, unsure if he should let them out, didn't do it right away. When Tiger Lily stood and threw her body against the door – Sam counted five times – he decided it would be better to let the girls out than allow Tiger Lily to hurt herself.

Tiger Lily accompanied Kali and Ko to The Drug Store, then hurried to CyberHealth, her assigned location.

Chapter 13: The Little Love Bunny Was Missing

At 1:00, Carlos and Jerry worried about Mr. Bean. The little love bunny was missing, and had been for an hour or so. This wasn't unusual, but they expected him during busy hours unless Annie had him. They knew Annie did not.

But they got a little rush about that time, with some locals coming in for a late sandwich and several guests from the Inn. They knew about the scavenger hunt, and sure enough, it looked like they all had the bags stamped with the In The Weeds logo, even a couple of guests that had not been in the play.

Carlos waited on this group himself. He gave them menus and told them the specials. "We don't have an extensive menu, but you can choose from any bread if you get a sandwich, and you can't beat our desserts."

Almost everyone ordered combinations from the special menu: Spanish grilled roast beef sandwiches with artichokes, roasted red peppers and olives, pepperoni-olive-grilled cheese sandwiches with provolone, asiago and mozzarella cheeses, stuffed red pepper soup and an especially thick and creamy New England clam chowder.

Before Carlos walked away, they ordered desserts to share after lunch: pumpkin and pecan cheesecake, white chocolate crème brulee, and warm apple crisp with a nutty topping and vanilla ice cream.

Each couple brought out their treasures. As their table was right in front of the counter. Carlos couldn't help but overhear the animated conversation.

Alec, looking around the table at the items they had gathered, said, "Between us, it looks like we have everything!

Guess that plan of keeping the secret of what to look for – and where – is going to be a failure."

"That's okay," responded Susie. "We can run in and get everything after lunch in plenty of time for the munchkins to get out of school."

Comments of "You're right," "Sure," and "It will give us the afternoon for other stuff," quickly went around the table.

They all laughed as the items were discussed and the couples told how they were found.

Alabaster picked up a brightly-colored cellophane package wrapped in pipe cleaners. "We found this snuggled – yes, I have to use that word – between fishing lures and tackle. It's a package of Duckweed Candlewicks."

Onstair showed the group an aluminum foil packet. "Doesn't this look like a packet of cocaine?"

The group laughed and Alec commented, "I'm not saying anything about how you might know that!"

"Well, of course, I watch police shows on television! That's how I knew it was Lily Spit. You'll have to go to the feminine products section."

Alabaster continued their story. "You have to spend some extra time at Bloomin' Crazy. She's got some beautiful arrangements of flowers – I know, not really a great thing to buy if you're just here for a couple of days – but she has some great gifts, too. I was looking at the Jim Shore collections. She had some Nativity scenes, Peanuts, even Wizard of Oz characters. Oh, but we found the Duckweed Desire in the refrigerator."

She held up an oddly-shaped and stoppered bottle. "They're inside pre-made flower arrangements."

Sparkle Shine took up the story. "I was happy to find the diet pills. I'm going to try them!" She picked up a green plastic bottle labeled "Get Thin With The Duckweed Diet." "We found these in the cell phone section at DoubleGood."

"Oh, and this bottle of Duckweed Sewage Cleaner was in the apple bin at Babar Foods." The glass bottle had a skull and crossbones behind the name of the product. "It's a good thing this stuff is fake. At least, I hope it's fake!"

Dr. Bong brought a packet of paper out of his bag. "The Duckweed Drawing Paper was the hardest to find. CyberHealth has a stationery section, and we spent quite a bit of time there. But she actually had packages in the gaming section. They looked like tablets for the gamers to use. We were ready to give up on finding anything, but the owner helped us. I didn't think they were supposed to do that."

Finally, Alec and Jessica showed the group their treasures. Alec pulled out a bottle of Duckweed Endurance. "Would you ever think to look for this in a church? You'll find it in the front display case of their charity shop."

Jessica jumped in. "You're going to love that antique shop, Antiques On Main. He had so many nice things there. He's not even open yet. He opened for the day, to help out with the scavenger hunt. He has the lingerie, and it's not in one place. He has them hanging on dining room chairs, lying on roll top desks, and I found this on a four poster bed!"

Jessica held up a cherry red bra and pantie set, and Alec pulled a black bustier out of his bag. "It's for a girlfriend," he said, with a blush.

As the lingerie was held up for inspection, Carlos and Jerry arrived with their food. Shy Jerry, who had not heard the conversation, nearly dropped a cup of clam chowder. Only quick action on the part of Carlos averted the disaster.

Tiger Lily noticed the group of guests gathering across the street at Mr. Bean's. Mommy and Grandmommy were still visiting with Mem, but she needed to gather the troops.

From the sidewalk she signaled her siblings – all of whom waited at windows – to join her at the Café. Trudie looked up in surprise to see seven cats rushing in.

Tiger Lily, taking a quick look around, headed for the back dining room, which was not in use at the time. She made sure to stand next to Little Socks. She had her reasons.

"Unfortunately, we aren't going to be able to hear from Jock, but certainly one or more of us saw the people that went to The Marina. Who wants to start?"

Sassy Pants jumped in. *"I starts. I seed two of those three ones that stay in the carry house."*

Little Socks opened her mouth to correct Sassy Pants, but Tiger Lily stepped on her tail.

"Ouch!"

"Go ahead, Sassy Pants."

"They comed in and gotted some bottles of stuff they founded at the front desk."

"I know you've been working on your report for a while and that you want to get it right, but skip all of that and just tell us if you heard them talk about anything else, anything that might help us figure out what they were looking for."

"Oh. That. They was talking about something when they comed in. That lady said she seed that Jeff guy and he was talking on a selled phone."

"*Anything else?*"

"*That guy, he said him walk past the attic store.*"

Tiger Lily interrupted her. "*Do you mean the antique store?*"

"*Yeah. That. Then he said something like they shoulda left the badge in the drawer. If the badge was still in the drawer, that Jeff guy might not be watching them.*"

Sassy Pants sat back and grinned at Tiger Lily. "*I does good, right?*"

"*Right. You did real good. Thank you. Did anyone else see this couple?*

Five cats shook their heads.

"*Okay. Who wants to go next?*"

Mr. Bean was anxious to get to his report. "*Me! Me! Me next! I saw the nice ones. The ones that like us and don't smell funny.*" He looked around with triumph.

"*Go on.*"

"*Oh, yeah! They petted me and she carried me through the grocery store. Laila didn't care. When they went to the back and Laila was in the front, that woman asked that man if he knew what was up with Spencer. I don't know who that is.*"

"*We'll figure that out later. Did he answer her?*"

"*Some other customer came in and looked at me funny, so they walked back up to the front, saw the stuff they needed and put me down. I didn't hear anything else.*"

"*Very good report, Mr. Bean.*" Mr. Bean beamed at Tiger Lily.

Tiger Lily continued, "*I saw the same couple, but before I say anything, did anyone else?*"

Mo said "*Trill!*"

Tiger Lily, frustrated, said, *"I have to learn your language, but for now, Kali or Ko will have to translate. Go ahead."*

Mo started trilling, and when he was finished, Kali and Ko said together, *"They were just talking about the rooms last night."* *"They said how strange it was that all the second floor rooms were gone through."*

"Did it sound like they had anything to hide?"

Mo trilled again.

Kali and Ko said together, *"He said he was glad they didn't bring their notebooks."* *"She said it was good she left her jewelry home."*

Tiger Lily said, *"They didn't say anything at Mem's. Mommy and Grandmommy were there. They just said 'hi' and did their shopping. So, there is one couple left. Who wants to go first?"*

Kali and Ko, originally hesitant to become a part of the team, were now proud to be able to give a report. They started to talk at the same time. *"The handsome guy..."* *"The big galoot..."*

Tiger Lily said, *"Stop! One at a time! Kali, you first."*

Kali said, *"He's so handsome. She's mean. They were looking around, and she said she was tired of the game. He said they had to keep playing."*

Ko stepped in here to say, *"I don't think he was talking about the scavenger hunt. I think he was talking about something else. He's not nice at all."*

Tiger Lily turned to Little Socks, who was still sulking about the tail incident. *"Did you hear or see anything?"*

"No."

"No? That's it?"

"No. Well, maybe. He was looking at some pretty flowers and said something about when she got her surgery."

"What kind of surgery?"

"He didn't say, but she said she was thinking about a Mary Monroe look."

Tiger Lily started to say something else, but she felt a presence and looked around. Mommy was standing in the entrance to the room with a puzzled expression on her face. Tiger Lily went up to her and purred, wrapping herself around a leg, to put her off guard.

Annie said to Trudie, I'm not sure why all of the kids decided to get together today, but I'm going to take them home early. Then I'm going to the hospital to get Henrie. On her way out the door, she ran into, of all people, Hank.

"Oh, for crying out loud. All of the blippin' cats are in the Café again. I'm going to find some way to stop this once and for all!"

"Good afternoon, Hank. We're always happy to see you here at Tiger Lily's Café. Trudie, you make sure he has the best of service."

"Yes, ma'am," Trudie said to Annie's retreating back.

As Annie settled Henrie in his suite, seven cats jumped into bed with him. Kali and Ko were at the front of the pack. Henrie gathered them as close as he could, whispering sweet nothings into the ears of each one.

Nancy and Sam were on their way to their romantic dinner.

Three guests of the Inn ate a private supper at Sassy P's Wine & Cheese.

Six guests gathered at The Escape to begin the second evening of their mystery play and the first of two evenings involving a cruise.

Most of the people in Chelsea were having an enjoyable evening.

Not Ray. Ray was angry. As he stormed from The Marina to The Escape, he tried to shake it off for the sake of his customers. He had just left Jock, desperate and whining, with Cheryl. Brad Spit had insisted "that damn dog" not come on the boat.

Chapter 14: The Perfect Little Black Dress

Instead of going to the hospital with Annie, Nancy spent the afternoon at a women's shop recommended by Mem. She found the perfect little black dress.

When Sam said, "I found a nice little restaurant that seems just right for two old lovebirds like us," she acted surprised.

"Let me just change into something more appropriate," she said, and now, in the car with Sam, she was feeling quite lovely. Sam asked about the dress, and she replied, "This old thing? I packed it just in case we went somewhere fancy."

At the restaurant, they settled in for a long evening. Sam ordered a bottle of wine and an appetizer to share. Nancy ordered a steak, medium, which was unusual for her. Sam ordered salmon. They flirted.

Nancy said, "I'm so glad we're having this evening alone. I thought we should spend it with Annie, but you know, we haven't had any time alone since we arrived, not really."

"I've been thinking about that. What would you think if we actually rented the bottom floor of that carriage house for a couple of months a year, once in the spring and once in the fall. That would give us time with Annie, it would keep Honey Bear out of the big house, and Annie wouldn't have to give up the income for us for two months of the year. And, best of all, we would all have some separation."

"Sam, you think of the sweetest things. Do you think Annie would like the idea?"

"The two of you have had quality time together. She loves being with you. But you both need some space. She doesn't need to be meeting you on the way up or down the stairs if she has a boyfriend with her."

"You're right. And she has given up some things for her cats with Honey Bear around. I don't understand why other cats don't just love him. He's so adorable."

Sam wisely kept his own counsel and took a bite of salmon, worried that he might be forced to talk about Honey Bear if nothing came along to rescue him.

He was so in luck. Nancy said, "Oh, look, Sam. They're doing their round two at this restaurant."

Sam turned, caught the attention of Chris and Ray and waved.

They were seated at a large table near Nancy and Sam. Sam asked, "Do you mind if we stay and watch round two?

"Please do," said Ray. I think it's more fun with an audience."

Ray had ordered ahead. Servers brought a selection of wines, craft beers and family style entrees and sides.

The tense atmosphere at the harbor had started to soften at the edges while Ray steered them to Marsh Harbor. Now that they were relaxing, enjoying good food and good drink, Ray began to enjoy himself again.

Nancy, doing something almost totally unheard of, ordered a dessert. She and Sam settled in, paying their bill and leaving a big tip so the table would be theirs for as long as the play went on. Sam said, "Just keep checking on the coffee and water, son," to the server.

Nancy, getting comfortable as dishes were cleared from the large table, said, "Oh, look, Sam. There's Jeff. Sitting by himself again, over there in the corner." Something kept both of them from waving. They looked away and concentrated on In The Weeds.

Chapter 15: In The Weeds, Round Two

Detective Brown started the second round of In The Weeds by setting the stage. "Something's going on between Sparkle and Onstair. I wonder what it is…."

Sparkle, bristling for a fight, looked at Onstair and said, "So. Women throwing themselves at you? And you can't tell them to just stay away?"

"I can't help it. I've got animal magnetism. Real women can sense it."

"Real women? An old hag and a mouse? You'll never change. You go for anything in a skirt."

"Well, let's talk about skirts. Mary's right. Whenever Spicy Pepper was around, your skirts barely covered the essentials."

"I have to make my clients feel special."

"Special. With special little meetings."

"There was nothing going on. But you flirted with Alabaster."

"There was nothing to that!"

"So I have to believe you, but you don't have to believe me."

"Oh for crying out loud! I don't know why I married you in the first place!"

As the argument drew to a close, Sparkle and Onstair appeared to just notice that everyone else had eyes only for them.

Chris was the first to ask a question. "Well, that was enlightening! You're married? Why are you keeping it a secret?"

Sparkle was the first to respond. "We've been married for about a year now. It's a secret because Onstair is more marketable as a single man. I told everyone it cost me a fortune to get him, but he's doing it for next to nothing. He needs the job, but really, using Onstair for Duckweed Spirits is a good business decision. He's a great front person."

Onstair agreed. "Sparkle is putting her company on the line for me, and I don't act like I appreciate it. I know she gets jealous, but I get jealous when men look at her. I still think she might have been having an affair with Spicy. And to top it off, Alabaster turned me down. I've been worried that I'm no longer able to attract women.

"Duckweed Spirits is working on several new products. One of them is Duckweed Desire. You can put it in someone's drink to loosen them up, or you can use it as a perfume to draw the opposite sex to you. When Alabaster turned me down, I saw a bottle in Dr. Bong's lab. I kind of picked it up, and I used it last night. I spritzed it into my hair. Dr. Bong, I think it's going to be a best seller."

Dr. Bong sighed several times, dramatically shaking his head and hands at the same time. "I have a confession to make. I've put the company in serious jeopardy." He had their full attention.

"I've been experimenting with Duckweed Candlewicks. Last night I set fire to my pants. Unfortunately my wallet was in the pants pocket. I kept the passwords and combination in the wallet. It was burned to ashes. We can't get to the recipes. We're ruined. I am so sorry. It was stupid of me."

Alabaster laughed. "I knew you kept those things in your wallet, Dr. Bong. A few weeks ago I lifted it and made a copy. I also added details about the products. I guess it's a good thing I did. Detective Brown, I present Clue #2."

The sheet of paper detailed every product currently marketed or in process of development, including the recipe names and passwords.

"See? Everything's right here."

Detective Brown inspected the clue for a moment. He then asked another question. "Brad, I got a call from the Chelsea docks this afternoon. They impounded a cargo of duckweed and said something about illegal drugs. Would you care to comment?"

Brad looked chagrined. "Well, okay. I know that cargo was stopped. It's only a matter of time before they come for me. I may as well tell you. Duckweed is the main crop from Spit City, but we have a secondary crop. There is a type of water lily that grows in the interior lakes of the island. We extract the sap, dry it and sprinkle it on some of the duckweed shipments. Duckweed has a horrid scent, so the dried sap goes pretty much undetected. Here in Chelsea, we have a little side business going. The dried sap is extracted from the duckweed, and we make a drug. And sell the drug. Yeah, okay, so I'm a drug dealer. It's kind of a date rape drug. We call it Lily Spit. Kind of catchy.

"Now that we're talking about it, let me give you some facts. People who use Lily Spit one time become uninhibited. If you're watching for it, you can see someone getting a little bit of a rush, and then, with another sip of whatever you're drinking, you get more and more uninhibited. Long term use, though, can bring on serious side effects. Headaches. Blinding lights. Last night my bottle actually had Lily Spit mixed in water. I slipped some into Alabaster's glass hoping she would loosen up for me."

Chris seemed to ignore this confession to making and selling drugs and went in another direction. "Alabaster, I was in the office the other day. You addressed an envelope to Mary, but you didn't put a letter in it. You wrote the word 'mom' in the middle of a sheet of paper and put that in the envelope. I see from Clue #1 that 'mom' is one of Dr. Bong's passwords. What were you doing?"

Alabaster sighed. "Okay. Mary promised to introduce me to some important business people if I got the password for Duckweed Desire. I mailed it to her. Now, I'm thinking I should have asked her why she needed it. Mary, why did you?"

Mary answered. "Alright, alright. I needed that password to hack into the system. Well, I hired someone to do it. I was losing Spicy to Sparkle Shine! I had to do something! I hired a young man I know from Marsh Haven. He got the recipe; I took it to Brad. He found someone to make it up, and last night I slipped some into Spicy's glass. I planned to slip him a little more throughout the evening and then offer him a ride home. And of course, then I would seduce him and he would be mine. Mine! Not Sparkle's!"

Mary, upset that Alabaster let her secret out, turned a hateful face in her direction. "Alabaster, I think you are a fraud. I'm going to make a telephone call to prove it." She pulled her cell phone out of her purse and hit a speed dial number.

"Hello. May I speak to Barry Goldfinger, please…. Hello, Barry, Mary Monroe here. Hope I didn't disturb you…. Oh, you're dining with Mitt Downey, Jr.? How interesting. I have a curious question. Have you ever employed an Alabaster Pearl as your secretary?…. You haven't? I thought as much. What about Mitt?…. He does not know her? Very interesting. No, that's all. Thank you."

Mary hung up and threw a pointed look at Alabaster. "Neither of your 'previous employers' have ever heard of you! What do you have to say to that?"

Onstair Royds challenged Alabaster as well. "Alabaster, when I was in the lab – okay, in the lab stealing stuff – I heard someone come in. I hid and saw you go straight to the safe. You unlocked it and took something out. What did you steal?"

Alabaster looked daggers at Mary and Onstair. She folded her arms, looked around the group and announced, "I have nothing to say."

Detective Brown said, "Ms. Pearl, when questions are asked, they must be answered."

Alabaster said nothing.

"Ms. Pearl, I must insist. Forged references and theft are very serious offenses."

"I have no comment to make."

"Ms. Pearl, this is a murder investigation. You were seen stealing from a safe where Duckweed Sewage Cleaner was stored. If you do not cooperate, I have no other option than to believe you murdered Spicy Pepper."

"No comment."

"Okay, then. I'm placing you under arrest. My officers will take you to the station, and I'll follow along to question you there."

"Before you arrest me, I want a word with you in private, Detective."

Detective Brown and Alabaster adjourned to the fireplace where they talked in low tones. The rest of the group looked at one another in puzzlement.

Detective Brown and Alabaster returned to the group where he made an announcement. "Ms. Pearl has been very helpful. I won't be taking her into custody. The investigation will continue."

Chris took up the questioning and challenged Sparkle Shine. "Sparkle, I'm a member of the country club in Chelsea. The other day I overheard some bankers talking about your company. It seemed they were ready to pull your loan. Is your company in trouble?"

With a beaten look, Sparkle said, "I've got an issue with liquid funds, and I can't always make my loan payments. I need cash. A lot of it."

Chris continued. "Dr. Bong, last night I heard you tell Sparkle that if you were in charge of the company you would double the marketing budget. With Spicy around that would never happen. Sparkle, did you think Dr. Bong could help you?"

"Sure, I thought he could help. For a minute, I hoped he would somehow get control of the marketing budget."

Chris kept going. "Dr. Bong, right before the toast was made, I saw you slip something into a glass of wine, then hand that glass to Mary Monroe. What did you give her?"

"Well, this seems to be the night for confessions. Mary's still here and kicking, so I don't mind confessing. This company was my idea. I was not about to stand by and watch that stupid woman ruin it. After that last board meeting, I decided to kill her. I knew Spicy would inherit her shares, and I knew he would agree to develop Duckweed Candlewicks.

"I had Duckweed Sewage Cleaner with me last night, in my jacket pocket. As a precaution, I also brought an antidote. Liquid Benzodiazepine was in my man purse. Just before the toast, I added the Sewage Cleaner to a glass of wine then handed the glass to Mary. Somehow Spicy got it instead, but I don't know how. If I had seen him take it, I would have given him the antidote."

Detective Brown asked if anyone had further questions for now. Finding they did not, he said, "We'll adjourn then, until tomorrow."

Nancy and Sam, as well as several other tables of diners, applauded the cast. As they left, Nancy noticed Jeff Bennett's table was already deserted.

Chapter 16: Annie Was Getting Used To Herding A Cat

At the Inn, Felicity and Nancy served a breakfast that included potato and prosciutto frittata, cinnamon roll bread pudding and berry strata. Annie was getting pretty good at herding a cat. She decided to sit down to breakfast before heading out for the day.

"Tiger Lily, get everyone off to work. Take Mo with you this morning."

Mo hung his head with a sad *"Trill."*

Tiger Lily looked at Annie and said, *"Mommy, he's a big boy. He can decide where to go on his own. He can even go to the Tap if he wants to. He can nap until George gets there."*

Mo looked at Tiger Lily with pride.

Annie looked at Tiger Lily and said, "Whatever it is that you want, big girl, you're sure awfully solemn about it. Come on, I'll open the door for you."

The dining room filled up with guests; Annie and Sam carried plates out to the back porch.

"By the way, Annie, Nancy and I saw round two of In The Weeds last night."

"You did? They had it at that restaurant?"

"It added quite a touch to our little celebration, and by the way, thank you for the recommendation. The meal was wonderful, the service impeccable."

"I'm glad you liked it."

"Is everything okay this morning?"

"I've just been thinking about the 'Geraldine' problem."

"What problem is that?"

"Her competing charity. The only reason she's having it is to keep us from raising money for real charity."

"Well, honey, you're going to have to let her hang herself. Every community has their Geraldines, and they learn how to work around them."

"I guess that's what I did before, but gosh, this is charity. She could ruin things for a lot of people who need the money we're planning to raise."

"Annie, I think you might be reacting to some overload. You've had a lot going on, and now this burglary, and you're playing host to two old folks…if you weren't pressed on so many fronts, it might be easier to ignore her."

Annie looked at Sam, wanting to be angry, but seeing the wisdom in his words. She sighed, "You're probably right. She's just not worth the worry, I guess. If we don't raise as much as we'd hoped, then we'll work harder at it next time."

"That's right, Annie. And just think, the block party has a great team working together. You do this six times a year. There's no way she can keep up."

"You're right about that."

Nancy and Henrie came to the porch with plates.

Annie asked, "Henrie, how do you like being served for once?"

"I will be back to work this afternoon, but for this morning, it is marvelous."

"Talk about marvelous," said Nancy, "have you seen those beautiful clouds over the lake this morning?"

Henrie answered, "They look lovely, but they could be a problem for us. It is October. We could get quite a storm. That reminds me, I probably need to make sure all of our storm supplies are set. That will be my first task this afternoon."

"I'll help," said Sam. I've never gotten a good look at that basement."

Sam stopped talking for a moment, then, looking determined, he said, "Now that the two of you are here – Henrie, and Annie – Nancy and I have a question. Or an offer. It depends on how you take it."

Henrie and Annie looked at one another, then back at Sam and Nancy. Annie said a cautious, "Yes?"

Nancy, warming to the topic, said, "You see, we really like Chelsea, and we'd like to make this our second home."

"Yes, but we don't want to completely move. We don't want to sell our home. We'd like to have a place to come, maybe for a month at a time, a couple of times a year."

"And we were thinking, dear, that perhaps we could rent the downstairs room in the carriage house, get on the calendar, and actually pay the rent…"

"…so you don't think you have to entertain us…"

"…and you aren't paying for everything, since we enjoy Henrie's breakfasts so much…"

"…and then, we'd all have some privacy…"

"…and Honey Bear would be safe in the carriage house …"

"…and you could come visit him, as well as your cats…"

"…and we could help you, Henrie…we could be here if you want to take several days or even a couple of weeks off…"

"…and we'd do everything the way you wanted it done…"

"…but we don't want to do it if it would be a problem for you."

Annie and Henrie looked at Sam and Nancy, then looked at one another, then looked back. When she was sure the duet was over, Annie said, "We'd love to have you!"

"Oh, Annie! How wonderful!"

"But you shouldn't have to pay rent."

"Yes, we should. Many of our friends have winter homes in Florida or Arizona or Texas, and they either own them or they rent them. We have enough money. We would consider this our vacation home, and it's only right we pay for the privilege. And we want to pay full rates."

"Well, Henrie, we have a special rate for weekly guests, right? Something a bit lower that still pays all of our expenses?"

"Yes, we do. Nancy, Sam, you could be assured you are paying full rates, but it will be a bit different than the daily rate."

Sam said, "That's just fantastic. Henrie, let's look at the calendar before the day is over!"

Annie smiled at her mother and said, "It will be wonderful to spend time with you all year round. You can have the carriage house whenever you want it."

"Thank you, dear. But you know, we don't want to take it away from those annual guests that love it so. Henrie told me about that group of men that come every summer to go fishing."

"We do have a few folks that come every year, but no regulars this time of year, or at Christmas, or in the early spring."

"Christmas. Now that sounds lovely. We'll have to think about that."

"We could plan Christmas here. The whole family could come. We'd just have to start planning it now, so the rooms are still available."

"Well, we really only need one more big room. Is the honeymoon room free over Christmas?"

"I'd have to check, but I don't think it's booked."

"Perhaps we could come for a couple of weeks then, and then come back for a month in the spring and a month in the fall."

From the kitchen, they heard Ray calling. "Henrie, Annie?"

"Coming," she said. Henrie insisted on taking the dirty dishes in, but Nancy followed him with the cups and glasses.

"Ray, what do you think about the weather?"

"I think it will hold off for us, but just to be safe, I'm not going out very far."

The original plan was to have In The Weeds during a moonlight cruise in the middle of the lake, far from the lights of any shore. Ray continued, "If we have to see lights in the distance, it won't ruin the ambiance."

Annie, following Ray back to the dining room, said, "We're going to make sure our basement is ready, just in case, and we'll have room for everyone. If the weather reports warrant, you head back here and get everyone downstairs. Tell Cheryl to come, too. If she's caught at The Marina, I'd rather she come here than try to make it home in that little boat."

"I think you're overreacting."

"Ray."

"I know that lake like the back of my hand, and it includes the weather systems. We're going to be fine."

By now, they were in the dining room, filled with ten hungry guests.

Brad Spit said, "We've been talking about the weather ourselves. Do you think we'll be okay out there tonight?"

"Sure. But to be safe, we're going to stay closer to shore than previously planned. We could leave a little early, too."

A quick look around the room and Brad answered for everyone, "That's a good idea. What time do you want to start?"

"How about 4:00? Annie, I'll call Felicity and make sure dinner will be ready early. Do any of you have any questions?"

Brad said, "I think we're set. We all have different plans today, but we'll meet here around 3:30 and walk down to the harbor. Should we bring rain gear?"

"It wouldn't hurt. Better to have it and not need it than, well, you know."

Annie said, "Ray, what's up with Jock?"

Jock was in the entryway, lying on his side, looking mournfully at Ray.

"He won't be coming with us. He didn't go last night. I think he's a little angry, actually."

"What's up?"

"It's my fault," said Brad. "I'm dreadfully allergic. Cats can be an issue, but being close to dogs is just impossible."

Annie touched Ray on the arm as she left and stopped to give Jock a supporting hug.

A big tail lifted from the floor and fell back down.

Once.

Chapter 17: She Calls It The 'Lick My Butt'

Annie stopped first at the yoga studio. Today was Saturday and Ginger expected to measure kids for costumes most of the day. Diana sent a text to Annie that morning that eight children were measured on Thursday and Friday after school.

As Annie entered, several children patiently waited for Ginger to finish a class so they could be measured for a costume. Well, one not so patiently, but her mother was apparently handling the situation.

Annie stopped. "Mrs. Jones, are the kids looking forward to the party?"

"You know, there were so many kids in the neighborhood that pretended not to care, but now that real costumes will be ready for them, they're excited. So often, they have to go as pirates or hobos, because it's easy to come up with old clothes for that.

"My Grace is looking forward to being a real character. They've been looking at the pictures Ginger put up, and I think she wants to be a ladybug."

"She'll be a cute one, that's for sure! I'm looking forward to seeing you and every little bug, princess and angry bird you can bring along."

Ginger was performing a new move. "What's that?" Annie asked Diana.

"She's doing the move Little Socks invented. She calls it the 'Lick My Butt.'"

Annie looked up with a question mark in her eyes and turned to look at the black bundle lying on the windowsill. Little Socks was curled into her tail, but one green eye was open and shining in their direction.

Diana continued. "Every now and then Little Socks gets into position with the instructor and does a particular move. I don't know if she has a name for it, but that's the name Ginger gave it."

From the windowsill came *"Ick! Ick! Ick!"* Little Socks was actually saying, *"The name is Lessiver Mon Derriere, or, for those who can't handle a foreign language, the Wash My Behind. Much more suitable than the name you've given it."*

Annie was a little shocked. "She doesn't actually...."

"Oh, no, Annie, Ginger doesn't take it that far! She stops at stretching the back muscles as far to the floor as possible, and she added a head and chin lift."

"You've ruined it."

"It stretches muscles you never knew you had."

"Cats have always known what muscles they have."

Diana continued, "Little Socks watches when Ginger does it. She tries to pretend she's not, but she does. I think she's secretly happy, but if she could talk to us, she'd never admit it."

Annie laughed, then turned semi-serious. "Diana, keep your weather radio on. If it starts to get bad, send your students home and close for the day. And get Little Socks home."

"Do you think it will get bad?"

"It doesn't look good over the lake, and the reports say there is a possibility of severe weather.

Ginger finished and came to join them, mopping her brow. She motioned to the children that she would be right there. Annie asked, "Have you lined up some help for sewing?"

"Yes. We're going to set up here in the studio. Diana emptied out a storage closet, so we can keep machines and costumes in process there until we get finished. Jolly, Laila, Diana and Mem all have portable machines, and they volunteered to sew.

"Henrie said he would help with hand stitching every evening he could. And Jerry said he'd help with stitching too. What a surprise! We'll be done in plenty of time. I just hope we have enough fabric."

"If you need supplies, go back to the fabric shop and set up a block party account. You can use my address."

"Thanks. What a relief! I think I might run out of red, yellow and green. Logs of ladybugs, angry birds and bad piggies will be running around Chelsea that night."

Annie turned to go, but looked back to say, "And Ginger, let me know if you need anything, anything at all. Thank you again for doing it. You know, you've started a new tradition."

"Let's hope parents put the costumes away so younger children will be able to use them next year."

"You know, that's an idea. I'll bet we could put a wardrobe in one of the basement rooms at the Inn. If kids turn in their costumes the next week, we'd have a starting point for next year."

"I'll put a note on them when they pick them up. We can ask that they turn them in or hold on to them for next year. At least plant the seed."

Annie, having remembered to say something about the weather to Diana, decided to stop by each of her businesses to say hello and pass on the warning. She backtracked to Sassy P's.

Sassy Pants ran to Annie to get a tummy tickle. Annie was happy to oblige. "You know, Sassy girl, your tummy just seems to get bigger and firmer. What's up with that?"

Sassy Pants just leaned into the caress and smiled.

Minnie said, "Good morning. How's Henrie today?"

"He's great. You'd never know he had a concussion. I think his head is made of cast iron."

"Good. He needed that protection. Has Pete been able to tell you anything yet?"

"You know, I haven't had a chance to check in with him. I should do that."

"Some of your Inn guests were in already today, the big guy and the — excuse me for saying it — the mousy woman. Onstair and Alabaster?"

"Yes, those are their character names. I am hopelessly lost about their real ones."

"They seemed to be having a bit of a tiff. I didn't hear what it was about, but they went into the back room where they could be alone. I wonder if one of them will turn out to be the murderer. Oh, and one of the other ones, the younger ones, was in here too. One of the twins. The guy."

"They don't usually split up. The one, Herb, I think, will sometimes be on his own playing computer games or whatnot, but I thought the twins traveled like Siamese."

"Not this morning. He came in after the couple, ordered a small plate and left when they did. He hadn't finished his order. Must be a little at sea when he's not with his twin. Guess they'll never get married, unless they build a house big enough for four adults and however many kids they want."

Annie's eyes went up and to the left. "Imagine what that would look like."

"Feel like."

"Be like."

"Ick."

"Thank you, Minnie, for that picture. I'll have a hard time getting rid of it. I had a reason for coming this morning."

"Shoot."

"Keep the weather radio on. If it sounds bad, close up, send people home, and get my girl here back to the Inn safe and sound."

"Will do. Every now and then I step out to take a look over the lake. Looks like we could be getting something."

Annie stopped at Mr. Bean's, apologizing for passing him up on the way down to Sassy P's. "I didn't forget you, little boy."

Jerry, standing at the counter, said, "He's been all droopy in the window since you passed him by. Twice."

"I waved both times."

"But you didn't hug. Either time."

"Mr. Bean, I'm so sorry."

"I know, Mommy. I love you. Carlos made some new treats today and he let me try one." Mr. Bean jumped off Annie's lap and stopped at the new treat section at the display case. He hopped up to touch the glass next to the treats Carlos let him sample.

"Is he trying to tell me something?"

"He must be. Those are the newest from Laila's recipes for cats. Carlos gave him one this morning. I guess he liked it."

"Why don't you get a bag and put some in it for me. If we have to go to the basement later on, we'll have treats for the kids. And you'd better put a few doggie treats in another bag. Just in case."

"Do you think the basement will be necessary?"

"Maybe. That's why I'm stopping in everywhere. To get a kitty hug and ask you to be careful. If it gets bad, close up and get the boy home to me."

"Will do." Jerry handed three bags to Annie.

"What's in the third?"

"Truffles. I made them up for you the first time you passed him by. I knew you'd be back."

Annie laughed, took the bags and turned to leave. Suddenly, Mr. Bean felt a tremendous urge to follow her out the door. She had treats!

"You stay here, little boy. You'll get some later."

At Mo's Tap, Mo sat on top of the bar, not a typical place for him. A sad face was trained on a table in the middle of the room. Four of the mystery crew sat there.

"Mo, what's wrong, big boy?"

George, from behind the bar, said quietly, "The big guy pushed him off the table."

"Pushed him?"

"It wasn't hard, not hard enough to hurt him, but I almost said something. If Mo had gone near the table again, I would have gone over to get him. When people like that come in here, I want to kick them out. But I know they're your guests."

"Everyone who comes here knows about the cats. If they don't like them, they should choose another place."

195

"I know. I've had that conversation in here a time or two. For the most part, our guests love Mo. There are the few idiots….Anyway, Mo wasn't hurt, but his feelings were."

"Thank you, George. I know cats weren't part of the deal when you first took over the bar for Dad."

"Lucky for you I'm a lover of all things cuddly."

"That's what I hear."

"Oh, no. Am I going to hear it from you, too?"

"Hear what?"

"How I need to straighten up my act and stop falling for…let's just call them cuddly things."

"Now, George. When have I ever gotten involved in your personal life?"

"Never. Well, never out loud. You have a way of 'looking' at me."

"Really?"

"Really."

"And you can tell from my 'look' what I'm thinking?"

"Absolutely."

"You know what, George, here comes a great big piece of advice that you have not requested, so I apologize before giving it. But give it, I will. When someone 'looks' at you in a certain way and you attach a particular meaning to it, you'd better listen to yourself."

George laughed. "You're right. Absolutely right."

Annie, on a more serious note, said, "Listen to the weather radio. If you think it's getting bad, close up and get Mo home to me."

"Will do."

Mo, after another hug from Annie, sadly watched her leave. Something was wrong with these people and his Mommy didn't sense it.

Chapter 18: Blended Groups Tend To Snipe At One Another

Annie stopped first at L'Socks' Virasana. "Little Socks, I didn't come over to say hello to you when I was here earlier."

Little Socks climbed into Annie's lap and curled up.

Annie was so surprised, she sat there for 10 minutes, allowing the warm bundle to sleep.

When Annie got to the Café, everything appeared to be running smoothly. She shared the weather warning with Trudie and Felicity then joined Pete and Clara at their table.

Annie was in a position to look around the Café, as was Pete. Unfortunately, Clara had her back to the room and had to keep turning to see what they were discussing.

Annie shared, "It's my belief that groups vacationing together should do it in shorter bites. By the third or fourth day, blended groups tend to snipe at one another."

"You see sniping?" asked Clara, looking around, ever hopeful.

"Well, one example of a nonblended group of one that isn't sniping at anyone is Jeff Bennett." Annie motioned with her head to a lone table. "What kind of business do you think he has that allows him to come to Chelsea and just hang out for several days? Oh, hey, look. Cyril is sitting over there with him."

Clara turned to look around the room. She gazed wistfully, looking for anyone who might be sniping. She saw Cyril standing at Jeff's table, looking blissful with his head in Jeff's lap.

Pete said, "He rarely does that. There must be something about that guy that Cyril likes. But back to the sniping, where do you see that?"

"There is the blended group of adult twins, male and female, vacationing with a grieving friend. Alec, one of the twins, was off by himself today. It's usually the friend, Herb, that stays to himself. But here you see Herb with Jessica. And how happy do they look?"

Annie motioned with her head to a table in the middle of the room. Clara turned again.

Pete added, "I've noticed them. Whenever a server walks close, they stop talking. Your girl is favoring them with a famous tabletop hop, and she's been there for several minutes."

Sure enough, Tiger Lily sat on one of her ledges in between the two, allowing Herb to stroke her back.

Clara said, "I'm glad you have animals in here. Gives me an excuse to turn around and see what you see. Next time, I get that side of the table."

"I wish Tiger Lily could talk. She could tell us what they were going on about. Pete, would it be illegal for me to install microphones at all the tables, so we could listen in to conversations that appear interesting?"

"Don't go there, Annie. I'd probably have to arrest you."

"That wouldn't be good. Okay. Let's move on to the next blended group. Look in the back corner. Those four folks were at Mo's just a few minutes ago. They started drinking early, but thankfully they came to the alcohol-free Café for lunch. It hasn't helped their mood."

Clara turned to look. "Well, I don't have an excuse to keep looking. No cat there. No dog there. You're going to have to tell me what you see."

Pete said, "I've noticed them, too. It doesn't look as if they are arguing amongst themselves. It looks more like they are discussing something of mutual disagreement."

Pete continued for Clara's benefit. "The couple that appears to be more wealthy and polished – Brad Spit and Mary Monroe – and the casual couple – Dr. Mortimer Bong and Sparkle Shine – they're angry about something."

"They didn't appear to be anything but pleasant at breakfast. Well, the same was true of the trio. No one was angry about anything that I could see. Again, Pete, I want microphones."

"You value your personal freedom too much," he laughed.

Before the mystery crew finished lunch, they were joined by the female half of the third couple. Mousy Alabaster Pearl strode in, all business. She spoke loudly enough that nearly everyone in the Café heard her.

"I can't find him!" she said. "He started drinking at that winery as soon as it opened, and then he just left! Said 'Give me some space!' Said 'Leave me be!' Said 'You'll see me when you see me!'"

Nearly spitting, she continued, "I didn't want to come on this mystery cruise in the first place. He'd better be back before we have to get on that damned boat tonight!"

"Well," said Annie. "There you have it. My theory is absolutely proven!"

Clara was finally on the correct side of the table to initiate a conversation. "Is anyone else worried about those clouds over the lake? Wind's picking up, too."

"I'd just be happier back at the Inn. Clara, are you still coming over this afternoon?"

"Yes. I was going to come right after lunch."

"Why don't you get Mem and Jennifer and ask them to come on over if they can. We can get to it and you all can get home before the storm hits. If it does hit. The weather people are still saying it's a possibility."

Pete added, "They should be saying probability instead of possibility, but I don't have a meteorology degree yet." Louder, he said, "Cyril, come on."

While Pete paid for his meal, Cyril and Tiger Lily compared notes.

Tiger Lily said, *"She's mad about finding the badge herself. She said, 'You said you searched that room, but I just opened a drawer and found it.' And he said, 'You should have left it there. Now he knows someone knows who he is.'"*

Cyril added, *"Jeff's nice. I can tell he's a police officer of some kind. He has that strength of character. I didn't smell fear on him, but I sense he's being really cautious."*

"I like Herb. I'm sorry he's not a good man. He likes cats and dogs."

Annie said to Trudie, "I'm leaving. I'm taking the big girl and picking up all of the others. If there is going to be a storm, I'd rather have them home well in advance."

Back at the Inn, Annie called all of the kids upstairs to the apartment. She locked the cat door and said, very seriously, "There might be a storm later today. I'm locking you in here so I can find you quickly and get you downstairs."

Seven cats seemed to hunch their heads into their shoulders.

"I don't know what's up with all of you. You just seem to go crazy when we have to do this."

One by one they slinked away to find hiding places.

Annie shook her head and pulled out seven cat carriers, setting them by the door. As she left, she called out, "If I have to come up to get you, you'd better come when I call."

Annie still had her purse with her and had picked up her notebook. She took them downstairs and called to her mother. "Mom, I'm going to put a few things down in the basement, my purse and notebook. Do you want to bring some personal things down before we get started on the decorating?"

"You know, I might do that. Let me get Sam's medicine and my purse. I don't like the look of those clouds, and the wind is getting stronger. Are they still saying a storm might not come?"

"They say a storm's coming and it passes to the north, or they say three feet of snow and six inches falls to the south, or they say sunny and warm and we get clouds and a cold drizzle. I'm not listening to them anymore. I'm going with my gut."

Annie walked through to the kitchen. "Henrie, are we stocked up on the basement?"

"We are. And just in case the electricity goes off, I stocked plenty of bottled water. We have food for cats, dogs and humans."

"Great. I picked up some of the newest treats from Carlos, so if we end up in the basement, we'll have them tonight.

Otherwise, I'll hold onto them until tomorrow for Sunday treats. Oh, Henrie, what kind of people stuff?"

"Protein bars, fresh fruit, and several meals. Packages from the freezer made up by the Café are now in the basement refrigerator. There are so many people on The Avenue without basements that we can always figure on a full house."

"Plates, napkins, extra toilet paper. Surely you checked that."

"Yes, and absolutely the most important thing, several – and I do mean several – gallon jugs of water so we can keep the commode flushed. Just in case we lose electricity. Oh, and litter. I didn't forget the litter."

"And…"

"Yes! Candles, matches, flashlights, batteries, LED lanterns, blankets, pillows, cushions, inflatable mattresses, cards and board games. Do you have any other questions?"

Annie laughed and said, "Once again, Henrie, are you sure you won't marry me?"

Nancy, Annie, Clara, Jennifer and Mem were in the basement by mid-afternoon. They were not ready to decorate for the block party; they were armed with cameras, notebooks, paper, pens and ideas.

"Let's start with the entryway and then move through the basement, room by room, in the same order we'll take our victims through. Let's not even look at a room until we're satisfied with the one before it," said Clara.

Going to the cellar entrance, they opened it from the inside and discussed the best, most eerie way to decorate it.

Jennifer, online, looked at images of spooky cellar doors, haunted house entrances and stairwell gore.

"We'll put string lighting on the wall at the step level, and tack lights into the base of each step. With a shrouded light at the top of the cellar, that should get them safely down. It has to be completely black when the get to the bottom of the stairs, though."

"We have to remember to put string lighting on the edge of the ramp, too, so no one falls off."

"We have to shut the door here to the left. We can't be letting our haunted house guests see what amounts to a well-outfitted apartment. Let's cover the door so it's not even visible, maybe a big piece of black plastic painted with glow-in-the-dark words of some kind."

"That'll work. So how do we move people through?"

Annie answered, "The rest of the basement is essentially a circle. We can go straight and end up here, or we can go right and end up here. And from here, they take these steps to the left or the elevator up. The steps go to the kitchen. The elevator goes to the foyer."

"We need to block that, too," said Clara. There has to be a light on, all the time, here at the landing to go upstairs. But we could hang a heavy curtain, so the light isn't visible until someone opens the curtain to escort the 'guest' up the stairs or the elevator."

"A ghost, or a zombie."

"Let's have the stairway attendant be a zombie."

"So we have our entry and exit. What's the most logical way to tour? Send people from the entrance to the right?"

"I think so. There are five rooms, each one opening into the next. The first room is fairly small, then there is a larger one, then the old coal room which is the largest, and another medium room, a smaller room, then we're back where we started."

"What in the world did they use this for?"

"I'm not sure. When Dad updated the Inn, he cleaned out all of these rooms and put all of the modern appliances, air handler, hot water tank, laundry facilities, in this suite of rooms to the left. It goes forward to the edge of the front porch and underneath the stairs. There's another door in there that opens up to the stairwell and elevator, but we never use it. We should probably block it off also, so no one ends up in the suite if the stairway attendant has to leave."

"Do you want to just lock it, or put something over it?"

"I like your black plastic idea. Words of some sort to maybe say they're lucky to be leaving the haunted house with their lives."

Annie had another thought. "You know, there's another door down here. It leads up to the library. It's in the old coal room. We'll have to figure out how to block it off as well when we talk about that room."

"So. We've finished with entrance and exit, and we're moving to the right. It's completely black, the only light they can see is on the stairway behind them. How do we get them to move in the right direction?"

"How about a skeleton here as they enter, to point them to the right? We could put a spotlight over the skeleton, one that is tripped when someone stands here at the landing."

"Maybe it's tripped to come on, but there's a 5-second delay, so they stand here in complete darkness for a little bit."

"How about this, the spotlight is tripped first, then the skeleton's arm a few seconds later. It rises – slowly – and the finger slowly lifts to point to the room."

"Do we need sound effects?"

"We could wait and add that in the first room."

Annie flipped the light switch and they went in. They stood there, not able to come up with a single idea.

Suddenly, Clara, said, "We need a library. I think the biggest room can be a library. That's the coal room, right? That would be room number three."

"After the library a room with medical appliances and tables and things."

"And after that, something that makes people think they're going to fall into a deep pit."

"You're all getting ahead of yourselves…"

"Okay, okay. We haven't gone into the rooms yet!"

"Before the library, a ghoulish dining room."

Then everyone was silent. Again. They stared around the empty room.

Annie sighed. "This room, then dining room, then library, then medical laboratory, then deep pit. What comes first?"

Jennifer hit her head with her hand. "Something beckoning you to enter. A ghost, or several, projected on the walls, set on a trip switch. Otherwise, darkness."

"Eerie pipe organ music begins, again, set on a trip switch to start a few seconds after the ghosts."

"Then a spotlight suddenly shines on a man, his back to us. He's standing by the door leading to the next room. Slowly he turns. Step by step. Inch by inch. Back hunching up more and more until suddenly, he's facing you. His eyeball falls out, and he has to reach for it…well, maybe it could be kind of like a yo-yo and it never leaves his possession, or he'll have to get down on his hands and knees and ask all the guests to help him find it."

"Oh, and then he has to point to the next room so they know to move on."

Satisfied with the effect they intended to create, they went into the next room. Annie flipped on the light.

"Now we're in the dining room. We have a long table and chairs, pushed every which way."

"Some are turned over."

"Cobwebs on the table, chairs, and candelabra. We have to have candelabra."

"The candles – we've got to have flameless candles – spring to life as they enter the room."

"Hollowed out skulls sitting on top of plates. Various levels of intestine pudding. Maybe some spoons still sticking in the skulls."

"The intestines have to be alive. They have to wiggle, like worms."

"Some of them reach up and down."

"Or try to reach to grab a guest."

"Glass goblets filled with blood."

"And after several seconds, maybe ten, a spotlight shines on a waiter, straight down, so nothing else is lit. He's dressed in black tie, but, you know, spooky somehow."

"He has a platter of eyeball appetizers, and he comes forward to offer them to the guests."

"There's a spotlight. How does he do that?"

"You're right. He has to beckon them forward. Of course, he's standing at the next door, the door to the coal room."

"How about sound in here?"

"I think we're too close to the eerie organ music. As some people enter this room, other people will enter the first room, and the organ will start up again."

"Oh, hey! This is an idea! The ghost or goblin or witch or whatever at the top of the cellar steps, the one that sends people down, how about this? She doesn't send anyone until the pipe organ music stops. Then she knows it's safe to send the next group down."

"Great!"

"So, no sound in here. How about putting something in their way?"

"Why don't we place the table so they have to walk around it, one way or another, and the edges on either side of the table are dark."

"We can have five or six people down here dressed completely in black, including ski masks, and they can poke at people or grab at them. Put two or three on either side of the table."

"They can say things like, 'I vant to drink your blood!'"

"Or, 'Vhat a tasty morsel!'"

"Fresh meat!"

"Let the feast begin!"

Eventually they ran out of ideas. Annie said, "Okay, then. Are we ready to go to the library?"

Annie stepped into the old coal room, flipped on the light, and stood stock still. If she were to move any further into the room, she would have to step over a body. A dead one.

Chapter 19: Once Again, Crime Techs Were On Site

By the time Pete arrived, it was nearly 6:00. Once again, crime techs were on site at the Inn doing what they always do. Dusting for fingerprints, looking for footprints, reconstructing the murder. Because it was murder.

One of Pete's officers, Marco, came inside to report on the attempt to collect evidence outside. Evidence that might have been left was long gone, washed away in the rain that grew steadily heavier.

Annie was punch drunk by this time. When Pete asked, "Can you tell me anything?" her response was, "It was Colonel Mustard in the library with a wrench."

Pete pulled Annie in for a hug. "Go upstairs. Try to reach Ray and let him know why he's missing a character. Which one is this?"

"Onstair Royds. And he really is in the library."

"You need a vacation."

Cyril licked her hand. He couldn't give her a vacation, but he could give her this.

Annie went upstairs, where Nancy, Mem, Clara and Jennifer sat, heads on the table or in their hands.

Henrie called Cheryl. "She said she would radio Ray and get back with us. He left at 4:00, and he must have left knowing he was missing a crew member."

"I'll try Chris, but they're probably out of range." Annie was right. Chris's cell phone message said the number was not available.

Henrie had the television on, tuned to the local news. "It doesn't sound good," he said.

Jennifer, Mem and Clara looked at one another. Clara said, "We're stuck here until Pete is done with us. You should be calling your families to let them know where you are."

Annie said, if you're all stuck here, I could sure use some help getting the kids down to the basement."

Nancy added, "I have to look for Honey Bear."

Five people turned out to be, well, not enough to get seven cats into seven carriers. Henrie, Jennifer, Mem, Clara and Annie scoured the apartment, looking under beds and sofa cushions, behind chairs and shower curtains, on top of the refrigerator and kitchen cupboards.

Annie had a sinking feeling. She had not locked the cat door to the patio. She opened the patio door, and around the corner, huddled together against the wind and rain, were seven cats. Cowering in the face of Having To Go To The Basement.

Annie called to her friends, asking that someone shut the pocket door from the kitchen to the dining room. Henrie did. Then Annie, carefully, paying no attention to the rain, walked to the corner of the deck, putting herself between them and the rail. She squatted down and said softly, "Come on, kids. We have to go inside now."

She moved slowly closer, one step, still low, then two. Tiger Lily finally led the way, giving Annie a leery look over her shoulder, toward the patio door and inside. When they were all in, Annie shut the patio door and locked the cat door at the bottom.

There they were, five humans staring down and seven cats staring up and around. The cats scooted together until they were in a circle, butts touching, the better to protect themselves.

Annie couldn't help it. She started to laugh, and so did the rest of the humans. The cats weren't having any of it.

"Grab who you can, and get the nearest carrier. They are mix and match. No one has their own. You're going to have a hard time getting them in.

They had a hard time getting them, period. Cats ran, jumped to the counter top, up to the refrigerator, back down again, to the top of the microwave, under the table and on top of chairs already under the table. Finally, each human got their hands on one cat, and then the fun really began.

Cats spread their front legs to stay outside the carriers. When humans tried to put them in butt first, the back legs were spread. There was hissing, spitting, loud meows, cries of absolute anguish, but eventually, five cats were in five carriers.

Tied for first place in eluding the humans who planned to torture them with basement time were Tiger Lily and Little Socks. They had, after all, had more experience in eluding capture.

By now the wind was howling and the tornado sirens had started to sound. "Why don't you all go down and take the lovelies with you. I'll get the last two by myself."

Annie put herself between the opening of the door as humans left and the two cats. If she had to, she would throw herself to the floor to catch either of them trying to escape.

Door safely closed, she reasoned with them. "Girls, we have to go downstairs. It's not safe up here."

She stared at two cats, furiously mewing. She was careful to maintain the stare, not allowing her eyes to waiver.

"Mommy, the food is up here! We'll starve to death down there!"

"There won't be any place for us to pee!"

211

"Treats! All the treats are up here!"

"Our friends are out there in danger! We have to stay here so they can find us!"

"All our toys are up here!"

"Mommy, please don't make us go!!!!!!"

Finally, they gave out. Mommy won the staring contest. They stood with heads hanging down.

Annie reached down. Little Socks allowed herself to be picked up and placed into the carrier without fighting. Then Tiger Lily, tail flopping between her legs without any energy, allowed it as well. Annie breathed a sigh of relief and carried her two oldest children downstairs.

When she turned the corner to the kitchen, she saw Nancy carrying a large case with a howling Honey Bear. "Mom, take Little Socks. Let me carry Honey Bear down the stairs."

"I'm not going to argue."

"Where did you find him?"

"He was in the library under the TV stand."

"Oh. That's a favorite place for Kali and Ko."

"Probably not anymore."

Henrie was in the basement on the Inn's hand held phone. When he hung up, he said, "Cheryl is going to come here with Jock rather than try to get home. And guess what."

"What?"

"The Escape cannot be reached by radio."

"Again? We have another murder and another storm and they are out of touch again?" Annie was of course talking about the scare they all had two months ago.

"She called the Coast Guard and reported it as an emergency because of the weather. She told them about the murder, so they are aware of all the circumstances. At least all we know of. I told her to come right away, but she wanted to make sure the harbor is secure.

"I always leave the kitchen door unlocked during a storm in the event our neighbors need shelter. She knows to enter there."

Inside the cozy basement room were Henrie and Annie, Nancy and Sam, Clara, Jennifer and Mem, Pete and Cyril and eight howling cats, still in carriers. If Cheryl and Jock were the only ones to join them, it would be very comfortable. Sometimes, several people from The Avenue joined them, but not always.

"Oh, my goodness!" said Annie. "The other guests!"

"My word!" exclaimed Henrie. "Stay here. I'll go check on them."

Henrie left and Annie asked, "Pete, where are all of your people?"

"They left fifteen minutes ago to start rounding up folks that we know need some extra help during bad weather. I stayed to rope off the 'library' so as not to contaminate that room anymore. But we're stuck with a body."

"You had to say that."

"It's true."

"Ducky. Just ducky. Did you call Janet?"

"Yes. She and the kids are already in the basement at home."

When Henrie returned, he had Alec, Jessica and Herb in tow. "Jeff is not here. Let us hope he found shelter somewhere else."

Annie introduced her guests to the people they might not know, and everyone got comfortable for what could be an hour or all night.

When the door to the suite was finally closed, cat carriers were opened. That was a mistake. The suite was too small for a dog and eight cats when one of the cats was Uncle Honey Bear.

At 4:15, Ray, Chris, Candice and five crew members sat on deck, waiting for the sixth. Alabaster Pearl said, "I tell you, he's not coming. He's impossible sometimes, and this afternoon, he just wigged out."

Chris spotted Jeff Bennett, taking an afternoon stroll around the docks. He turned to Ray, "Why don't we ask Jeff if he wants to sit in and read Onstair's part?"

"That's a great idea, that is, if you all don't mind."

"It's a great idea," said Brad Spit. "He took that investigator spot. Maybe he'll be willing."

"It will mean a free moonlight – well, there won't be any moonlight tonight – but a free cruise and free dinner."

Chris hailed Jeff and ran over. Ray kept an eye on Chris while the two men talked. Soon they both headed to The Escape.

Chris said, "Everyone, I'd like to introduce you to Onstair Royds."

Ray took The Escape out, cruising for a short time, and by 5:30, they stopped at a point fairly far out, but not too far.

Lights from Chelsea were beginning to come on and could be seen in the distance. Ray cut the engine and joined the crew in the comfortable lounge.

Bottles of wine and a chiller with iced craft beers were in the middle of the table. As Ray walked in, Candice was saying, "I have to remind you of the Captain's rules about drinking. While we're on The Escape, no one drinks to excess. If we cut you off, you need to accept it, and accept it graciously."

"No problem." "Yes, ma'am." and "We'll be careful." were heard in response.

As Ray sat, Candice served the first course, chicken fricot, a chicken and vegetable soup spiced with savory and dotted with dumplings.

Ray said, "We'll enjoy a good meal, courtesy of Tiger Lily's Café, and then we'll finish the play. Unfortunately, I think the weather will keep us from going any further or staying out very late."

"Are we safe out here?" asked Mary Monroe.

"Yes. I think the storm is going to pass us by."

The group relaxed to enjoy dinner, everyone getting to know one another on a personal level. Ray was surprised at how easily Jeff fit into the group.

Candice served the second course, pork tenderloin rubbed with fennel and salad made with escarole and apples. By now, no one worried about the wind and rain outside. They believed the worst of it would pass them by. Then the waves got just a touch bigger.

Ray said, calmly, "Why don't we start the play while we're having dessert."

And there was Candice, serving moist apple cake with a toffee crust, caramelized apples on the side, vanilla bean ice cream and butterscotch sauce on top.

By now, it was 6:00. Candice, having cleaned plates and silver after every course, stood by to take away dessert dishes, glasses and bottles as they were finished. She placed a carafe of coffee on the table and used the less formal – but unbreakable – cups she found in the galley instead of the china from the Café.

Chapter 20: In The Weeds, Round Three

Ray handed the booklets around and said, "This is a short round. We discover the murderer, make the arrest, and then we can head for shore. We'll have some wind, rain and waves, but we'll be safely back to shore before anything dangerous comes in."

Then, as Detective Brown, he started the round. This will be our final night. If you have questions, get them ready. Who wants to start?

Chris had a question for Mary Monroe. "Ms. Monroe, after Dr. Bong passed you the poisoned glass of wine, what did you do with it?"

"I had a glass already. I noticed Onstair didn't have a glass in his hand, so I passed that glass to him."

Chris continued. "Sparkle, earlier you said you gave Spicy liquid aspirin. Did you actually see him take it?"

"I saw him take it just before the toast."

Chris kept going, "Dr. Bong, I heard about an argument you had with the manager of Mo's Tap. What was that about?"

"I needed something out of my man purse. I dug around inside the purse but couldn't find it. I thought the manager had allowed a thief to enter the bar. I realize now I must have picked up Onstair's man purse."

Chris said, "I think I'm on a roll, Detective Brown. I'm going to ask another question. Earlier, Brad, you confessed to slipping Lily Spit to Alabaster. You spiked Spicy's glass with the same bottle. Did you plan to get frisky with him as well?"

"Not frisky. Spicy knew about my drug smuggling. He used this knowledge to blackmail me into supplying duckweed to him for nearly nothing. I'd had enough of this and I tried to kill him by running him over. Unfortunately, I failed. But that was Plan B.

"I've been working on my A Plan for the last few months. I have been secretly dosing him, hoping to make him an addict. This would give me power over him. The dose in the wine was just a continuing effort.

"I wish I had killed him. With him dead, my smuggling would have been a complete secret. Spicy was the only person connected with Duckweed Spirits who knew about it."

Alabaster Pearl stood up and announced in a smug voice, "Thanks. That's all I needed to know."

She moved to stand in front of Brad. "I'm with the State Narcotics Task Force. We've been watching the Lily Spit shipments for a long time, but we needed to know if you were working alone or if others in the company were in on it. I was planted in the company to get close to you.

"We were particularly interested in your Duckweed Desire. The useful purpose of that product was essentially the same as the drug you make; we thought you were using Lily Spit as one of the ingredients.

"I took a sample and sent it to be analyzed. There were no traces of the drug in Duckweed Desire. I had reached the conclusion no one else in the company was involved, but you just confirmed it.

"Now I can act. Brad Spit, I'm arresting you for drug trafficking. You have the right to remain silent. Anything you say can and will be used against you in a court of law. You have the right to speak to an attorney, and to have an attorney present during any questioning. If you cannot afford a lawyer, one will be provided for you. Do you understand these rights as I have explained them to you?"

Brad appeared broken. He looked at Detective Brown, hung his head, and remained silent. Detective Brown said, "Stand up, now, Brad. I'll have to search you."

He conducted a search of Brad's body and appeared to find Clue #3 in his jacket pocket. He read it aloud.

"This appears to be for a recipe named "Camel." There are ingredients and a method for mixing it. And there's a handwritten note, asking that the finished product be mailed to Sparkle. Can you explain this, Brad?"

"Sparkle came to me with a recipe she said was for Duckweed Endurance. She asked me to find someone to make it and to mail it to her marketing agency. I don't know why she wanted it, but I got it made and mailed it to her."

Detective Brown turned to Sparkle. "Is this true?

"Spicy told me about Duckweed Endurance. I thought it could help Onstair with his Olympics bid. I told Onstair and he asked me to get it for him. I bribed Alabaster to get the recipe. I told her I would introduce her to some influential people. I picked up Brad's package just before the party the other night. I gave it to Onstair when he got to Mo's Tap."

Dr. Bong jumped in. "Alabaster, why did you do it? Why did you steal that recipe for Sparkle?"

"Well, as you now know, I was investigating everyone in the company. I decided to play along with her, hoping to find out more."

Chris had another question. "Onstair, maybe you cheated at the World games after all. Well, that's another story. What did you do with the Duckweed Endurance?"

"Well, since this is all going to come out anyway, you're right. I did cheat. That was then. This is now. Duckweed Endurance is new. It would not be on the list of banned substances. It would never be discovered in the mandatory testing process. I thought it could help me win gold. When Sparkle gave it to me, I put it in my man purse. I slipped it into my wine during the toast. You all saw how it affected me. I dumped the glass of red wine and got a glass of white. I'm afraid to try it again. I'm going to have to win without cheating. If that's possible."

Detective Brown announced, "Well, ladies and gentlemen, I think we have heard enough evidence to solve this mystery. In a moment I will reveal all. But first, it's your turn. You'll have three minutes in which to come to your own conclusions. We'll go around the group for a quick tally to see who receives the most votes, and then we will go around again and ask for your reasoning.

"Remember, the guilty party does not know that he or she is the one that committed the murder. If you think you might be the guilty party, you can vote for yourself."

Detective Brown allowed three minutes to go by. "Okay. Let's have a vote for who-done-it."

"Brad Spit, who do you say?"

"I say Dr. Mortimer Bong."

"Dr. Mortimer Bong?"

"I say Brad Spit."

"Mary Monroe?"

"That fraud, Alabaster Pearl."

"Alabaster Pearl?"

"Sparkle Shine did it."

"Sparkle Shine?"

"It was Brad Spit."

"And finally, Onstair Royds?"

"Dr. Mortimer Bong is guilty."

Detective Brown concluded the voting. "You've heard it. Brad Spit and Dr. Mortimer Bong are tied with the highest number of votes. Now we'll go around one more time to hear your reasoning. Let's start with you again, Mr. Spit. Why did you choose Dr. Mortimer Bong?"

"Mortimer is not the famous scientist he believes himself to be, and deep down, I think he knows that. He had to get control of the company, one way or another, in order to have his big break and really become famous."

"And Dr. Bong, why did you choose Brad Spit?"

"Brad doesn't have the brains that God gave a goose, and here he was, dropping what he thought was a date rape drug into Spicy's drink. I think he got the drug mixed up with the poison, or he believes he can convince a jury that he got mixed up. He poisoned Spicy, accidentally on purpose."

"Ms. Monroe, why did you choose Alabaster Pearl?"

"She's a fraud. She's a fake and a phony. She stole something from the safe, and I think it was Duckweed Sewage Cleaner. Spicy must have found out she was a fraud and she knew she had to shut him up."

"Ms. Pearl, why did you choose Sparkle Shine?"

"Talk about frauds, fakes and phonies, that's Sparkle all over. She's going broke. She needed money. She knew that Spicy wouldn't increase his marketing budget, so she had to get him out of the way.

"Ms. Shine, why did you choose Brad Spit?"

"Well, now I'm thinking it was Alabaster Pearl! But I really did – at first – think it was Brad Spit. Brad and Spicy were both playboys of a sort. I think Brad is not nearly so well off as he pretends to be, and I think he was coveting the financial resources of Mary Monroe. No, that didn't come out at all with any of the questions and clues, but I'm quite insightful. I am a marketing success because I can read people so well."

"And finally, Mr. Royds, why did you choose Dr. Mortimer Bong?"

"Dr. Mortimer Bong is an incredible idiot. He thought he had developed the perfect stamina drug, but it was a complete bust. I must admit he was onto something with the love potion, but, for the love of Pete, look at his list of products. Diet pills. Lingerie. Candlewicks. Sewage cleaner. He's grasping at straws. I should have recognized the folly of the stamina drug before choking on it the other night. He was going to be found out, and the great and famous scientist had to have an excuse. Somehow, he was going to link the death of Spicy Pepper to the problems of the company to shroud the real reason for controversy, his ridiculous product lines."

Detective Brown listened thoughtfully to each and every reason, then he sat back to review his notes.

"Remember how you voted and your reasoning for those votes as I tell you how Spicy Pepper met his death. See just how wrong you really are. As you will soon see, I am the greatest detective in the state, quite possibly the world."

The silent mystery crew plus investigator stared up at him, expectantly.

"This was a difficult case, with lots of subplots and attempts to use people for nefarious ends. It was difficult to sort out the red herrings from the real clues. But we are limited in the number of suspects. Only six people could have poisoned Spicy Pepper.

"Every crime needs a motive. I first studied the relationships between the six suspects and Spicy Pepper. I came to the conclusion that of these six people, two were anxious to keep him alive, one was indifferent to his existence, and three people had a motive to kill.

"The two people who wanted him alive were his very good friend, Dr. Mortimer Bong, and his, um, let's just say lady friend, Mary Monroe.

"Dr. Mortimer Bong wanted the next commercial venture to be Duckweed Candlewicks. He was so determined for this to happen, he was prepared to kill Mary Monroe to achieve it. With her death, her shares in the company would go to Spicy Pepper, and Dr. Bong was counting on Spicy to then develop the candlewicks.

"Mary Monroe realized Spicy was the man with whom she wanted to spend the rest of her life. She was so desperate to seduce him that she spiked his drink with Duckweed Desire.

"Alabaster Pearl frankly didn't care whether Spicy lived or died. However, since she was investigating his company, ideally she would have preferred him alive.

"Now let's turn to the remaining suspects.

"Brad Spit has been importing illegal drugs into the country, hidden in the duckweed. Spicy knew this and was blackmailing Brad.

"The jealous Onstair Royds suspected Spicy was having an affair with his wife, Sparkle Shine.

"And Sparkle, whose business urgently needs a cash infusion, was told by Dr. Bong that he would write a check if he had the power to do so. This could only happen if Spicy was dead.

"So, having worked out who wanted Spicy dead and who wanted him alive, let's take a look at all the ways the Sewage Cleaner could have been administered. Let's start with Brad Spit.

"Brad spiked Spicy Pepper's drink what he said was Lily Spit. He says this was part of a long campaign to addict Spicy to the drug. But do we have any evidence to support this?

"Well, the answer is yes. Alabaster Pearl received the same thing. She's still alive. When drinking the toast, she got a little rush, a sign of just one dose of Lily Spit.

"Brad is also telling the truth about his campaign to make Spicy an addict. Spicy was having headaches and was seeing blinding lights, symptoms of long term abuse of the drug.

"Brad did not kill Spicy Pepper.

"Let's move to Sparkle Shine. Spicy told Sparkle he had a headache; she gave him a liquid pain killer. She told us he took this just before drinking the toast. Could this have been Duckweed Sewage Cleaner, and is Sparkle the killer?

"The answer is no. If Sparkle had poisoned Spicy, why would she tell us she saw him take the medicine immediately before he died? If she were guilty, it would be far more sensible to lie and say that he took it early on during the evening, long before the murder.

"And Sparkle found out only on the night of the murder that with Spicy dead, Dr. Bong would bump up the company marketing budget. The use of Duckweed Sewage Cleaner in a public restaurant surely proves this murderer came prepared to kill. Sparkle Shine is not the killer.

"We know someone who did go to the restaurant prepared to kill with Duckweed Sewage Cleaner. Dr. Mortimer Bong. He had every motive for keeping his very good friend alive, but could Spicy have died due to the planned murder going horribly wrong?

"Dr. Bong poisoned Mary Monroe's wine with Duckweed Sewage Cleaner, but Mary did not drink it. She passed the glass to Onstair Royds. So why didn't our Olympic athlete fall lifeless to the floor?

"The answer is that Onstair Royds is the luckiest man alive. By a miracle, fate stepped in that night to prevent his death.

"Onstair is prepared to cheat. He persuaded Sparkle to get Duckweed Endurance so he could win in the Olympics. Sparkle gave it to him when he arrived at Mo's Tap. He put it in his man purse.

"Now remember what Dr. Bong told us. He said he took Duckweed Sewage Cleaner to the restaurant. But he also told us that, as a precaution, he took something to act as an antidote, carrying it in his man purse.

"When Onstair and Dr. Bong were at Mo's Tap, they picked up one another's purse. Just before the toast, after Mary unwittingly handed him the poisoned glass of wine, Onstair, thinking he was adding Duckweed Endurance to his glass, actually added the antidote to it!

"This explains his illness and swift recovery after the toast. He was poisoned and resuscitated all in one mouthful!

"But if Onstair Royds drank the poisoned glass of wine, how did the poison get into Spicy Pepper's wine? And who administered it?

"Here we come to the final irony. Spicy Pepper was killed by the person who most wanted him alive. Spicy Pepper was killed by Mary Monroe."

Mary Monroe gasped, almost fainted, and was caught before falling to the floor. She was settled into her chair with a glass of water while Detective Brown continued.

"We know Mary was worried that Spicy and Sparkle were involved. To seduce Spicy, she took the reckless step of adding Duckweed Desire to his wine. But let's take a look at how she came into possession of this seductive elixir.

"She persuaded Alabaster Pearl to send her the password. Then Mary paid a hacker to obtain the recipe. She gave the recipe to Brad Spit who had it made for her."

At this point, Detective Brown paused to pick up the list of passwords sent to Spicy Pepper by the computer security company.

"Remember, there is nothing on any of the product recipes to indicate what the recipe is for. When the hacker obtained the recipe, he typed in the password supplied by Alabaster Pearl.

"Now let us consider very carefully how Mary Monroe received that password. Alabaster wrote the password in the center of a plain piece of paper and mailed it to Mary. If we look at Clue #2, we see the password for Duckweed Desire is 'mom,' a simple, nonsense word.

"Here it is, on Clue #1. You can see it among the other passwords. Now imagine it was written in the center of a plain piece of paper, folded up and placed in an envelope. What would happen if the recipient of that envelope opened it up and took out the paper upside down? Keep your eye on the word 'mom' and watch what happens when I turn the list of passwords upside down."

Detective Brown slowly turned the list over as the suspects crowded around, staring at the paper.

"You will see that it becomes 'wow,' another simple, nonsense word. By tragic coincidence this was the password for Duckweed Sewage Cleaner!

"When Mary's hacker broke into the system, he entered the wrong password. There was nothing on that recipe to warn Mary of the mistake. Believing it to be a love potion that would make Spicy forever hers, she added it to his wine.

"Mary Monroe killed Spicy Pepper, but it was a tragic accident."

Mary, dazed, seemed to babble. "I can't believe it. I killed Spicy. And I loved him! I really believed he was having an affair with Sparkle. All those late night meetings, and the way she acted. I thought I would lose him forever!

"And now I have! I killed the only man I have ever truly loved. I can't believe it. I've killed my only chance at happiness."

Mary collapsed into her chair and sobbed, "Oh, won't someone just put me out of my misery!"

Detective Brown wrapped up the mystery session. "And now we know how Spicy Pepper died. Give yourselves a round of applause for your efforts."

Even Mary Monroe smiled and applauded.

"And now, my friends, it's time for us to head for shore."

Indeed, the wind howled, rain pelted the boat, and waves had begun to toss The Escape about as if it were a rowboat.

Candice had everything stowed with the exception of the last carafe of coffee and a few unbreakable cups. She moved to the table to take those away while Chris took the precaution of breaking out life jackets.

Ray headed to the wheelhouse, but before he got out of the galley, a strong wave hit The Escape. Everyone but Ray was close to something to hang onto. Ray was thrown to the side, and his head met the countertop with terrific force. He lay on his back on the floor, unconscious and bleeding from a deep cut in his forehead.

Chapter 21: It Was A Large Pile Of Fur

The electricity went out. Annie and Henrie lit candles and put some LED lanterns around the room.

Nancy asked, "Annie, do you think we ought to put the cats back in their carriers?"

"No, they would just set up a racket. At least they're quiet now."

They were. They were scared, but they were gathered around Cyril for comfort. It was a large pile of fur, huddled and shaking.

Cheryl and Jock arrived, having driven from The Marina to the Inn, a distance of about two city blocks. In the short time they were outside – from The Marina to the car and from the car to the Inn – they were soaked. She found her way to the basement using a flashlight and used the flashlight to knock on the door of the suite. "Is it okay to open the door?"

"Come in quickly. The cats are in a pile on the other side of the room, but they could run."

She did it quickly, pushing Jock in front of her. With the door safely shut, Cheryl slumped to the floor, back to the door. She opened her purse and took out a portable radio. "We can stay in touch with the Coast Guard."

Annie said, "It's a good thing you have that. A while ago we tried our cell phones; the tower must be down."

"Which one?"

"Apparently all of them in our radius," said Pete.

"Well, we'd better try the radio." She was able to raise the local Coast Guard station. The second in command told her volunteers had been called out. Not only was The Escape at stake, their boss, Chris, was out there. They were going to get him.

By this time, Annie was next to Cheryl with a bath towel and a blanket. Pete dried Jock with another towel.

Annie asked, "How bad is it?"

"Bad as I've seen it. I was fool enough to try to make sure boats were secure. Good grief! I could have been killed out there. Jock finally took hold of my pants leg and started pulling me back. There were lots of cars in the parking lot, and I could swear they were moving in the wind."

A telephone rang. Everyone looked around, and Henrie pulled out the Inn's land line, safely tucked into his jacket pocket. "Oh, my!" He pulled himself together and answered, "The KaliKo Inn, Henrie speaking."

"Henrie, it's Felicity. Is Annie there?"

"Certainly, Felicity. One moment."

He handed the phone to Annie, who said, "Felicity? Is everything okay?"

"Yes, but George, George was called out to help find The Escape. He's a volunteer, you know."

"I'm sure all the volunteers were called. Are you worried about Mo's Tap? Certainly they're closed right now, but Candice will be fine on her own later on."

"Then you don't know. When Ray pushed up the time of the dinner, he thought it would be nice to have someone serve. Candice volunteered to go. George didn't seem to mind, you know, the two of them being kind of crosswise."

"So Candice is out there, too?"

"Yes. I just wanted you to know that Trudie and I will open up Mo's as soon as the warning is lifted. People will want to drink."

"Thank you, Felicity, thanks to both of you. I certainly hope this evening ends on a positive note."

Nancy was confused, having heard only Annie's side of the conversation. "What was that all about?"

"Well, Candice volunteered to serve the meal for the mystery crew, so she's out there with Ray and Chris. And George is a Coast Guard volunteer, just like your volunteer firemen at home. He's one of the people that will be out there looking for The Escape."

"Oh, my. Well, what we need to do is offer up our prayers for everyone out there on that lake tonight." She continued, "Annie, it is awfully crowded in here. Isn't that a bedroom behind Pete? Can we open it up for the cats and dogs?"

"Sure, Mom, that's a good idea. We can put their carriers in there too, just to get them out of the way."

Humans got up and tried to rearrange ten companions. It wasn't easy. Knowing they were "supposed" to go somewhere made it worse. Eventually, it was accomplished, although the only thing that could possibly happen with Uncle Honey Bear was to leave him in the room with the humans. He stretched out on the most comfortable chair, leaving floor space available for a human.

With sighs of relief, twelve humans sat down on less comfortable chairs, cushions, mattress pads and the floor. Annie looked at Alec, Jessica and Herb and said, "Welcome to the madhouse."

On the companion side of the door they could hear howls, yowls and meows of fear and anger. On the human side of the door, complete silence.

Annie finally said, "Henry, please tell me the cat and dog food, water and litter bins are in the bedroom."

"The food, water and litter bins are in the bedroom."

"Thank you."

"However, they have not been served, so to speak. The bowls and litter bins are empty, and the bags are safely closed inside the wardrobe."

Annie closed her eyes and sighed. Pete said, "I've got it."

He made his way into the bedroom without losing anyone. The longer he was in the room, the quieter it became. Finally, he came out without having to rush, shutting the door behind him.

"I swear, they were not afraid of the storm at all. They were afraid they were going to starve to death. As soon as I put the cat food in bowls on top of the dresser, they jumped up to eat as if they were never going to eat again. And the dogs dug into their food; I put that on the floor, of course.

"I put out three bowls of water and filled one litter bin. I left that beside the bed. And you had pee pads for the dogs. Thanks, Henrie. I put that in front of the door on the other side of the room.

"By the way, where does that door go?"

"It just goes back into the basement. Everything goes in a circle around here."

"Hmm. I probably should have fingerprinted in here, too."

Alec, Jessica and Herb looked up at him. "Fingerprinted?"

"Oh, yes, you didn't hear. Cheryl knew before she got here, but by the time you got here, we were only concerned about shelter. I hate to tell you, but there's a body over on the other side of the basement."

"Oh, my," said Jessica. "Never a dull moment in Chelsea."

"Or, apparently, at the KaliKo Inn," added Alec.

Henrie leaned over to whisper to Annie, "There go our ratings. Straight into the cellar."

In the other room, finally relieved that food, water and toileting supplies were supplied, the companions settled down to discuss the situation.

"Well," said Jock, *"We might be here for a while. It's awfully bad out there. The wind and the rain, waves…Cheryl said something about tornado warnings."*

Sassy Pants said, *"What's a tanordo?"*

Little Socks sighed.

Cyril answered. *"A tornado. It's a really bad wind, and it tears things up."*

"Trill!"

Cyril looked at Mo and said, *"I'm sure everyone on The Avenue went somewhere safe."*

Cyril then looked at Jock and said, *"Why aren't you on The Escape with Ray?"*

"That one man they call Brad Spit didn't want me."

"And you let him go without you?"

"I didn't have a choice. I was able to keep Cheryl safe. That's important."

"Yes, it is."

Mr. Bean asked, *"So are we safe down here?"*

Cyril and Jock looked at one another. Cyril responded, *"We're safe from the storm, but I don't know if we're safe from all the people in here."*

"What do you know?"

"Pete has been doing some investigating. Because of that break-in, he sent all the fingerprints he found. There are a few people at the Inn that are wanted for several things."

"Who?" "What?"

"The three that are down here, two of them are wanted for lots of different things. The twins. Mostly related to drugs, but some other stuff, too."

"No! They're nice!"

"Especially that Herb. Is he wanted for anything?"

"Pete couldn't tell. His fingerprints were found, but it came back as something private, so he couldn't get any information."

"What does that mean?"

"It could mean he's in witness protection."

"What's that?"

"That's a program where a criminal turns against his friends, and the police hide him, because he helped. He's still a criminal, though."

"What about the other people, the ones that are on the boat with Ray?"

"Two of them are wanted, too. One for fraud and the other for drugs."

"Who are they?"

"Both are men. I'm not sure which two of the three; I couldn't see the pictures while Pete was on the phone."

"What about the body? Is that a bad man or a good man?"

"*I think it might be a bad man. Pete didn't say anything to the other officers, but he was looking through his pockets awfully close.*"

"*This isn't good. We're on the wrong side of this door, if those three people are bad.*"

"*Pete's in there.*"

"*But he's still in danger. They're all in danger.*"

Jock got up to sniff at the door on the other side of the room. "*I don't know if it will help, but maybe we can get out of this door. It doesn't look very sturdy.*"

"*If we can get out of that door, what good would it do? There's another door that's closed. We'll still be shut out.*"

"*One door at a time, my friend. One door at a time.*"

With that, Cyril and Jock began working at the door, digging their paws between the door and the latch. For some reason, Annie's dad hadn't upgraded this door as he had the others. It wasn't sturdy at all, and within fifteen minutes, they had cleared it. The door opened with a squeak, but the humans didn't hear it.

"*You stay here.*"

"*No!*"

"*Yes! Well, one of you can come. Tiger Lily, you have to stay here and keep the rest in line. Push the door mostly shut, just in case any of the humans come out. We don't want them to know we're out. Little Socks, come with us.*"

Jock and Cyril didn't know what they were looking for, but they slipped around the corner, Little Socks close behind. Jock said, "*Little Socks, go to the door and see if you can hear anything.*"

Chapter 22: Things Went From Bad To Worse Fairly Quickly

Things on The Escape went from bad to worse fairly quickly. Ray was unconscious and bleeding. The storm was stronger than before. The lights of Chelsea were no longer visible in the distance. They would have to rely on instruments to get into the harbor safely.

Chris took charge. "Does anyone have medical experience?"

No one did, but Candice and Jeff knelt to see if they could help. Chris said, "It would be best not to move him at all. Jeff, find what you can to hold him steady on the floor; Candice, see what supplies Ray has to tend to that wound. The rest of you, get on the floor around him and hold him steady until Jeff can get him stabilized. Does anyone have experience with a yacht?"

Several people, in scared voices, said, "Don't you?" You don't?" "Oh, my God!"

"Don't worry, I was just looking for help. I've been out with Ray several times in the past, and I certainly have experience in Coast Guard boats. I was just hoping to have a second person up there with me."

Chris went to the wheel room by himself and looked around to make sure he was familiar with everything. He sent a silent prayer up that the instruments were in good condition, since he could not see to navigate, and went to the captain's seat. He checked the kill switch and did everything he knew to do before turning the key.

He turned the key. Nothing.

He turned the key again. Nothing.

He looked around to see if he was supposed to do something else first, but couldn't find anything.

He tried the radio. Nothing.

He took a steadying breath to calm himself and looked for a glove compartment. Glove compartment? he thought. I'm losing my mind. But where in the world would the manual be?

He looked everywhere, and realized Ray might keep manuals and records in his stateroom. He had to pass through the galley to get there.

As he walked, holding on to walls and railings on his way through, he waved off shouted questions.

He got into the stateroom and looked through all the drawers, closets and cupboards. Nothing.

Chris had to face the group.

He went back to the galley, came close to the group, all huddled on the floor around Ray, and said, "Now we really are in the weeds."

Chris explained the situation to them. He could not start the engine. Everything was in fine shape on the way out, but it's not working now. The radio was completely out of commission. It's possible the radio was not working before they left the harbor, there's no way to know.

"We need to get the raft and some safety gear out. We have one option, folks. We stay here and wait for the Coast Guard. If they don't come, and if things get worse, we go over the side into the raft and hang on for dear life."

Chris thought he dropped a bombshell. Not even close. Jeff stepped to the plate and dropped the real one.

"Now that the play is over, and now that we find ourselves in this situation, allow me to introduce myself. I work for the FBI. I'd show you my credentials, but they were stolen the night our rooms at the Inn were burglarized."

Brad Spit said, "You're daft, man! This is no time for jokes!"

"Not joking."

Alabaster Pearl said, "The play's over, honey. I'm the undercover officer."

"Not joking."

Mary Monroe, finally getting it, said, "Oh for God's sake, Hirsch, I thought you said we were in the clear!"

"Shut up!"

"The frickin' FBI is here, Hirsch. You said we were free and clear and no one would be looking anymore!"

"I said shut up!"

As Chris watched the scene unfold, it was almost comical.

The Brad Spit and Mary Monroe pair, whose names he was beginning to remember were Hirsch and Linda Stone, were confessing to some kind of crime. It appeared, from the look on his face, that Special Agent Bennett — if that was his real name — was actually amused!

Dr. Mortimer Bong and Sparkle Shine — another couple, but with different last names, thought Chris — moved back several feet to put distance between themselves, the injured captain, the possible FBI agent, and this couple with whom they booked the cruise.

The lone woman, Alabaster Pearl, the mousy secretary cum undercover State Police Officer — recently left in the lurch by her handsome real-life husband – sat like a lump. In shock, he thought.

"In shock!" Chris said. "She's going into shock! Someone get some blankets, get her into a chair and keep her warm!"

Candice jumped in response, ran to the stateroom corridor and came back with two blankets. She handed one to Jeff to put over Ray and went quickly to Alabaster Pearl. "Here, Hannah, let's get you up and into a chair, hon, and I'll wrap this around you."

Hannah, thought Chris. That's her name. I need to write this down.

Chris, realizing he was, actually, still in charge and that their situation was desperate, rallied.

"Jeff – is that your real name? Jeff?"

Jeff gave a quick nod.

Stay with Ray. Candice, stay with Hannah. I'm going to get that safety gear. Dr. Bong – I'm sorry, sir, what is your name?"

"Tom Mollar."

"Tom, thank you. Please come with me. I'll need help carrying it up. Everyone else, sit tight."

As they went to the emergency supply area, Tom said, "Really, whatever is going on out there, I'm not a part of it. I've never done anything illegal in my life! Well, I smoked pot a few times, but I regret it now. Boy, do I regret it now. Will they be giving lie detector tests?"

"Tom, please, just stay calm. I have no idea what the FBI is doing here, but I'm sure we'll all find out at the same time."

They returned, and as Chris stowed the gear in an easy-to-reach location, Candice retrieved more blankets. She handed them around to keep everyone warm. The heating system wasn't working, and the temperature was dropping. What else could go wrong?

"Did you all bring rain gear?" asked Chris.

Hirsch pointed to some bags in the corner. "I brought our bags in before you got to the harbor this afternoon. There is gear for six of us, because Hannah packed for Spencer."

"If we need to use it, I'll take Spencer's gear for Ray. Jeff, how is he doing?"

"He's breathing steady, the bleeding has stopped. The cut doesn't look serious, but who knows what got hurt inside."

Chris kept his gaze on Jeff. "Now, Mr. FBI. What in the world are you doing here?"

All eyes turned to Jeff.

"Well, I thought I knew what I was doing, but apparently I'm in the weeds. I guess the best thing to do is start talking and see what happens." He turned to the Stones. "Hirsch and Linda Stone, correct?"

Hirsch and Linda nodded, a bit sullen.

"Well, of course I know about you because I had to check out everyone at the Inn and other people around town with whom you all communicated. You don't exist. Or at least you didn't exist before a couple of years ago."

Linda turned to Hirsch and said, "You dimwit. If we're going to hide in plain sight, we have to have a story. You didn't make a story for us?"

"I didn't have time, dear. I just didn't have time."

Tom and his – wife? partner? companion? what in the world is her name, thought Chris – looked at one another in confusion. "You've been our next door neighbors for two years. What do you mean you don't have a story?" asked Tom. "You told me who you are. Retired. Living the good life. Who in the world are you, really?"

"You don't want to know who we were. And you don't want to know how we got the money we use to live the good life. I'll tell you we were in witness protection, and we got tired of all the rules and the 'you can't go here,' and 'you have to get permission,' and 'don't stand out,' and 'just blend in.' You have no idea how boring suburban life is to us. You're happy. You live in your little blissful life with 2.4 kids, a dog, a cat and a barbecue grill. Egad, man! Doesn't it drive you crazy?"

Sparkle Shine said, "Linda? I thought we were friends? I thought you liked the neighborhood?"

"Oh for goodness sakes, Susie!"

Chris thought, Susie, Susie, Susie, I have to remember that.

"I hate that neighborhood. I hate that church you drug us to. I hate the annual barbecue. I hate those kids of yours, especially when they make all that noise on a Saturday morning. And most of all, I hate you! You are such a goody-goody. Don't you ever get tired of it?"

Chris, half believing he was still in a mystery play, turned to Jeff again. "So, are you here because of them or not?"

"I'm not here because of them, but, during the course of my investigation," he turned to Hirsch, "I sent your photos to the Federal Marshals. They recognized you. I asked that they wait until tomorrow to pick you up, because I'm working on something else."

Linda screamed at Hirsch, "You idiot!" She looked at Jeff and said, "If we aren't there tomorrow, they won't know where to find us. So you just put yourself in a pickle, mister."

"No, I didn't. Everyone in town knows you're on this boat, and the only way you're getting back is by Coast Guard rescue. You're still going to be picked up. And I'm not the only one tracking you."

"What?"

"Someone, and I think it was that quiet, unassuming police chief here in Chelsea, also sent photos of every one of you to the FBI, the Federal Marshals and the CIA. Everyone is talking about everyone, so if you all aren't squeaky clean, you have something to worry about."

"Do they worry about a little pot in college?"

"No, Tom, they won't worry about that. Didn't come up, actually, so just keep your mouth shut."

Tom relaxed into Susie with relief.

Candice asked, "Why did you think Pete, I mean the Chief, sent pictures out? Why him?"

"I recognized him. He was career Marine, and he worked in their criminal investigation division. I was Navy, doing the same work. We crossed paths once. I'm pretty sure he recognized me. I knew him, for sure. He was always good."

"Huh," said Chris. "So, what are you working on?"

"Something that involves Hannah's husband."

Hannah sat up straighter.

"But he's not here, and I thought he was being targeted for murder by his colleagues. It appears this was the weapon of choice for them."

Jeff looked at Hannah. "I believe your husband's partners saw they could wait for round three and the weather to collide. I think they sabotaged the engine and the radio. I think they were pretty smart about it. I think your husband was smarter and got out before they could get to him. But he left you. That wasn't part of the plan, was it?"

"We were supposed to leave together. Instead of going home with all of you, we were going to take off in the middle of the night tonight, drive up the coast a ways, get a boat and go across the lake to another state. Pick up our new identities. Move on again."

"So, what were they looking for in the rooms?"

"Spencer thought they were looking for the money he stole from them. He wouldn't be so stupid as to keep it on him, and he surely wouldn't leave it in the bedroom of a bed and breakfast. Those idiots. They wouldn't have known the money was missing, except I did something stupid."

"What'd you do?"

"I bought a car."

Susie broke in, "Your new Lexus? I wondered about that. I told Tom if you could afford one, I could too, and he wouldn't hear of it."

Hannah just looked at her.

Susie added, "Did you guys have secret names and everything too? Were you living secret lives?"

Hannah just looked at her.

Linda said, "Of for goodness sakes, Miss Goody Goody Susie. Of course they had secret lives! They're criminals!"

Jeff cut in, "But not criminals in witness protection. Just criminals. Spencer had a good position as the middleman in a drug operation. He was smart enough to not touch the stuff. He didn't use drugs, and he literally didn't touch them. He brokered them on the darknet."

Tom asked, "The darknet?"

"Darknet. I'm not going to go into the technical stuff. Suffice it to say it's an anonymous way to connect sellers and buyers of particular products. Let's just say he was dealing in Lily Spit and leave it at that. Except, in his case, he was shaving a little bit from every deal. Not enough to raise suspicion, but enough to make Spencer and Hannah very rich. Very rich indeed."

Chris said, "So, let me see if I have all of this straight. Correct me if I'm wrong. Tom and Susie are really Tom and Susie, living in a suburban community with 2.4 kids, a dog and a cat. And a barbecue."

Susie said, "Three, actually."

Chris, head spinning, said, "Three barbecues?"

"No, three kids."

"Three kids, right. One barbecue. And the two of you are blissfully unaware that one set of neighbors, Hirsch and Linda, are criminals on the lam from the witness protection program, and that another set of neighbors, Spencer and Hannah, are drug dealers getting rich by stealing from other drug dealers on an anonymous website."

Jeff said, "You've got it."

"And the rest of the story is that some of these drug dealers, angry about the missing money, wanted to, apparently, get the money back and then kill Spencer, and in so doing, they're trying to kill all of us as well."

"Yes."

"So, if you knew this, why did you get on the boat?"

"I hadn't figured that part out yet. I was just keeping an eye on Spencer, but I lost him late this morning. I was trying to pick up the trail again, and figured, where Hannah was, pretty soon he'd show up."

"So, who are the bad guys?"

"The three young folks staying in the carriage house at the Inn."

Chapter 23: Some Semblance Of Peace Descended On The Humans

In the basement, some semblance of peace descended on the humans. Sitting on the floor around a coffee table, Clara, Jennifer, Pete and Herb played a game of Scrabble by LED lantern light.

Henrie, Cheryl and Annie sat cross-legged in a circle with dice coming out of a monkey barrel, playing Yahtzee.

Sam, Hannah and Mem, the most mature of the group and therefore the wisest, napped while they could.

Alec and Jessica politely declined invitations to get into the games and talked quietly to one another, sitting on the floor with their backs against the door.

Little Socks crept back to Cyril and Jock. *"The bad people are sitting by the door. They don't want to get caught and get blamed for the body down here. They're going to try to get Pete's gun away from him."*

Cyril started to lunge for the door but Jock stepped in front of him. *"You can't do anything. It's just like me with Ray. I can't do anything because he's there and I'm here. Pete's on the other side of that door and you're here. We have to think."*

Little Socks said, *"We have to get the doors open."*

"These doors are newer and solid. How do you think we can do that?"

"We have to make the humans do it."

"Which door?"

"I think the one inside. Those bad ones are closest to this door; Pete's closest to that door. If we do something to make them come in the bedroom, it will probably be Pete. We can get him away from them."

"But how do we keep them from coming after him?"

246

"I don't know! I had the first part of the plan. You have to have the rest of it!"

"Let's go in and talk about it with everyone."

They weren't quick enough.

From the door, Alec said, "Herb, it's time."

Herb, sitting on the gun-side of Pete, slipped his hand in quickly, snapped the strap and had the gun in his hand before Pete knew what was happening. "Sorry, man," he said.

No one moved. Pete finally said, "What's going on?"

Jessica said, "It's unfortunate there are so many of you, so we're going to have to talk about what we're going to do. Typically we don't leave any witnesses. We didn't count on this, though."

Pete, remaining calm, said, "Why would you need to get rid of witnesses? We're just down here, keeping safe from a storm."

"You said something about a body."

"Yes. There's a body in there."

"I'm sure our fingerprints have already been sent away because of that little burglary. With a body, you'd probably start detaining people. We can't let that happen."

"So let's just be calm. There's no need for you to be concerned about witnesses. If your fingerprints are already going to expose you, killing a bunch of people isn't the smart thing to do. You can lock us up in here and get away. That would be the wise thing to do."

"You could be right, but just be quiet, okay? We need to talk, and we need to do it without having to listen to you."

Alec said, "Herb, bring him over here. Let's take his radio and search him good, tie him up somewhere else down here."

On the other side of the door, the quick ears of the cats and dogs picked up the conversation and realized they would have to go with the current situation. There was no time to make a plan.

Jock said, *"Let's just make them open the door, then we'll go from there."*

Tiger Lily said, *"Mommy always opens the door when I throw myself against it. She thinks I'll hurt myself if she doesn't"*

"Let's try it. We dogs will do it, though. We'll make more noise."

Jock and Cyril threw themselves against the door, over and over, and all they got for their trouble were shouts. Alec and Jessica shouted for them to "Quiet down in there!" Pete didn't shout, but in a fairly loud voice, he said, "Down, Cyril!" while Cheryl yelled, "Jock, stop it!"

Finally, they stopped. Jock looked at Tiger Lily and asked, "Do you have any more bright ideas?"

"Maybe," she said, and she started to shriek. She kept it up, as if the dogs were killing her, and soon six other cats joined her. Well, five joined her and another added a melodious *"Trill!"* to the mix.

Eventually, it worked. Jessica and Alec couldn't stand the sound. They took Pete, now handcuffed, out the front door of the suite. Jessica had a bedsheet in her hand. She found the cellar door and made Pete sit on the steps. "Put the handcuffs in front of him, so he can raise his arms."

She tore several strips from the sheet and wrapped them together, then through the handcuffs and through the metal handle of the cellar door.

Cyril started to go through the back door, but Jock stood in front of it to stop him. *"We can't let them know about this door. They only have one gun, and it's in that other room with all the other people. Let's wait and see what happens."*

With Pete out of the way, the twins went back to the room to discuss their options. Jessica must have had a touch of bloodlust. She argued for killing everyone. "No one will hear it while this storm is going on."

Herb argued forcefully the other way. "That cop was right. We just need to keep them down here so we can get away."

Human voices rose with each passing minute, probably because the cats' shrieks continued to annoy them.

Cyril saw his moment. *"We have to get him!"* Jock agreed, and together, they nosed the back door open and crept around, looking to see if the twins could see them. The twins couldn't, but Herb could.

Cyril looked Herb full in the eyes for a few seconds, then continued. Jock followed on faith that his friend knew what he was up to.

Pete, knowing when to keep his surprise to himself, kept his mouth shut. Jock and Cyril nosed around the strips of sheet and they soon found the weak point.

The old cellar door had not been replaced. The metal latch was loose. Not a lot. Not so that Jessica would have noticed. But loose, none the less.

Jock and Cyril got a mouthful of sheet on either side and started to pull. Pete pulled, too, and in 20 seconds, the latch was loose. Pete was still handcuffed, but he was mobile. With the noises made by the cats and the storm, Jessica and Alec didn't hear them.

The three made their way back to the bedroom via the back door. Cyril stopped to nod a thank you to Herb, and Pete, confused, did the same.

The cats wanted to show Pete how much they loved him, but Tiger Lily said, *"Don't stop! Keep up the racket!"*

Pete said, "Cyril, I love you, but this night just keeps getting stranger and stranger."

The noise made by the cats had several benefits. One was that Jessica and Alec couldn't think clearly. Pete's shoulder mic was still with him. It was difficult with handcuffs, but he was able to key the mic and tell his men about the situation, noting there were several hostages and where in the basement they could be found.

Then he made sure the back door looked like it was closed. He leaned back into the corner to rest and think.

Chapter 24: Ahoy The Boat!

"Ahoy the boat!" With relief, Chris heard the shout. Well, to be honest, he didn't hear the shout. He heard the horn of the Coast Guard cutter.

"Thank goodness," he said. I'm going out to discuss our rescue. I'm not sure how we're going to do this."

He was happy to see his second in command, a seasoned sailor, along with George and another volunteer, both with several years' experience.

"We have no power!" he shouted.

"Do you want us to give it a tow?"

"I think it's too rough for that."

"It's rough to transfer people, too."

"Which do you think is the better option?"

The four of them surveyed the situation. They had to hang on to railings to keep from slipping into the lake, but getting these two boats any closer was going to be dangerous for both of them.

"We have to do something and get these two further away from one another! I'll get the raft!" Chris turned and went back inside the galley.

George said, "What did he say?" and received shrugs in response.

Soon, it was clear. Chris came out with the raft, pulled the ripcord and threw it into the lake, tying it fast to the rail. Jeff, Hirsch and Tom came out in rain gear, carrying Ray, covered by a slicker.

Chris had to yell, "One of you has to go down first, we'll hand him down, then get as at least two of the women in the raft. Whoever goes down is going over with the first round."

251

Jeff said, "I'll go first, and I'll stay in until everyone is on board the cutter. It's going to take a lot of body strength to keep it steady in between the two boats."

He jumped down and looked up at the cutter. They were ready with a weighted rope to throw. Jeff caught it and tied it to the raft. As soon as that was done, the cutter powered up and moved further away.

Jeff turned to The Escape and reached up to steady Ray as he was lowered. Once Ray was safely in, Chris sent Susie and Hannah down.

Hannah went first. She climbed over the railing and jumped to the raft, backwards and feet first. She nearly fell into the lake. Jeff caught her and made sure she had a handle firm in her hand. He then turned back to Susie, who dropped in hard but straight.

With hand signals, Chris let out his rope while the Coast Guard pulled in theirs. George, down the side of the low end of the cutter, dropped into the raft and helped the women first. Susie climbed up fairly easily. He had to stay behind Hannah and push as she climbed painfully over the side.

A halter was thrown down for Ray. George and Jeff struggled together and finally secured it. Giving the cutter crew a the thumbs up, they steadied Ray as he was lifted.

George shouted, "I'll wait here," and climbed back on the side of the cutter.

Using the same rope-pulley system, Jeff went back to The Escape; Linda, Candice and Hirsch waited to board. The three of them boarded without incident and were pulled to the cutter.

George, seeing Candice safe, gave her a fierce hug before sending her into the cutter. Next was Linda, then Hirsch. Again, George stayed on the side of the cutter.

Jeff returned to the escape to help Tom in, then turned to get Chris. Chris looked at the situation, set the rope so he could pull it free, then came down quickly. "We're too close!" he shouted.

"Then let's make it quick!"

The Coast Guard crew pulled, and Chris and Jeff pulled as well, hand over hand, working hard to get to the cutter before the two boats collided.

Once there, Tom went over the side, then Jeff. Chris yelled to George, "Go!" But he shook his head, motioning Chris to go first. Chris was just over the top as George, hands on the top rail, screamed in pain.

Chris grabbed for him. A wave had pushed The Escape sideways into the cutter, with George in between. When the wave subsided, Chris, Jeff and Tom grabbed two arms and a belt and pulled. Chris was conscious but in severe pain, and they didn't know how much of his body had been crushed – full legs, top half of legs, legs and back – they didn't know, and he couldn't tell them before he blacked out.

The cutter was in motion as soon as George hit the deck. They needed to protect the cutter and The Escape from further damage. Unfortunately, whatever damage The Escape sustained would not be known until later. They roared away, leaving its fate in the hands of the lake.

Chapter 25: There Was No Real Chain Of Command

The Chelsea Police Department was on full alert. That meant six police officers surrounded the Inn while all three dispatchers kept vigil at the radio.

The officers huddled in yellow rain gear, wind gusting and water pelting first from one side, then another. They knew better than to have their guns drawn at this stage of the game. You don't want to go into a fight with wet powder, or so they say.

They knew they were out of their element. They were waiting for the Sheriff's Department and the State Police. Marco assumed command. Because he could. There was no real chain of command in a department so small. It came down to seniority. Marco had that.

Marco grew up in Chelsea, and he was inside the Inn two times recently, investigating the burglary and the murder. As much as anyone here, he knew the lay of the first floor and the basement. He stationed one officer just outside the cellar entrance and sent another around the building to look for additional outside cellar exits.

Before getting to the Inn, he asked the dispatcher to call someone, anyone, who worked for Annie and to get that person here. That person turned out to be Carlos. He stood outside with them, without rain gear but with a jacket and umbrella.

They maintained radio silence from Pete. He requested that, fearing for the safety of all inside. In fact, he turned his radio off.

The Sheriff arrived with 5 cars, silent entry. They stood quietly while Marco brought them up to date. "There are three perpetrators and nine hostages. Everyone is in the basement, in a room on the northeast corner. Pete said we have to take the perpetrators alive. He said he has his reasons.

"Oh, and he wanted me to make this really, really clear. Between the three of them, there is only one gun, and that gun is his. And – now this is the strange part – he said it's likely the one that has the gun is not going to use it, so don't shoot him. Just arrest him with the other two.

"Oh, last thing, he said the three are guests of the Inn."

The Sheriff, a large blustery fellow, said "Let me talk to Pete."

"No, sir. He turned his radio off. He was able to get us a message, but he has to remain silent now."

Just then, a deputy came up to say, "That town cop that's sitting on the cellar door, he swears there's someone screaming down there."

Marco said, "No. That would be the cats."

"The cats?"

"The cats, sir. I could hear them too, when Pete was on the radio. I thought someone was being tortured. Pete said it was the cats."

The Sheriff shook his head. He looked around the group and said, "I've heard a lot about these cats. You never know what's true and what's a long, tall tail. And I spelled that t-a-i-l."

Carlos smiled for the first time. "With those cats, anything can be true. They must have a reason for doing it. Oh, and I remember something else, Marco. They always leave the kitchen door unlocked during storms this bad. Lots of folks don't have a basement. They want anyone that needs shelter to be able to come in."

"Which door is that?" asked the Sheriff.

"This one here at the corner."

"How do you get to the basement from that door?"

"Straight ahead, then at the end of the kitchen, there are two doors. One door goes into the dining room. It's always open. The other door, that's the basement. It's usually closed, but they might leave it open during a storm so people know where to go."

Carlos continued. "There's another entrance to the basement from the library." He pointed to the left. "If someone goes in the front door, then to the left, all the way to the end of that room, the door is on the right. It's a long room. The door is on the north side of the house."

"Those three perps. Pete said they were guests at the Inn?"

"Yes, sir. He said 'the twins and the other guy.'"

"How are we supposed to know who they are?"

Carlos said, "Oh, that's so sad. They seemed so nice, those young people. They are staying in the carriage house, to the left over there, and back behind the Inn. There's a big room upstairs and a big room ground level. They're ground level."

"Who are they?"

"Their first names are Alec and Jessica – those are the twins – and Herb. They've been here, oh, this is their third or fourth night. I'd have to think about that."

"And all three of them are in the basement?"

Marco said, "That's what he said."

The Sheriff called a deputy over and arranged for the carriage house to be searched immediately.

The State Police arrived and the Sheriff thought it his responsibility to bring them up to date. Marco kept his head in the circle and – once or twice – corrected something the Sheriff said.

"Oh," said Marco, as the group broke up. "I suppose I should tell you about the body in the basement."

Everyone within earshot stopped, turned, and looked – with expressions ranging from confusion to exasperation to outright anger.

"Yes, I believe you had better do that."

Marco told them what he knew, which wasn't much. The body was discovered by the owner of the Inn, who called it in. Several officers were on scene to investigate the murder – well, yes, they assumed it was murder, what with a bullet hole in his head and all – but then they had to leave, because, you see, there are only six of us, and that's if everybody's working, night shift on day shift and what not, and this storm came up, and we had to go help the old folks get into shelters.

By the time Marco was finished, neither the Sheriff nor the detective had a word to say, so they motioned their officers into position.

And then a car roared down the street, screeching to a halt. Two men, tall, well dressed but soaked to the skin, got out of the vehicle. The younger of the two said, "Who's in charge here?"

Chapter 26: He Gave The Sheriff A Thumb's Up

Both the Sheriff and a State Police Detective stepped up at the same time and said, "I am."

"Well, then, I'll talk to both of you. I'm Special Agent Jeff Bennett of the FBI. I don't have my credentials. They were stolen while I was working undercover. Have one of your boys call the FBI and check me out while I'm talking to you here."

The Sheriff motioned with his hand and a deputy – happy to be out of the wind and rain – made the call. In a couple of minutes he gave the Sheriff a thumbs up. But he decided to stay in the car as long as he could get away with it.

Jeff laid out what he know about the three perps, which was, frankly, a lot. He, too, wanted them to be taken into custody without a gun battle, but he didn't share his reason.

The Sheriff looked at Jeff and said, "What can you tell us about the body?"

"What?"

"The body that was found here right before the storm hit."

Jeff looked at Chris, who saw Carlos standing at the side. "Carlos, is Annie okay?"

"I think so, Chris. I didn't hear about this body until just a few minutes ago, but it's not Annie. These officers say it's a man, but they don't know who it is."

Marco said, "Annie was being flip with Pete and she said something about the guy being on steroids."

"Oh, that's my missing guy. Well, now he's found. Where is he?"

Marco pointed to the left and said, "In a room on that side of the basement, nowhere close to the hostage situation."

Jeff looked at the two men in charge and said, "The body's not important. Let's go."

Two town officers got into position at the cellar door. They would not attempt to enter; they would stop anyone trying to exit.

Two town officers got into place outside the kitchen door for the same reason, and the fifth town officer and a deputy were stationed at the main entry. To prevent exit by anyone making it to the first floor, two deputies were stationed at the back porch entry and two more were outside the exit coming from the downstairs guest room.

Two state troopers went through the kitchen door. One stayed there, the other went around, through the dining room, and opened the front door. That trooper and two deputies moved to the basement door at the library, opened it and waited for orders.

When they were in position, another trooper, a deputy and Jeff joined the first trooper in the kitchen. They got into position at the open basement door and waited for orders.

Marco and the Sheriff stayed with the Detective, who had finally taken command of the situation.

The Detective ordered Chris and Carlos to stay in Chris's car. He emphasized they were not to get out for any reason.

Certain the noise of the storm had shielded their footsteps up to this point, the Detective prepared to give the "go" order. Everything had proceeded in an orderly fashion. He was confident.

Suddenly, a town officer stationed at the cellar door ran around the corner and yelled, "Someone's being killed down there! Go! Go! Go!"

Bedlam ensued, not so much on the part of the disciplined state troopers or the county officers, but on the part of the five town policemen whose chief was down below.

Three entries took place simultaneously, two of them in full view of the shocked Marco, Sheriff and Detective.

The officer remaining at the cellar door shot through the lock and entered, not prepared to be met by total darkness and not prepared for the ramp that had been constructed on the right side of the stairwell. He ran and landed half on the ramp and half on the steps, broke a leg and fell into the stairwell. The officer who had given the alarm came around the corner at a dead run, tripped over the downed officer and landed halfway down the stairwell. Of course, he was unconscious by the time he stopped sliding.

The town officer who should have stayed at the main entrance ran into the Inn, through the library, and through the group of troopers waiting for the "go" order. His counterpart, the deputy at his station, followed him, wondering when their orders had changed.

They went down the stairs at a full run, followed by the troopers, without benefit of the flashlights the troopers would have trained on the stairs if they had responded to the order to "go." One by one, they went down. The first one tripped on a dead body. The second one tripped on a dead body and a police officer. The third one...well...you get the picture.

The two officers who should have stayed outside the kitchen door rushed through, forcing the others to go before the order had been given. In this instance, those originally stationed at the door were in the lead and one of them managed to get his flashlight on before they hit the bottom.

They stopped short, unable to grasp what they saw.

Pete stood in the middle of the entry to the basement, handcuffed but holding his gun on two perpetrators. Two dogs helped to hold them.

One, a Portuguese water dog, held a young woman by the collar of her shirt, growling when she threatened to move.

Another, an English Setter, sat across the lap of a dark-haired young man, licking his face every now and then but not allowing him to move.

As they cleared that area and moved around the corner, they saw a third man sprawled half in and half out of a doorway. Light shone from the room, probably from LED lanterns. The man's face, neck and arms were severely scratched. Blood showed through the back and sleeves of his polo shirt. One cat, a black one with white socks, lay across the man's neck, one of his ears clenched firmly between her teeth. Two very large gray and peach colored cats were on either side, claws dug into flesh through the shirt. A large gray long-haired cat sat proudly on the man's butt. And finally, another large cat, this one orange and long-haired, lay across the man's ankles, teeth sinking into blue jeans.

Several humans and a few more cats peered from the lighted room to the scene before them, now glowing from the light of several flashlights.

Jeff was the first one to speak. "Annie, Henrie, is everyone alright in there?"

"Yes. Is that you, Jeff? What are you doing?"

"I'll explain later, Annie. Pete, are you hurt?"

"Only my pride. Can someone get me out of my own cuffs, please?" An officer moved to oblige, taking the gun out of Pete's hands first, just in case.

A couple of officers entered from the library entrance. They looked a little worse for the wear, but they were alert and ready for action if necessary.

"Stand down," said Jeff. "Can one of you let the Detective know we're clear down here?"

Pete said, "I heard some noise at the cellar door over that way." He motioned with his head. "They shot through the lock and, I'm not sure, maybe fell on their way down."

Pete continued, "It's going to take some time to sort this all out, but for now, we need to take these three into custody, and then I need to re-secure my original crime scene. It sounds like you guys messed it up.

"And if it's all clear, and the warnings have expired, I think the rest of these folks would like to go upstairs."

"Can you tell us what happened down here?"

"I can tell you part of it, but you won't believe me."

Jeff smiled, "We'll just have to give that a try."

Before he turned away, Jeff looked again at Pete and said, "You knew me when you saw me."

"No, I recognized you. But it didn't come back to me until I stared at your picture for a little while. Then I knew."

"That dog of yours knew, too."

"He surely did. He surprises me more and more every day."

Cyril looked up at Pete with absolute joy, looked at Jeff the same way, and turned to lick Herb's face again.

Chapter 27: Their Words Were Not So Oblique

When the "all clear" signal was given, Chris jumped out of the car. The Detective waved him back. "You aren't going anywhere until I tell you. Marco, stay with him."

Detective and Sheriff together walked through the kitchen door and down to the basement to see just what in the Sam Hill had happened. But their words were not so oblique.

Pete asked officers to first clear the animals and let them back into the safe room. It was easy to get Jock and Cyril up and moving. All it took were two officers armed with handcuffs on either side of their prey. Cyril jumped up with a final lick to Herb's face and Jock, with one last, low growl, let go of Jessica's collar.

The cats were another matter. Mo enjoyed sitting on his captive so much that he did not want to move. Kali and Ko just dug their claws in deeper, leading to moans of pain coming from the man just waking up.

Pete said, "Mac, pick up the gray cat and carry him into the safe room. He won't bite. He's a lover."

Mac picked Mo up. Mo gazed at him with joy and jumped into the room once Mac reached it.

"You two," Pete looked at two troopers, "get an arm around the stomachs of those big calico cats, they're big enough and soft enough they won't hurt you. Now, just take hold of one paw at a time and unhook them. Gently, gently, that's it, now just take them to their Mommy."

Kali and Ko, once they realized they had committed battery, were happy to get into the room and hide under a table.

"Annie, I'm going to need you to come out here and get Honey Bear. Do you think you can get him to let go?"

Annie did as he asked. Honey Bear displayed no emotion but he was also in no hurry to let go. It took several seconds for Annie to convince him to give it up.

"Now let me get down here to get Little Socks."

Pete got down on his knees and put his face close to hers. He whispered, "Now, pretty thing, you did a wonderful thing, bringing this man down so he wouldn't hurt me. But now, see all these men? They're going to take him into custody, and he won't be able to hurt anyone again. Do you understand?"

Big green eyes looked up at Pete, teeth still firmly attached to the ear.

"Big girl, you haven't drawn blood yet, but if you do, they're going to have to test you for rabies. That will be very painful. And they'll lock you up until they get the results. You don't want that."

Big green eyes looked up at Pete again, but this time they blinked. She slowly unclenched her teeth and let the ear fall from her mouth.

"That's right. Let me take you to your Mommy."

Little Socks allowed Pete to pick her up and carry her to Annie, anxiously waiting in the doorway.

The Detective came to the door of the room to say, "Make yourselves comfortable. You're going to stay right here until we've cleared this room and taken all the evidence we need. Then we'll probably all go upstairs to begin the questioning."

"Can we call our families?" asked Mem.

"Make it quick. Don't say anything except that you're alright."

As officers tended to the business of making arrests and roping off the crime scene, Jeff went into the safe room.

"Annie, everyone that was on The Escape is okay. The Escape itself is still out there on the lake, but everyone got onto the cutter and back to shore."

"Oh, thank you! Was anyone hurt?"

"Well, a couple went to the hospital." Looking at Cheryl, he said, "You're Ray's wife, right?"

"Yes. Is he hurt?"

"He probably has a concussion. I fear that's been going around a bit," with a nod to Henrie on that note. "He was awake when we got back to the station, and an ambulance was waiting to take him to the hospital. Perhaps you can ask the Detective to let you go now, answer questions later."

Cheryl left the room, said something to the Detective and while Annie watched, she turned and waved good-bye. "Keep Jock for me, will you?"

Annie turned back to Jeff. "You said a couple. Who else was hurt? Is Chris okay?"

"Chris is fine. He's outside, and I'm certain they've had to place him under guard to keep him from coming in here. The other person that was injured was a Coast Guard volunteer; I believe he's your bartender."

"George? How bad is it?"

"His injuries have the potential to be severe. The server, Candice, went with him to the hospital. You can call her to check."

Henrie took the phone from his pocket and realized as he did so that the trio had neglected to take any of the phones from them. Of course, no one thought to try to call anyone, perhaps because of that infernal racket the cats kept up.

Goodness, he thought, that racket kept the trio from thinking clearly also. Henrie turned to look, and Tiger Lily was staring straight at him. It was a wise, knowing stare. Then she closed her eyes, licked a paw and calmly started to wash her ears.

Henrie made the call to Candice and, as he was talking, shared information with the group.

"They do not know much yet...there is severe bruising...x-rays show nothing is broken...they are not sure of internal injuries or perhaps some crushing of the spinal cord...swelling will have to come down...they are inducing a coma for at least a day, perhaps longer. Now, Candice, what do you need?....Oh, do not worry about work. We will make sure to cover everything for both of you...Someone will bring you some warm and dry clothing...Yes, yes, I'll take care of it."

Henrie, turning off the telephone, said, "I will just make some calls on Candice's behalf."

"Certainly. Mom, could you help me when we get back upstairs? I think we should have some hot drinks ready for our guests. And maybe some snacks."

"Oh, no!" Annie turned to Jeff. "We have to tell Mrs. – what is her name? – about her husband. He's down here, in the old coal room. He was murdered!"

"I just heard, and I need to talk to Pete about that. And actually, about taking care of the rest of your guests, I think only two will be coming back to you. The rest will find accommodations elsewhere."

Annie's eyes narrowed, and she said, "Start talking. And let's begin with just who in the world you are."

Chapter 28: Sunday Dawned Bright, Clear and Beautiful

Sunday dawned bright, clear and beautiful. Wasn't that always the way after a big storm, thought Annie.

Annie wanted to sleep in, but it was her turn to make the coffee and serve snacks before church. In the kitchen, she made a pot of coffee, drew out a couple of boxes of cereal, milk, bowls and spoons.

She went to the cupboard to get cat food for the bowls. Seven cats heard "that" cupboard door open – how do they know? – and came click-clacking into the kitchen, around the corner of the island, and then….

It sounded like Godzilla versus Mothra.

The fight woke Jock, who ran into the kitchen, sliding on the quarry tile to collide with the table for two in the corner. Salt and pepper shakers, a napkin holder and a vase with a silk flower crashed to the floor. Something shattered on impact.

Annie sighed, shoulders slumping, eyes closed and head lifted to the ceiling. Chris came around the corner. "So this is what it sounds like when Uncle Honey Bear visits."

"Yes."

"I'll take him downstairs. Get a cup of coffee ready for me, please."

When he got back upstairs, he said, "Nancy said to take your time. She knows how to get the coffee and snacks out, so she and Sam will go to church early. She wanted me to remind you that had you followed her lead and taken a nap, you would have already been up today and had a walk."

Annie's eyes, which had brightened at the "take your time," narrowed at the "had a walk" part.

"I know. Take the good half and run with it."

She did. She and the cats took their time.

Chris had to go home to get clothes that had not recently been washed in rain water. He took Jock so he could run up and down the beach while he cleaned up.

When Chris and Jock returned, they all walked to Soul's Harbor. The procession included Henrie, Chris, Annie, Jock and seven cats. Tom Mollar and Susie Benton joined them. Annie thought they looked none the worse for wear. Actually, they looked invigorated.

As they walked, others from The Avenue joined them as well.

"Do we have to wait until after church to hear the whole story?'

"Yes. And I don't think we know everything yet. At least, we don't know who killed Onstair Royds. Henrie, what is his name?"

"Mr. Smith."

"Oh, yes. Mr. Smith. Spencer Smith."

"How about getting together for lunch. You can tell us then."

"We'll know more about everything tomorrow. Maybe. And maybe by then, I'll have the names straight. They're all swimming around in my brain right now."

Today was the twentieth Sunday after Pentecost. One of the texts was from Psalm 90.

> So teach us to count our days that we may gain a
> wise heart. Turn, O Lord! How long? Have

269

compassion on your servants! Satisfy us in the
morning with your steadfast love, so that we may
rejoice and be glad all our days. Make us glad as many
days as you have afflicted us, and as many years as we
have seen evil. Let your work be manifest to your
servants, and your glorious power to their children.
Let the favor of the Lord our God be upon us, and
prosper for us the work of our hands-- O prosper the
work of our hands!

Annie thought, once again, Teresa seems to be in sync
with the words in my own heart.

Sunday afternoons were typically lazy days for Annie and
the cats. Today, it was lazy, it just included some additional
people.

Tom and Susie, who had planned to leave today, were
asked to stay in town until investigators were finished with
them. Instead of spending the day as tourists, they spent it as
part of the loose knit family of the KaliKo Inn.

Henrie and Nancy worked together to heat up the
individual meals from the basement refrigerator. Annie and
Susie set up picnic tables, got drinks, paper plates and plastic
silverware. Sam, Chris and Tom pulled the grill from the
storage barn and made hot dogs, hamburgers and brats, beers
in hand, looking for all the world like neighbors of long-
standing.

Jock raced up and down the beach with Mo, Mr. Bean and
Sassy Pants. Tiger Lily, Little Socks, Kali and Ko stretched
out in the sand, soaking up the heat from the sun and sand in
the cool autumn breeze.

Pete and his family joined the group, bringing Jeff along with them. Linda helped Nancy and Henrie. Ginger herded the younger children down to the beach to make sand castles.

Pete and Jeff found a place with the other men, standing around the barbecue with bottles of beer in their hands. Annie could hear Chris, Tom and Jeff laughing about the silliness of the night before, both the mystery cruise and the ridiculous nature of the conversation once people were actually acting as themselves.

Before too long, Cheryl arrived. She picked up a wine cooler and told everyone about Ray. He would be released from the hospital tomorrow morning if all went well, and a couple of men who tied up at The Marina year round rescued The Escape this morning. There was very little damage. Some cosmetic repair would be needed where the unfortunate incident with George occurred.

The group wasn't complete, however, until Laila and her children arrived. The children ran to join Ginger while Laila gave Annie a tremendous hug. "I hardly saw you at all this week, and you've gone through so much in just a few days."

Food and drink flowed smoothly. No one ate at any particular time, just when hunger demanded. Chris put out the badminton game; some of the older kids played beach volleyball without a net.

Cats and dogs mingled where the mood suited. They received treats in the mid-afternoon, when Annie brought out the bags that were never opened in the basement.

Susie said, a few times, that she wished her children could be here. Now <u>this</u> was a block party.

The lunch and laughter drug on well into the afternoon. It was a perfect day. White clouds now dotted the bright blue sky and the scent of bonfires further up the beach wafted on the breeze.

Perfect, thought Annie. Just perfect.

But then she heard, "Hello! Is anybody home? Hello!"

Annie closed her eyes to shut out the sound of That Voice. Geraldine.

Chris, ever the gentleman, took care of it for her. "We're on the beach, Geraldine. Come on around."

Geraldine, dressed as she always dressed, including a perfectly tailored Sunday dress with perfectly styled hair, perfectly applied make-up and perfectly matched stilettos, walked around the house on the sidewalk. That worked out well for her. The brick and concrete sidewalk allowed her to walk without issue.

Once she reached the end of the walk, however, she stood, uncertainly, looking at the group.

"Annie…Annie, could you come here, please, so I can talk to you?"

Annie saw the perfect opportunity, but her mother saw if first. Nancy brought out her sugary sweet voice and said, "Why, Geraldine! It's so nice to see you. Why don't you come on out here and sit in the sun. We have wine coolers, and here's an empty chair. We must have just known you would be coming."

Sam, knowing that voice as well as Annie, decided to move a little further away. He said, in a welcoming voice, "Why don't you come sit here in my chair, right here between Annie and Nancy. It's much more comfortable that that old one. I'll sit there instead."

Geraldine, looking uncomfortably at the sand, realized that when in Rome, one must do whatever those silly Romans do.

She gamely stepped out, shoes picking up sand and ankles wobbling painfully.

Annie suggested, "Take those shoes off and come on out barefoot. It will be much easier for you."

Geraldine had to comply. There was no getting around it. She hobbled on one foot after the other until finally, strappy shoes dangling from one hand, her purse from another, she stepped gingerly forward, looking down to make sure nothing dangerous was in her path.

When she got to the chair, Nancy had a wine cooler ready for her. "Here you go, dear. Sit for a while."

Geraldine sent a withering smile in Nancy's direction. "Do you have a glass?"

"Oh, I'm sorry, no."

"Then please keep that bottle." She turned to Annie.

"Annie, dear, you know all about my charity ball, right?"

"Yes, I do. How are your plans coming?"

"Oh, well, they're coming along well, thank you. I just wanted to stop in and say that, well, I'm afraid I made a dreadful mistake. You know the ball is invitation-only?"

"Yes…"

"Well, I was cleaning out my office yesterday and I realized your invitation was still sitting on my desk. Here," she reached into her purse, "I brought it along with me."

"Thank you, Geraldine. I'm very pleased you thought of me. I can RSVP right now. I will not be able to attend due to a prior commitment."

"Well, I'm aware of that commitment, and I'm so sorry we mistakenly chose that day. It just didn't cross my mind at all in the planning stages that your block party was that very evening."

Annie wisely held her tongue and stared a dagger at her mother to do the same. Nancy sat back with a triumphant shake of her head. Unfortunately, it was lost on Geraldine who still looked straight at Annie.

"Well, now that we have that out of the way, I was hoping I could count on your for a sizeable donation. You are one of the premier business owners in the community, you see. Your example would be so noteworthy."

"I would be happy to consider making a contribution. Tell me, what is the charity?"

"Oh, about that. We talked and talked, and we couldn't settle on any one charity. There are so many needs in the world, you see, so instead of one charity, we decided to create a foundation."

"A foundation that will support…"

"Oh. Well. The foundation will support so many charities, you see. There are children, and, um, starving people in Africa, and, let's see, oh, the homeless…"

"The homeless here in Chelsea, you mean?"

"Certainly. I'm sure there are many."

"What will you call the foundation?"

"We've tossed around so many names, but the one that comes up the most – from all of our supporters – is the Geraldine Foxglove Charitable Fund."

"Great name. Who will be on the board?"

"The board? Well, let's see if I can remember them all. Hank has agreed to serve, and my mother. My ex-husband will play a role, probably as funds manager. I, of course, will be the face of the organization, and the, I suppose you would call it the Executive Director. Or possibly President. We haven't decided. And the state senator from over in Marsh Haven. And I'm working on our US Congressman, but we haven't heard back from his people yet. And so many more I just can't think who they are right now."

"Geraldine, this sounds like a fascinating opportunity. I'll have to get back to you, though. When the foundation is established, get a prospectus to me and I will certainly consider making a contribution."

"I was so hoping you could contribute before the ball, so we could announce it to the community. Or at the very least, during the ball itself, to add to the grand total I'm certain we will receive."

"I'm sorry, Geraldine, but I won't be able to move that quickly. You see, once you have a prospectus, I'll have to give that to my accountant, and then wait to hear back. This isn't a decision I can make before the end of the month."

"Oh, well, I see. Chris? Are you interested?"

"I haven't been invited."

"Oh. Well. It's been so nice chatting with you all. I'll see myself out. Well, back to my car."

Geraldine stood, brushed sand from the back of her dress, and walked carefully back to the sidewalk. She nearly stopped to put on her shoes then decided to do that at her car. Or at least around the corner of the Inn.

Annie leaned her head back in the chair to catch a slice of sun and smiled. "Perfect ending to a perfect day."

Chapter 29: Back To Business Monday

It was "Back to Business Monday." Staff at the Café and the Winery scrambled to cover shifts at Mo's for Monday through Wednesday. Once again, Annie was amazed at the camaraderie. They took care of it and let her know how they had done it.

Henrie was pleased to have no guests on the schedule until the weekend. He couldn't wait to get those police officers out of there so he could clean out the rooms once and for all.

Of course, Jeff, Tom and Susie extended their reservations, but they were hardly guests anymore. Henrie put out a sumptuous breakfasts, but, as he told Annie without a trace of ego, "I can do that in my sleep."

George would be fine. He had a good deal of internal bruising, and it would take time to heal, but no permanent damage would ensue.

And Candice. Well, that was another story. The short story was that Candice and George were once again a couple.

It took the entire day to get back on track, but by Monday evening, The Avenue pulled together once again to hear "the rest of the story."

As they gathered as Sassy P's that night, the group included Jeff, Tom and Susie, and of course Pete and Chris, who were, after all, significant members of The Avenue even though they didn't live there. When Ray and Cheryl arrived, they were welcomed with a rousing cheer.

Annie thought, sadly, how lonely Mem looked. Frank should be here, too, but they had not yet reconciled. Frank was still, as far as Annie knew, planning to accompany that dreadful Geraldine to what she hoped would be a dreadful ball.

To round out the group, Nancy and Sam were there. This was a going away celebration for them as well. They would leave on Wednesday to return to their home.

Nancy and Mem spent several minutes at a separate table. Annie was glad they had become such good friends. Sam, taking a quiet moment with Annie, thanked her for the hospitality and told her they couldn't wait to get back in a couple of months.

"Annie," he said, "I just have to tell you how very much you resemble your mother. I've loved her for so long, and I see all of her good qualities reflected in you."

"Thank you, Sam. I've always wanted to be like her."

"Well, you are. And I have to tell you, the bitter comes along with the sweet."

"What?"

"Well, you know that voice of your mother's?"

"The viper-getting-ready-to-strike voice?"

"Yes. That very one. Well, sweetheart, you can sound just like your mama."

Annie gaped, then laughed, remembering the Sunday afternoon chat with Geraldine. "I can. I'll have to be careful how I use it."

"Yes. I was keeping an eye on Chris while you chatted with Geraldine. I think his eyes were opened just a tad. Use it sparingly."

Pete rapped on the table with the bottom of a bottle of wine to get everyone's attention.

"Are you ready for the rest of the story?" he asked.

"Yes!" came the resounding reply.

Pete, Chris and Jeff had positioned themselves at the 'head' of the conglomeration of tables in order to share in the telling of the several tales. Ray, while an integral part of the story, sat back to listen.

Almost everyone knew parts of the story by now, so Pete went through it quickly – with help from Chris and Jeff – until getting to the lesser known bits. Together, they told this tale.

'Hirsch and Linda Stone' – not their real names but as fake as Brad Spit and Mary Monroe – were on the run from witness protection. Hirsch had been an accountant for a small crime family. They were large enough that Hirsch got rich, and he was frankly doing a little skimming.

About the time he thought he would be caught, he was approached by federal agents and asked to become a witness. Hirsch and Linda figured their odds and decided they stood a better chance if he took the deal.

However, they found life in witness protection to be stifling. They shook their handlers, assumed new identities and hid in plain sight where they figured the Marshals would never look. Small town suburbia.

When Tom and Susie invited them to come on the cruise, it was the most exciting opportunity to come along in years. They could travel, see a new part of the country, and again, they were hiding in plain sight.

Unfortunately, Hirsch and Linda were now going to have to take their chances in the same system in which Hirsch's former employers now resided.

Spencer and Hannah Smith – Onstair Royds and Alabaster Pearl – were another story. They both craved money and the lifestyle they could have, "if only." Spencer was bright, and he had connections, both high and low. He heard about the darknet and found people that could tell him what he needed to know. He set up advertisements about brokering deals and once the first deal was made, the rest was history.

Spencer had sticky fingers, though, just like Hirsch. He accumulated a great deal of wealth, putting his ill-gotten gains into bearer bonds. Those bonds were spread in safety deposit boxes in several banks in a three-state area. He and Hannah kept enough cash to live a substantial but not flashy lifestyle.

Until Hannah wanted more. She bought a Lexus, and the walls started to crumble.

When Tom and Susie approached them about the cruise, they realized an opportunity was at hand. They made plans to leave Chelsea, headed for a new life with new identities instead of returning home.

They did not know they were already under investigation. They also did not know that Spencer's problem with sticky fingers had been detected.

When they arrived in Chelsea, a veritable parade traveled with them. They were not very smart crooks, after all. The FBI set an undercover officer in place, and the people from whom they had been stealing did so as well.

The trio had orders to find the money then get rid of him. They tried to find the money, but couldn't. In the process of looking for the money, they realized Jeff was an undercover agent. They decided to just get rid of Spencer and get out of town.

Sometime during the late morning on Saturday, Spencer took off, or so almost everyone thought. Jeff couldn't locate him, so he kept his eye on Hannah. That's how he arrived at the harbor in time to take the role in the murder mystery.

Also that morning, the trio took advantage of the confluence of events, the weather and the cruise.

Herb was a bomb expert. He got into the engine and set a bomb to go off two hours after it was started. They hoped Ray wouldn't start it until the mystery crew boarded to leave.

Alec got into the radio and cut almost all of the wiring, again, hoping Ray would not try it before leaving.

The plan was to leave town that night after dark, sneaking away before anyone heard about the boat blowing up in the middle of the lake.

"And now," said Pete dramatically, "you'll hear the rest of the story!"

From the end of the table, Clara shouted, "That's not how he said it! He said it at the end, and he said now we <u>know</u> the rest of the story!"

Mem, in the middle of the group, looked at Clara to say, "I don't know what to be confused about first. That you, born in Haiti in the late twentieth century, listened to Paul Harvey, or that you, I think a liberal, listened to Paul Harvey."

"Just be confused, Mem. I live to confuse my friends!"

Pete rapped the table again. "Well none of you are going to hear it or know it unless you let us tell it!"

"Tell it!"

"Okay!"

Pete continued with the story. First of all, Spencer and Hannah were not a happy couple. Not happy at all. Hannah told Spencer she wanted to show him what she found in the basement, going through that door from the library.

"I'm going to lock that door!" shouted Annie.

She told him there was a safe, and it just had a padlock on it, and there might be something in it of value. She took their pistol to – as she told him – shoot the padlock off. Once in the basement, as he looked around for the safe, she used the pistol on him. She then joined the group and made up the story that he took off.

The trio heard this story and realized their plan was going to be a bust, and they would end up killing a bunch of people that didn't have anything to do with their problem. There was a chance, however, that Spencer would show up.

They decided they had to find out if he made it to the cruise. They watched from a distance and realized he wasn't on it, but the undercover FBI guy was. At this point, they couldn't stick around any longer. They would have to leave town and pick Spencer's scent up at a later date, and hopefully he would have the money.

They had to wait until dark, though, because they wanted their departure to be a secret, and several women had come to the Inn for some reason. They didn't want to be taking off and have them see it.

"And then…"

"The storm!"

"Yes, the storm."

Henrie and Annie, concerned that their guests be protected, brought them to the basement. Okay, they thought. We can stay here, it's safer here anyway, and leave as soon as it's clear.

Then they heard about the body, and they knew they would be detained and questioned, and it would all come out. Especially after the town went into palpitations about the boat blowing up.

"So why didn't the boat blow up?"

"For the same reason I'm still standing here today," said Pete.

Herb, the supposed bomb expert, really was a bomb expert. But he set one that would only kill the engine, not blow up the boat. It had to look as if he set it, but something went wrong.

Pete continued, "It was pure luck that he was chosen to be the one to grab my gun. He's the only one of the group that wouldn't use it and the only one that would protect everyone in that room."

At this point, puzzled faces stared at the head of the table.

Jeff said, "Herb had been deep under cover for six months. He infiltrated the group selling drugs on the darknet, but his job was not complete. He had to pretend to be a really bad guy while, at the same time, protect the innocent. He tried to maintain his cover all the way through his arrest Saturday night, but his handlers got him out of there. He's back with his family in a state I won't mention here."

"But his wife died," said Annie. "What…"

Jeff cut in, "It wasn't his wife. A 'significant other' was under cover with him. He was operating as a married gay man, and his partner was killed in a car crash. The crash was not an accident. The dealers gave Herb the dirty work, setting him up to commit murder, because they were testing him. That was another reason for his handlers to get him out of there. He got out with a lot of information."

"And with his life."

Clara, always the antagonist, said, "So do we know the whole story yet?"

Pete looked down the table at Annie. "Do they?" he said.

"They wouldn't believe the rest of it."

"Tell!"

Pete and Annie looked across the room at the pile of friends, cats and dogs, mostly sleeping. Two faces looked up at them. Cyril and Tiger Lily. Both were sending long, cool gazes toward the humans, holding the eyes of their special humans, Pete and Annie.

Pete, looking at Annie again, said, "Let's just say we had a little help from our friends."

As Annie got ready to go upstairs that night, she asked Nancy, "Did you and Mem have a good talk tonight?"

"We did. She is so heartbroken over Frank. He's tried to talk to her a few times, but she says he is still going to that ball with Geraldine. She just can't handle it."

"Did you tell her about Geraldine coming here?"

"Yes. We both think the RSVPs must be very slow coming in. It might even be worse than that. If she is courting you, she must think she needs to put a prettier face on the event."

"I wonder," said Annie as she kissed her mother goodnight.

Chapter 30: Halloween Block Party

Halloween dawned sunny and warm. A few clouds dotted the sky, but wind and rain were not in the forecast. Annie thought of Mem. Darn. Mem had wished so hard for a polar vortex to screw up Geraldine's big bash. Oh, well.

The people of Chelsea loved Halloween. Annie's businesses had been decked out for a week. On the day itself, Annie started early. She planned to stop at each place before going back to the Inn to finish preparations for tonight's block party.

They all walked up together, one cat after another peeling off to go to work. When they passed Mo's Tap, Mo looked longingly at Annie. She stopped and looked down at him. "Mo, do you want to go in, even though no one's here?"

Mo's face turned hopeful; he stood a little straighter.

"Okay. Go on in. You're going to give George a scare when he unlocks. You know that."

Mo curled his tail around Annie's leg once and scampered into the Tap to take a nap.

Tiger Lily's Café was decorated with colorful paper Mache jack-o-lanterns. Each pumpkin represented the feeling associated with the color. There were sad blue ones, angry red ones, scared green ones, happy yellow ones, excited orange ones and tender purple ones.

Today, Felicity, Trudie and the servers wore masks depicting the same color and feeling combinations. The cooks wanted to, but after an accident due to impaired vision, Felicity banned masks inside the kitchen.

Trudie wore a purple half mask with bright red hearts beside both eyes. As Annie and Tiger Lily entered, Trudie was placing a mask display on the hostess stand. "Look, Tiger

Lily," she said. A full face mask, glittery, purple, and tall enough that Tiger Lily could peer through the eyes if she sat straight up, allowed even the hostess to "wear" a mask for the day.

Tiger Lily may or may not have understood the concept, but she understood a hiding place when she saw it. She walked behind the display and sat there, looking through the eyeholes. "I wonder what she's thinking," said Annie.

"No one will know I'm here. Cool."

Annie stopped to say hello to everyone in the kitchen, stood for a while at the servers' station until she had greeted every server, and walked through the Café, talking to customers at every table. This was one of her favorite ways to begin the day.

When it was time to leave, she stopped at the hostess stand, leaned against it and looked around the room. "I wonder where Tiger Lily is," she said. "I wanted to say good-bye and get my hug."

Annie could hear a purr start up behind the mask.

"My goodness. Maybe I should ask Trudie where she got to."

The purr intensified.

"Trudie," she called, "I wanted to say good-bye to Tiger Lily but I can't find her. Have you seen her?"

Ignoring all logic, as Trudie was looking at the back of the mask and could see every inch of the big girl, she answered, "No, Annie, I haven't. Do you want me to look in the kitchen?"

"No, that's okay. If she wants a hug, she'll come. I'll just stand here for a minute."

Tiger Lily let it drag on for several seconds, then one paw, part of a tail, and finally an ear appeared from behind the mask. Annie said, "Oh, my, what is this?" She reached past the ear and stroked Tiger Lily's head, which finally came out from behind the mask.

"Big girl. Give me a hug." Tiger Lily pressed her head into Annie's chest. "I'll see you this afternoon. Don't be late. Tonight's the party."

Annie headed for L'Socks' Virasana. Little Socks had already claimed her favorite window sill and was curled into a nap. Annie saw clients duck every now and then to keep from hitting a ghost with their head. She laughed with them.

Ginger and Diana used poster board and added color with markers to create yoga ghosts, ghosts positioned in various yoga poses. One ghost, proudly positioned at the favorite window of their namesake, performed the Lessiver Mon Derriere. Well, it caught the eye of passers-by, and that, after all, was the name of the marketing game.

Ginger was a plump yellow angry bird today and Diana a tall slim ladybug. "You had some extra fabric, I see," laughed Annie.

"We are merely acting as role models," said Diana. "We're modeling to children of all ages that whimsy is wonderful."

Little Socks was not disposed to open an eye or move a tail as Annie stroked her, so Annie finally leaned over and whispered, "Tonight will be your night, Little Socks. You're the only black cat of the bunch. Don't be late coming home."

Annie had to use her key to get into Mo's Tap. Neither George nor Candice were there. George was on light duty, but he typically opened up and left by suppertime, grudgingly allowing other staff to do the heavier tasks, at least for a few weeks more.

As she entered the cool, dark room, she stood for a moment to let her eyes adjust. She saw Mo at the back of the room. He had apparently been napping on a back table but now he sat straight up. His first customer, and it was Mommy!

Mo jumped down and started to run, remembered the importance of being "the only" staffer in the place, and walked at a more lordly pace until he was standing at Annie's feet. She looked down at him, then looked around at the ghoulish containers.

Everywhere. Canning jars filled with red watery liquid, eyeballs floating around. Clear wine bottles with gross green jelly-like substance and something that looked like finger bones. Covered old-fashioned candy dishes stuffed to the top with squishy wormy stuff.

George came in, a little worried to find the door unlocked.

"Oh, Annie, thank God! I thought someone had broken in!"

"Nope. Just me. I came in to make sure Mo was getting things set up. He decided he wants to be here before you from now on."

"Oh, that's great news," said George, looking down at Mo. "I'll feel a lot better knowing you'll be opening."

Mo looked first at one, then the other, with absolute pride in his eyes. Then he licked his privates.

Annie turned to leave, "I'm so glad you're feeling well enough to work, George, but don't you dare do too much."

"Not me. Taking it easy. Thanks, Annie."

"I can see how you're taking it easier. I see your handiwork all over the bar."

"You haven't been in all week, or you would have noticed it earlier. I may have graced your drink with an eyeball or a finger straw."

"I think I'll stay away for another few days, if you don't mind."

Of course, Annie's next stop was Mr. Bean's Confectionary. Jerry set out fresh, free truffles throughout the Halloween season. The only catch was that the person or persons wanting to partake had to navigate a sea of skeletons to get to them. The skeletons rattled and clanked, except for the ones that had sloppy, damp flesh attached. In short, it was not for the squeamish.

Mr. Bean, however, loved it. He offered his services to everyone who came in, if they only knew to ask. And if they didn't mind tooth marks in their truffles. Annie did, and she didn't.

"Mr. Bean, could I please have a truffle?"

He scurried from his windowsill, scampered through the skeletons, rattled and swished his way around, jumped to the table, then looked the tray over for the best truffle. Selection made, he grabbed it in his mouth and brought it to Annie.

"Oh, thank you! Both slobber and tooth marks this morning. Thank you so much, darlin'."

Carlos and Jerry were both at the counter when Mr. Bean presented his treasure to Annie. "Would you like a clean one?" asked Jerry.

"No. I get his kitty kisses every morning. There's nothing here that I don't already have floating around inside me. Did you guys make dog and cat treats for tonight?"

"Yes, we did," said Carlos. He brought out a couple of boxes to show her dog treats in the shape of skulls and cat treats that looked like black mice.

At Sassy P's Wine & Cheese, she knelt down to give a tummy tickle and served herself a witch's brew from the caldron in the middle of the room. It simmered, smoked, bubbled and hissed, and tasted like apple-cinnamon heaven.

Minnie put the final touches on a cheese flight headed to a table in the back of the room and offered a bite to Annie. Annie could never resist a good bite of cheese, and this was Wensleydale with cranberries. She munched happily on her way out the door.

At the Inn, she was greeted by Kali and Ko. They looked frazzled. They looked up at Annie with worried faces and talked. And talked. And talked. Finally, Annie said, "Girls, let's go up to the landing. We can discuss it there."

Kali turned and started to walk up the steps; Ko followed her. No, Annie thought to herself. Then she reconsidered. Stranger things have happened. She followed them to the landing. They were already seated on the coffee table facing the most comfortable chair. Annie said, "I guess I'm sitting here."

Kali and Ko started talking together. Annie listened, looking at first one, then the other.

"You have to get rid of that awful thing at the front door."

"We're going to have guests tonight, and it just looks horrible."

"Have you seen what's on that tray?"

"It has those horrible eyeball looking things, and people are <u>eating</u> them!"

"I think it's supposed to look like a man, but it has all of those awful bandages."

289

"At least, if we have to have a man like that at the door, can't it be handsome?"

"Henrie doesn't even seem to care!"

"Yeah, what's up with Henrie? He's putting these weird things all over the tables."

"And downstairs! Have you even looked downstairs in the basement?"

"Gross! There's just gross stuff going on down there!"

While they talked at her, Annie tried to consider the best way to answer. Obviously, they were telling her something important. She didn't want to minimize it. They deserved a serious answer. But a serious answer to what, exactly?

She was saved by Henrie.

"O, Annie, hello, I didn't hear you come in. Girls, I finished cleaning the second floor without you this morning. You have shirked your duties all day. What is it you're telling your mother?"

Kali and Ko turned their concerned faces and their worried voices to him. After a few seconds, he said, "And this is what you've been telling her?"

They looked at Henrie, expectantly.

"So, Annie, our girls have been quite concerned about all the activity going on these last few days, as you can tell." Looking at Kali and Ko, he said, "I'm sure she'll be able to explain all of it."

With a knowing look, he went downstairs. Annie sat still for a minute, straightened, looked at Kali and Ko and began to talk.

"Kali, Ko, have I forgotten to tell you we're having the block party here tonight? I know it's usually in the little park behind the Café, but tonight, we're going to have everyone here."

"Then you have to get rid of that guy at the door!"

"That guy at the door" was a mummified butler holding a tray of eyeballs. The eyeballs were cherries surrounded by cream and covered with dark chocolate. Some of the eyes still had stems, looking for all the world like eyeballs with bloody sticks poking them.

Of course, Annie didn't know this is what concerned them. She punted. She gesticulated. She made it up as she went along.

"We don't always decorate for Halloween here, and if we do, it's usually pretty tame. But this week, we've put out some pretty strange looking things, and we've moved furniture, and Henrie is getting ready to have a lot of people in to eat, and, you know, those tablecloths are different…"

Annie realized she was hitting the nail on the head. Their lovely Inn was being turned into a freak show.

She looked straight at them, hands in her lap. With all seriousness, she said, "We have gone overboard with our decorations, haven't we? It's because humans can be silly. They like things like this for Halloween. I know you don't, and I know the Inn should be held to a higher standard. On my honor, I promise you that within two days, everything – absolutely everything – will be back to normal. I promise. I pinky finger promise."

Mem was downcast. "I so hoped it would be too cold for that fancy affair at the community building."

Annie gave her friend a hug and said, "It's going to be a bust, no matter what the weather."

"I hope so. That's not kind, I know."

Annie and Mem were putting the final touches on the outside decorations for the haunted house. Everything else was ready.

Several community volunteers stepped up to handle serving and attendant duties, so the core group, normally busy for all the block parties, would be able to enjoy the festivities. Annie set up shifts for each station. This would be a relaxing evening.

Ginger and her crew of seamstresses made over twenty costumes. Little Grace Jones was indeed going to be a ladybug, and she had asked to help at the bobbing for apples event. If you teach them young, thought Annie, they will always be givers.

Trick-or-treaters accompanied by parents trolled the streets of Chelsea in the early hours of the evening, stopping at every home with a porch light on. By the time darkness fell, porch lights would go out, and cars from all over town would begin to stream toward the KaliKo Inn.

Annie and Mem acted as the first guests to make sure all was ready. They walked as far up the sidewalk as Sassy P's, then turned to walk back.

As they approached the Inn, knowing the sky above was nearly cloudless, they heard thunder and saw lightning streaking across the top of the building. They reached the Inn and were presented with two options. A witch guarded the turn at the sidewalk and beckoned them to move to the right, into the Inn, or to the left, around it. She said, "To the left is certain doom."

Annie and Mem chose the right. They followed the sidewalk up the steps to the porch. The sidewalk was lit by jack-o-lanterns. On each side, three jack-o-lanterns together spelled the word "Boo!"

On the porch, they were forced to walk through a forest of headless horsemen, each holding a pumpkin with only part of a face carved. An eye here, a nose there, a crazed mouth on another.

Inside, the mummified butler held a tray of eyeballs in one hand and gestured to two jars with the other. Chest high, one was labeled "UNICEF" and the other "Winter Outerwear For Chelsea Residents." They dropped their checks into the jars and decided it worked.

"Okay, let's try the haunted house. We'll be the first victims!"

They left the house and, without walking all the way to Sassy P's, got past the turn of the sidewalk and tried again. The witch offered them the choice of right or left. Again she said, "To the left is certain doom."

Annie and Mem chose certain doom.

Solar-powered lights, dim in the fall evening, showed the edges of the sidewalk. As they got to the side of the house, they found themselves in a ghostly cemetery.

Fluttery white things danced in and out of their vision. Fog rose up from the ground. A chill, wet wind hit their faces. From the left, a pirate rose from the ground and sent his grim laughter to the sky.

Even knowing what was in store, Annie and Mem huddled together. The sensations, in the dark, were eerie.

At the back of the house, the annex to the cemetery continued, again, dim solar lights leading the way. A coffin stood open, its resident standing on the sidewalk. A vampire, not the classic Dracula, but a seedy looking creature from the

14th century, blocked their way. His teeth suddenly grew large and sharp with a loud click! Bats flew around his head.

The vampire looked them over carefully, up and down. Not liking what he saw, his teeth retracted and he backed away from the sidewalk. With a long, slender arm, he gestured to instruct them to continue their journey around the house.

On the other side of the house, they saw nothing but the dim solar lighting until they reached the cellar door. There, three semi-friendly goblins offered to help them down the steps or the ramp. When they refused the offer of help, the least friendly of the goblins spat, "Just go on down. Be very careful. One false step and you will never return."

The light just inside the cellar was shrouded in black. Small shimmering lights outlined the edges of the ramp and the edges of the steps. As Annie and Mem walked further and further into the cellar, the only lights visible were those tiny twinkles that kept them from falling.

Spider webs brushed their faces, arms and hands. When they reached to steady themselves against the wall, their hands came away with slick, slimy goo. The handrail was dry, but the slimy goo on their hands picked up what felt to be centuries of dirt.

At the bottom of the steps, they looked to the left and saw faint words gleaming on the wall. "Fear for your lives."

Suddenly a skeleton appeared, spotlighted in front of them. The skeleton didn't move. Then, slowly, an arm came up. When it was shoulder high, the hand rose, and a finger slowly pointed. As the finger straightened, lights came on in the room to their right.

Annie and Mem turned and walked through the door.

The lights from several ghosts flickered on and off, first on this wall, then on that. Sometimes nothing. Then music. A pipe organ in much need of repair played ghostly chords.

Annie and Mem walked further into the room until a spotlight came on, illuminating a man, his back to them. He was dressed in common workman's clothing of the 18th century. He turned, slowly, very slowly. As he turned, his left shoulder facing them, that shoulder went down, and his right shoulder went up. By the time he faced them fully, he was hunched into a painful looking position.

Huge pores on his face oozed with slimy yellow liquid. His right eye popped out. As he opened his mouth, rotten teeth coming bare, the door behind him suddenly opened. They rushed through it.

Once in the next room, the door slammed shut behind them and again they stood in darkness.

"This is really scary," said Annie. "Do you remember we found a real body down here?"

"Shut up!" said Mem, and the lights to the candelabra flickered on.

They stood by a long oaken table, long enough for five sets of candles. Chairs looked as if they had been vacated quickly, some overturned. Spider webs hung from the candlesticks, the table, the chairs, and the goblets of blood, still fresh and watery. Plates around the table held skulls, the tops cut off, and some kind of pulsating food danced in them. Tendrils reached out to try to grab them.

On the other side of the room, and the other side of the table, a spotlight turned on. A waiter carrying a tray beckoned them to come forward.

"Shall we walk together, or walk separately, one on each side."

"I don't want to let go of you, but we have to try both sides."

"Okay. I'll go right."

Annie went to the right around the table and toward the waiter while Mem went left. Hands groped for them in the dark. They heard voices that sounded barely connected to bodies saying things like, "I'm hungry!" "Catch them!" "Fresh meat!" "It's been so long!"

When they reached the end of the table and were once again clutching one another, they looked at the waiter who offered them eyeball appetizers. "Oh, ick! Those look like real eyeballs!"

Mem and Annie politely refused and were beckoned to go through the door that had just opened.

Once again, as soon as they were inside the next room, the door behind them shut and they stood in darkness for a few seconds. The next light to flicker on was a warm fireplace light. A Victorian chair sat in front of it; a woman, her back to them, stood beside the chair.

Lights played around the room, showing walls full of bookshelves. Bookshelves lined the wall on either side of the fireplace and on both walls coming toward the entry.

The woman was dressed in the finest fashion of the mid-19th century. As she turned slowly, Annie and Mem saw a beautiful face, until she turned far enough that they could see the other side. That side was scarred with what appeared to be dragon claws. The claws reached deep enough to expose bone and sinew. In her hand was a derringer.

She slowly contorted her face, pointed the derringer and screamed, "GET OUT OF MY HOUSE! GET OUT OF MY HOUSE! GET OUT OF MY HOUSE!"

As she screamed, a hidden door on the opposite side of the room sprung open.

Annie and Mem literally ran to the next room and saw two doctors and a nurse huddled around a medical cot. They turned toward the disturbance at the door. Their smocks were smeared with blood; their faces and hands dripped blood. Each held an instrument, a bloody scalpel, a hatchet, a drill.

On the hospital cots around the room were severed heads and limbs. One live person was in the bed in the middle of the room, the bed surrounded by the medical staff. A long gash ran from his throat to his stomach. One of the doctors had hold of his heart.

He was still alive. Blood pumped with each beat of his heart. He screamed, "HELP ME! GET ME OUT OF HERE!" Once again, as he screamed, an exit door opened. Annie and Mem ran for their lives.

They stopped short, backing up to lean against the wall before falling into the deepest pit they had ever seen. Clinging to the wall, they inched around the room. But then, the door behind them closed! They were in complete darkness again! Sick laughter drifted from the ceiling to their ears. Oh, my goodness, would they get out of this house alive?

In a few seconds – it seemed like hours – the door on the opposite side of the room opened, allowing weak light to penetrate. A zombie entered He stepped gingerly, keeping his back to the wall, and made his way to Annie and Mem.

"Follow me, and step exactly where I step."

Slowly, slowly, slowly, they inched around the wall, out the door, and into a dimly lighted foyer.

Words glowed through the darkness. "You are lucky. Most do not make it this far."

The zombie guide asked if they preferred stairs or the elevator. When they chose the stairs, he laughed a sick laugh and said, "Good luck getting out of here!"

Annie and Mem fairly flew up the stairs and were welcomed by the scents and sounds of a party that only folks on The Avenue could throw.

"Do you think we went too far?" asked Annie.

Mem laughed. "Oh, no! This will be tame for the kids! They'll love it. The goblins will not let children of a certain age in without their parents, and if they believe it warranted, they'll send a message down to the actors to tone it down a little. I think we got the full blown effort."

"I guess so! I'm not allowing any of <u>my</u> kids to go through it!"

"Let's eat."

Henrie had gone all out. Of course, Kali and Ko had already complained about this. Tables and buffets had a collection of coverings ranging from the standard black and orange Halloween theme to crocheted pieces that, upon further inspection, appeared to be a collection of spiders strung together with webbing.

Kali and Ko took their typical stations in the dining room. One sat on either end of the drinks, set up on the buffet usually holding breakfast items. They guarded ghoulish punch for persons of any age and vampire sangria for anyone over twenty-one. Of course, Henrie had supplied chilled bottles of water and carafes of regular and decaf coffee also. Kali and Ko tried to steer people to these "regular" drinks and were confused when most people tried the weird ones.

"Even Mommy got that vampire stuff. Ick!"

Tiger Lily and Jock stuck close to the food. They sat under the dining room table, in the center, as far away from feet as possible. Every now and then they got lucky. Especially when children helped themselves. Before the end of the evening, they knew the names of the items they were eating. Vampire bat wings, spider web pizza, cheesy skeleton bones, monster claws with bloody dipping sauce and barbecued monkey's ribs.

"It's funny," said Tiger Lily to Jock. *"Most of this stuff tastes like chicken."*

Desserts were on the tables to the side. Mr. Bean liked his sweets, and he wasn't about to stay on the floor underneath the table. He climbed on top and sat like a centerpiece on the table with the slices of caramel apples. He was very careful to not drop any hairs on them. Well, not too many.

Another table held funny sounding stuff, so he stayed away from it. From his perch, when he heard a new name, he would call down to Tiger Lily, *"What's dirt pudding?"* Another time he asked *"What's s'lime swamp cake?"*

When Tiger Lily couldn't help him, it reinforced his belief that the apple table was the place to be.

Annie made sure her children in the dining room knew she had seen them. She gave long pets to Kali and Ko and told them again that things would be back to normal very soon. She complimented them on handling the crowd so well.

Annie bent to look under the table at Tiger Lily, who looked back with complete innocence. Tiger Lily purred, *"I'm not eating anything at all, Mommy. I'm just cleaning up when someone messes up."*

Annie said, "Yeah, right."

Tiger Lily and Jock looked at one another in amazement.

She saw Mr. Bean and shook her head. She started to the table to pick him up. Henrie stopped her. "No one seems to be the least bit bothered by this sweet thing. If anyone complains, I'll take care of it."

Annie thought she should look for the others in the library. Several activities were going on in there.

At the entrance to the library were tables with candy dishes. Small trick-or-treat bags were available for the children – of any age – who thought going home with candy was the only way to do Halloween right. Not a cat in sight.

At one end of the library, tarps were laid to protect the floor from jack-o-lanterns being cut by children of all ages. Adults and mature children helped, using patterns for designs ranging from a simple smiling face to intricate spider webs.

Well, there was a cat. Sassy Pants, for some reason, had decided to roll in the gooey, messy pumpkin innards and seeds. Good heavens. She will drag it all over the house, Annie thought. I just won't look.

Additional tarps were under the bobbing-for-apples tub and the guess-the-monster-parts tub. To guess the monster parts, children wore blindfolds and placed their hands inside. They pulled out and identified by feel a variety of body parts. The parts included intestines (cooked spaghetti), eyeballs (large grapes), teeth (candy corn), hearts (Jell-O jigglers), and ears, (dried apricots).

Little Socks was entranced by children pulling slimy hands out of that – Annie couldn't call it anything but "awful" –

tub. Thank goodness this was handled by the girl scouts, and they were armed with towels and washcloths.

At the far end of the library was a mini-bowling alley. Small pumpkins, stems removed of course, were rolled toward empty plastic liter bottles painted to look like tombstones.

That's where she found Cyril and Mo. Cyril stayed at the end, catching tombstones as they flew up in the air. Mo rode the pumpkins-in-waiting. When a pumpkin was needed, players would have to move a tail or a leg or a butt to get to it.

Annie was surprised none of her cats were on the four-season porch. They liked hanging out with Chris. He was there with his artwork, and he helped Sam, who Skyped in at the driftwood table. As customers picked up pieces of his driftwood art, he explained how he made it or the inspiration that drove him to design it.

Chris looked at Annie when she walked in. "Sam's a natural salesperson."

Chris's charcoals were going like hotcakes. Most of his sales were commission sales. He displayed photographs of the charcoals he had time to finish, using them as examples. He talked to families about their own companions and how they would like to have them portrayed. Several discussed family portraits, humans and companions together.

Chris asked that they supply a photograph of the companion – and any humans to be included – and he commissioned the concept with a down-payment, the check made out to Soul's Harbor, which served as the clearing house for the block party charities.

His finished pieces included Tiger Lily on her hostess stand, crushed purple day lily at her feet; Little Socks with a brilliant red torch flower in her teeth, looking for all the world like a Spanish dancer; Kali and Ko bookending a vase of flowers, mostly in charcoal but with a bright blue rose in the center; Mo dancing around a candle glowing orange and yellow, fluffy tail coming dangerously close to the flame; Sassy Pants on her back, tummy extended for a tickle next to a deep red glass of wine; Mr. Bean dancing in a window with a slice of luscious lemon meringue pie in the background; Cyril sitting in a regal pose in front of the police station, gold badge emblazoned on his chest; Jock running on the beach in front of a fiery sunset; and the famous turtle that almost closed the Café, sitting inside a bright green bowl of soup.

Chris said, "I didn't have time to do any of the other local companions, so I'm using these to sell others. And believe it or not, I'm also taking orders for some of these. People in town love your cats. All of them have sold. I'm not going to tell you who's in the lead. I will tell you Diana asked for Little Socks in her signature pose."

As the evening drew to a close, Annie, doing a shift at the front door, welcomed a black-tied Frank. With a sheepish look on his face, he gave Annie a quick hug and dropped a check into each of the contribution jars, having to give them a push as they were both filled to the brim.

"Annie, I'm so sorry. I never, ever meant to do anything to be unsupportive of this event, or of you, or of anyone here on The Avenue. I got caught up in a situation, and then I couldn't get out of it."

"Frank, you don't have to explain anything to me."

"I do. I know what Geraldine tried to do to you, and I should have kept my feet on the ground when she came to me with an offer."

"An offer?"

"Yes. She offered to help me set up stores throughout the region, using her connections, financial and political. She said many of her connections would be at this event, and that I should plan to attend. Before I knew it, she told people I was her 'date,' and things went from bad to worse after that. The more I tried to explain my position to Mem, the worse it sounded, to me as well as to her. I just couldn't figure a way out of it."

"Why aren't you still there?"

"At the faux charity ball, you mean?"

"Yes."

"It was a complete bust. Total money raised, $500, and I imagine those folks will be asking for the return of their money."

"This is a gauche question, but it's getting ready to jump out of my mouth anyway. Did you give anything, Frank?"

"Let's see. I haven't made a contribution per se, but after fronting the money to set up the event, I am now out $7,500. $5,000 to pay for food and drinks to feed 100 people and the rest for a small chamber orchestra."

"Wow. Expensive food and drinks."

"She insisted spending about $50 per person, given the size of the contributions she hoped to receive, was necessary."

"And why were you paying for all of it?"

"Supposedly, I was giving her a loan, because her funds are not currently liquid."

"And you do realize the last infusion of cash she received was from your purchase of that building, right?"

"Belatedly, yes, I realize that."

"But what about the charity? What about the Foundation?"

"I've been so busy setting up the store, I paid no attention at all to the 'charity,' this bogus Geraldine Foxglove Charitable Fund. I saw a brochure tonight, and my name is actually on it as a board member! Along with, of course, her ex-husband, who, I understand now, is not ex-anything."

"So you paid for all of this food and drink, you're on the board, and you're here?"

"Everyone else saw through her. I was blinded by the possibility that my business could blossom at an unreasonably fast pace. The attendees were Geraldine and me, of course, as her 'date,' while her husband and her parents looked on, Hank the baboon, a State Senator and his wife, and about ten other people, all of whom left as soon as the dessert was served."

"After eating all that food and dancing to a chamber orchestra?"

"Well, 'all that food' turned out to be something rubber – probably chicken – fake mashed potatoes with lumpy beef gravy – tell me, how do you get lumps in beef gravy? and why beef gravy with rubber chicken? – canned asparagus – have you ever eaten canned asparagus? – an iceberg lettuce salad – and that was it, just the lettuce, with some kind of red dressing – and, let's see, what was the dessert…oh, yes, they called it apple cobbler, but it was the kind of dish that you make with Bisquick and the Bisquick rises to the top."

"Drinks?"

"Water, pre-sweetened iced tea, and lemonade. Not even coffee."

"And did she order food for 100 just to serve, what, 20 of you?"

"Oh, no. The caterer, if you can call them caterers, came with exactly the right number of servings."

"Was the orchestra at least good?"

"They didn't show up."

"They cancelled?"

"They didn't cancel. They just didn't show up. I don't think she hired anyone in the first place. I think she took my $7,500 and used it to pay personal bills and buy a very expensive dress."

"Oh, my. Frank. I'm sorry. Well, I'm not sorry for Geraldine, but I'm sorry this experience has been so expensive for you. And you realize it's been expensive in more ways than one."

"Yes. I have some personal repairs to make. Repairs to relationships, one in particular, and repairs to my reputation."

"If you want to start on that personal relationship, I suggest you go into the library and look for the pumpkin bowling alley."

"Do you think I have a chance?"

"To be frank, Frank? This is just me talking. Mem has said nothing of the kind. But I think knowing that Geraldine's affair was a complete wash-out may help you get back on track with her."

"Annie, I will never understand women."

"Nor should you."

Annie went to the porch to see how sales were going and to take Chris a glass of wine. "This isn't the vampire stuff. Jesus brought a few bottles of his best."

"Thank goodness. Hey, Sam said Nancy would like to talk to you."

"Hi, Sam, you've been on this thing all night. And you thought you wouldn't use it."

"You're never too old, Annie. You're never too old. Let me get your mother."

Nancy came on, wanting to know "everything."

"Chris has of course told us what a great time you all have had, and how successful everything has been, but I want to know if you've heard about that snazzy ball."

"Oh, have I!" Annie laughed with Chris, Sam and Nancy as she told them everything she knew. "And I hope Mem will find it in her heart to forgive Frank. But that's between them."

"Yes it is, dear, but now, I want to talk to you about a problem."

Annie sat up straighter. "What's up, Mom?"

"It's Honey Bear. You know, that night in the basement, I'm not sure at all how everything happened, but there at the end, he was biting that man's ankle."

"Yes…"

"I think it's affected him. He bites the ankles of just everyone now. Oh, not Sam and me, but our friends, and the plumber, and last week he bit the ankle of Pastor Jones. Do you have any idea how to stop it?"

Annie thought back to her conversation with Kali and Ko. "I think so, Mom, but I'm going to have to ask you to do something for me."

"What's that, dear?"

"Get Honey Bear in front of your computer, and you and Sam have to leave. Leave the room and shut the door."

"What?"

"Mom, do you want my help?"

"Alright. Let me see if I can find him."

Chris said, "Annie, what are you up to?"

"Just roll with it, and if you ever say anything to anybody, I'll swear you're lying or crazy."

Chris took a drink of very good wine and decided to roll with it.

Eventually, Nancy came back with Honey Bear. She put him on the table in front of the computer. "Now, you're sure I have to leave?"

"Yes, Mom, please leave."

Annie waited until she heard the door close, and she looked into the camera. In the most sincere voice she could muster, she said, "Honey Bear, you did a very brave thing that day in the basement. You helped stop a bad man from hurting all of us. You did it the only way you knew how, by biting him. Now pay attention. It was important that you do it for that one time, but biting ankles doesn't make you a hero. Only biting ankles to save someone makes you a hero. Do you understand?"

Annie hadn't realized Tiger Lily was in the room, but she jumped to the table and stood close to the monitor. Tiger Lily said a few quiet words to her Uncle Honey Bear. He said a few quiet words back to her. Tiger Lily hissed and jumped down.

In a voice less sincere and, truth be told, a little strident, Annie said, "I don't know what that was all about, but here's the rest of the story. If you bite someone and you draw blood, they'll have to quarantine you and do all sorts of tests to make sure you don't have rabies. It will be a long and painful process. So if you believe Mom and Sam are in danger, bite away. If not, stop it."

Nancy stuck her head in the door. "Annie, are you finished?"

"Yes Mom...."

It had been a long day. The companions found themselves on the four-season porch, close to Chris and close to the portraits.

The portraits – in effect, the companions – were still getting a lot of buzz. It was heady, frankly.

But frankly, they were just too tired to care.

Epilogue

Pete and Janet, Ray and Cheryl and Chris and Annie gathered with their companions in the large dining room of Annie's apartment. At the end of the room stood an easel draped with a sheet.

Annie opened a bottle of champagne and poured a glass for each human. She solemnly placed silver trays, each with three treats, in front of the companions.

Chris raised his glass in a toast, including humans and companions in the sweep of his arm. "And now, we toast the heroes, for whom, unfortunately, the finale of the story must forever remain a secret."

He pulled the sheet from the easel.

It was a lovely charcoal. Annie's intelligent brood of cats sat in a row. All held regal poses. Tiger Lily was in the center, flanked on the right by Kali, Ko and Mo and flanked on the left by Little Socks, Sassy Pants and Mr. Bean. Behind them were Cyril and Jock. Honey Bear peered around Jock's hind legs. Each companion wore a glittering red ribbon from which hung a gold badge. The name was "Friends & Heroes."

Two weeks prior to this unveiling, swearing everyone to secrecy, Pete and Annie shared their common secret with this small group.

Pete and Annie were the only humans to know everything, because in the minute or two the heroes acted, everyone else closed their eyes, or covered their faces, or ducked for cover, or did some combination of those three things.

Most of the other humans knew "something happened," but only Pete and Annie knew the whole story. Pete and

Annie, eyes wide open, stared in shocked silence while the action unfolded.

In the basement on that stormy night, Pete sat in the corner, amazed at the rescue just performed by Cyril and Jock. He stared at the chorus – that was the only word he could use – of cats. They screeched, screamed and yowled as if they were being killed. However, there was a conductor.

Tiger Lily called the shots. He was certain of it. When he first sat back and noticed it, Tiger Lily, Little Socks and Mr. Bean were lounging – actually lounging – in front of Kali, Ko, Mo and Sassy Pants. The four screeched – well, to be honest, three screeched and one added a melodious trill – while the others rested.

One at a time, they got up to drink from the water bowl, taking time after their drinks to wash behind their ears, or, in the case of Mr. Bean, his privates. In a couple of minutes, Tiger Lily gave a motion – he was certain of it – and they took up the chorus while the four took a rest.

After the four had taken drinks and washed their ears – and Mo his privates – she motioned again, and they exchanged places.

From here, Annie took up the story. Herb and Alec were close to the bedroom door while Jessica stood at the entrance to the safe room. Jessica at first, and then Alec, argued for killing the witnesses. Herb, who thankfully had the gun, argued forcefully against that action.

After several minutes, Alec seemed to break. He started yelling at the door, "Shut up! Shut up! You're driving me crazy!" This was the point that everyone else took cover.

When Alec made a lunge for the door, Annie stood up, wanting nothing more than to protect her cats. What she saw, though, stopped her in her tracks.

Alec didn't make it inside the bedroom. He screamed as seven cats leapt. They clawed every inch of his body they could reach. Jessica made a run for it out the front door and Herb followed her.

Pete saw the rest of the action. He had barely gotten off the floor and out the back door, while Cyril and Jock were already on their way around the corner. Jock tackled Jessica, keeping her head on the floor until the action subsided. Cyril stuck his nose in Herb's crotch. Herb sat down, back against the wall, and slid the gun in Pete's direction. Cyril then "captured" Herb by sitting across his lap, going down slowly and carefully so that both man and dog would be comfortable.

While the dogs made their captures, Alec tried to escape the cats. He passed out, probably in pain, as he reached the door to the safe room, seven cats continuing the attack.

Once Alec was down, Tiger Lily called off – Annie insisted that's what she saw – the younger cats, Sassy Pants and Mr. Bean. At that point, Honey Bear got in on the action. He sauntered over to the downed man, lay down on his ankles and grabbed one between his teeth.

The human friends knew they could not discuss this with anyone else. But they could commemorate the heroic actions of the companions in another way.

This charcoal with bright reds and golds would be their private memorial.

Tiger Lily left the group celebration, jumped to the dining room table and gazed at the picture. She felt a surge of pride that they had been able to save Mommy and everyone else, and that Mommy finally understood her. Kind of.

Looking at the picture, she tried hard not to cry. She kept her thoughts to herself, not wanting to ruin an otherwise wonderful evening.

That picture would be perfect, except for that hateful Uncle Honey Bear.

Thank you for reading <u>Boo!</u>, the second installment of the Tiger Lily's Café Mystery Series. It will be followed later in 2015 with the third installment, <u>Phishing</u>.

About The Author

Kathleen (Kathi) Thompson was raised on a small livestock and grain farm in northwest Indiana. She has an undergraduate degree in Sociology and an MBA. She served as a probation officer, parole agent and juvenile residential counselor before moving into administrative, marketing and fund raising positions in human service organizations.

Kathi and her mother discovered an injured kitten of indeterminate age at the family farm. The kitten decided to make Kathi her guardian. She wrapped herself around an ankle, started purring, and wouldn't let go. Against the advice of her mother, Kathi took the kitten home, vowing that if the kitten lived through the night, she would take her to the vet. She lived; the vet diagnosed road burn serious enough to take all the fur from the left side of her face, and the kitten – Tiger Lily – eventually healed and took a huge part of Kathi's heart.

Tiger Lily was joined by the rest: Little Socks (thank you, Aunt Mary); Kali, Ko and Mo (thank you, Connie Hall); Sassy Pants (thank you, Ant Sherwy, better known as Sherry Simpson); and finally, Mr. Bean (thank you, Pulaski County Animal Control).

Tiger Lily's Café has been rattling around in Kathi's brain – there isn't much else up there – for all of the years since, sometimes as an actual café and sometimes as a book. It was less expensive to write the book.

A Note From The Kids

This is Tiger Lily. I want to tell you about writing books. I help Mommy write the books. We all do. We work as a team.

Ko is especially good with papers. She rearranges all of the papers on the desk so Mommy has a better idea where to find things. When Ko has finished her work, I lie down on the papers, because Mommy really does a better job if she can't see anything.

Little Socks helps by lying in front of the laptop, head and paws on the keyboard, moving ever so slowly until she is on the keys, helping to type. Sassy Pants and Mr. Bean keep the excitement going in the house, so Mommy has to take a break every now and then to see "what that noise was." Kali sleeps or cries to be held, because Mommy has to take a break every now and then.

Precious Mo is no longer a part of the family in body, but he lives on in spirit and in these books.

I hope you enjoy reading this book as much as we enjoyed writing it.

Find us on the web: www.tigerlilyscafe.com

Find us on Facebook: TigerLilysCafeMysteries

A List of Tiger Lily's Café Mystery Series Books:

- Turtle Soup
- Boo!